## CUFF 'EM AND CAN 'EM

Normally it's not good bail enforcement agent policy to hit a guy on the head, as it usually does not work out the same way it does on TV. After his eyes roll up in his noggin, he may be in a coma for a year, while you're fighting a lawsuit for excessive force.

But this seems the exception.

Butch, being no trained knife-fighter, comes in high, with the knife overhead. Mistake. I swing my chair up and get the seat between me and the knife. The blade buries deep in the black upholstery, I twist, and the cheap blade snaps. Then I crack him a good one to the bridge of his wide nose with the butt of the Smith and Wesson. I sidestep, spin, and while his eyes are still doing an Orphan Annie imitation, give him a low side-kick to the knee with the cowboy boot. The knee folds inward with a crack like a Louisville Slugger hitting a home run—folding in a way knees don't normally fold. The knife goes spinning across the floor, and he goes on his face in a growing puddle of bubbly nose blood.

The hell of it is, his brother, my FTA, has made it out the door and is on the run.

I may have won the battle and lost the war.

# BOOK YOUR PLACE ON OUR WEBSITE AND MAKE THE READING CONNECTION!

We've created a customized website just for our very special readers, where you can get the inside scoop on everything that's going on with Zebra, Pinnacle and Kensington books.

When you come online, you'll have the exciting opportunity to:

- View covers of upcoming books
- Read sample chapters
- Learn about our future publishing schedule (listed by publication month *and author*)
- Find out when your favorite authors will be visiting a city near you
- Search for and order backlist books from our online catalog
- Check out author bios and background information
- Send e-mail to your favorite authors
- Meet the Kensington staff online
- Join us in weekly chats with authors, readers and other guests
- Get writing guidelines
- AND MUCH MORE!

**Visit our website at
http://www.kensingtonbooks.com**

# CRIMSON HIT

# BOB BURTON

**PINNACLE BOOKS**
Kensington Publishing Corp.
http://www.kensingtonbooks.com

# Prologue

You'd think a guy with a name like Reginald Winfield would be a high class, old-money Boston type, but the guy who's standing ten feet from me, a half-head taller than my six feet two, pointing and shouting at me through a shaggy blond beard, is anything but. The good news is he's shouting, not swinging. The bad news is he's pointing with a machete.

Remind me not to approach a skip while he's working on his woodpile.

"Reggie," I say in my most calm demeanor, "this is the second time you've missed your court date. Max put up your bond in good faith, and he's not going to forfeit it just because you want to go to some motorcycle rally in Sturgis."

"Come on, Dev." His growl softens a little and I'm hoping he's going to come peacefully. "It's only once a year and my bike is tuned and ready to go." His volume increases as he talks, and I can see by the vacant look in his eyes that it's probably meth speaking, not good old peaceful Reggie. This is the third time I've had to hunt the old boy down, and the other times he walked over and stuck out his thick wrists for the cuffs. It looks like the third time he won't be so charming.

"Screw him, honey." The shrill cry comes from over my shoulder on the porch of the broken down single-wide trailer. It's Fat Thelma, whom I've met before, whom I think is most of Reggie's problem. She's a down and dirty doper, the type who's been the downfall of many a good man.

This is getting out of hand, so I reach under my T-shirt and pull my .38 Police Special from the small of my back. "Reggie, you brought a knife to a gunfight. Now lay it down and get your head on straight so we can go in and take care of this."

His eyes actually look as if his brain is suddenly on fire. He takes a couple of steps forward, growling and dripping spittle like a pit bull, swishing the big blade back and forth.

My fee for bringing this bad boy in is twenty percent of ten grand, a lousy two. I'd hate to shoot a guy, particularly a guy who's almost a friend and a steady source of income, as I've picked him up so many times, for a lousy two grand . . . hell, for two hundred. I don't like shooting people. But I may have to. I take a wide stance firing position with both hands on the nicely blued revolver, aiming it mid-chest, which is easy to do as Reggie is almost as wide as an ax handle.

"Reggie, remember I bought you and your old lady a beer the last time I ran into you guys. Now, put it down."

"Up yours, asshole." The voice is behind me, close behind.

The blow damn near takes me off my feet. I'm on my knees, head swimming the backstroke, then . . . all goes black.

It's dark when I wake up, my mouth tasting like the cat box. I guess the residents of Reggie's trailer park are used to seeing someone sprawled out in the dry Bermuda grass with blood leaking, as no one's bothered to call a cop or even turn their hose on me. I roll over, head throbbing, and sit up. The good news is I have all my limbs and Reggie has not gone to work on me with the machete. The good and bad is he's long gone. The bad is the back of my head has a twenty-stitch gash, presumably from the Sears steam iron lying nearby. And it's ruined my favorite *Life Is Too Short To Drink Bad Wine* tee shirt.

I know better than to turn my back on the most deadly of the species. It appears Thelma has clocked me with her iron; tell-tale blood's smeared on its stainless bottom. I guess approaching a guy chopping wood is only slightly less stupid than a woman doing her laundry—that's bound to make one a little grouchy.

His Harley is gone. Fat Thelma is gone. I probably should phone the Sturgis, South Dakota, Chamber of Commerce and warn them these two are on their way. But my head hurts too much.

I get to my feet and brush off. Santa Maria's Marian Medical Center is only a few blocks away, and my health insurance is current.

Win some, lose some. All in a day's work.

# Chapter 1

There are times when life is just too easy.

Those times don't come along nearly often enough.

To be truthful, when things come easy, I get a queasy tingle down my spine. Of course, living in Santa Barbara, California—especially on a converted fifty-five-foot fishing boat—produces more tingles than, let's say, Newark, New Jersey.

After my run on the beach and my return to the boat, I am leaning far back in my desk chair with my newly donned deck shoes resting on the chart table that serves as a desktop. I'm a little off balance when I chuck a dart at the cork-covered bulkhead across the main salon that doubles as an office. It bites and I drop feet to the floor, shooing Futa, my ten-pound Siamese, off my lap, and pad across the office to find the dart poked dead center in the second C of CONFERENCE CALL. There are almost a hundred skip-tracer techniques on the list, but this is a good one.

Okay, so Conference Call it is. Studying the info sheet on Julio Sanchez as I pick up the receiver, I hit the button on the old reel-to-reel tape recorder perched on the credenza behind my desk; then, with the surround-sound speakers lit up with the chatter and clatter of a typical busy office playing in the background, thanks to a sound-effects tape, I dial Oxnard and Julio's blessed mother, Petra Sanchez.

Futa leaps easily to the desktop and sits, eyeing me in anticipation. He's been around so long he can sense the hunt, and the hunt is on. Sometimes I wish he were a pit bull.

"*Hola,*" Petra answers.

"*Hola, Señora* Sanchez. *Habla Inglés?*"

"*Sí,* Yes, yes, I speak English."

"This is the AT-and-T operator. Hold for a call, please."

I hit the hold button and quickly dial Julio's ex-wife, Yolanda. She answers on the first ring and I give her the same tripe.

Then I hit the conference button on the phone as well as the record button on the little device connected thereto, and the ladies are together and being recorded for posterity.

"You're connected," I say, and kill the recorder so they think I'm gone. Now if they just don't speak in Spanish, of which I only have a smattering, and which I'll have to have accurately translated. Of course, that's no problem in Santa Barbara.

"Who is this?" Petra asks. "This is not collect, is it?"

"It's Yolanda. Are you all right? You called me."

"I didn't call. . . . Where are you?"

"I'm home, Mama, home with the children, where your son should be."

There's silence for a moment as both women try to figure out what's going on. But their being women, talking is the first option.

"So, have you seen Julio?" Mama Petra asks.

"Not for a week. He don't care nothing about the kids."

"He cares, Yolanda. He just has his troubles right now."

"Where is he?"

The moment I'm waiting for.

"He's not far," Petra says.

Damn.

"Where?" Yolanda presses.

Atta girl.

"Near."

"Oh, hell. I'm not going to give him up, Mama. He called day before yesterday . . . Saturday. The son of a . . . *friento* . . . Sorry, Mama. He said he was going to a Blood, Sweat and Tears concert. We got no food in the fridge, I'm out of smokes, and he's going to a concert. I bet those tickets cost fifty dollars."

Thank God Futa waits until now to cut loose with a howling meow like only a Siamese can reverberate. I manage to cover the receiver with my palm and eye him with my best rottweiler imitation before he's halfway through his yowl. As if he cares. He flops down and curls up, purring sleepily. I hit the mute button on the phone, which I should have done in the first instance.

"You got a cat?" Petra asks.

"That's not my cat."

There's a fairly long silence, and then the women are jabbering again.

But I've already got what I called for. I wait until the ladies ring off, happy that Mama has said she'll bring a couple dozen homemade tamales over for the kids, then hang up.

In moments I have Googled Blood, Sweat and Tears and have a Web site up on the computer with David Clayton Thomas's chubby bearded face smiling at me. I find the band is playing at the Paso Robles County Fairgrounds, a hundred miles or so up the coast, tomorrow night. Google, the premier search engine, is the bounty hunter's best friend.

I spin my Rolodex and come up with a number for another bail enforcer, an old friend, in Paso Robles. "Oscar?" I ask, when the gruff voice answers.

"Yeah?"

"This is your old buddy Dev, in Santa Barbara. You want an easy five hundred?"

"Do seagulls crap on your boat?"

"Okay. I'm e-mailing you booking pictures and a rap sheet. Julio Sanchez is an FTA . . . he skipped from a DWI, evading arrest, and assault with a deadly weapon—his car—in Costa Mesa County. He totaled a black-and-white with a buddy's low-rider. You transport him."

"No sweat."

"He'll be attending a Blood, Sweat and Tears concert tomorrow night at your fairgrounds. His rig is a bright yellow eighty-six Chevy Bel Aire two-door, down on the ground. Typical *chingaso*. You can't miss him. No record of him carrying anything more than a pig sticker, but he can run like a coyote. It took a half dozen of L.A.'s finest to run him down, so be ready."

"Slam dunk."

"Call me on my cell right after you buckle him into the backseat."

"You got it. Hey, Dev, thanks for the work. Things is slow around here."

"My pleasure."

Sometimes, life is a bowl of cherries. An easy two thousand, less five hun for my old friend Oscar.

My phone rings almost as soon as I recradle the receiver.

I check out the number on the caller ID as I answer, so I'm a little less professional than usual. "Dev. Jump bail, he's on your tail."

"I've got an interesting one," the sultry voice announces.

I feel the twinge in my groin that I always seem to get when Cynthia Proffer lays that voice on me. I should be running for the woods, as I know she wants something big time, and whatever it is it won't be easy. Cynthia, with auburn hair to the middle of her tan back and legs all the way from the sidewalk to heaven, is one of Santa Barbara's more successful P.I.s, and oftentimes my partner in crime. Crime-busting, that is.

"Why am I always wanting to run for the closet when you say you've got 'an interesting one'?"

"Is a hundred thou apiece interesting?"

I take a deep breath. There's this Porsche Boxster I've been admiring. . . . Then of course, there's also the boat payment and the phone bill. . . . "Okay, I'm out of the closet."

"The hell you say. I've heard a lot of interesting things about you, but out of the closet?"

"Of all people, you should know that's b.s." Cynthia and I were, at one time, an item. "Tell me about the gig."

"Stolen child. Off to Spain, if the client's info is right."

"So, I risk the *guardia* chaining me in the dungeon, and you sit on your patio overlooking the Santa Barbara Channel, sipping sangrias and reminiscing about what a great guy Dev was . . . and we split even?"

"It's my gig, big boy. And don't count on me crying in my beer over you."

I sigh deeply, but she knew when she called I couldn't resist. "When do we meet?"

"How about right now? Get to Brophy's and get us a table on the balcony before the *turistas* hit."

"Be there by eleven forty-five."

"I will, but make it a table for three. I'm bringing the client. And you know I'm never late."

I laugh as I hang up. Never late to a woman is any time within thirty minutes of when she promises to arrive. But hell, this woman's definitely worth it, even if she wasn't talking a hundred thou.

Life, so far today, is a bowl of cherries. And Cynthia is bringing me a cherry pie. But there was a certain edge to her voice. Why do I suddenly get the feeling I may end up with nothing but the pits?

# Chapter 2

Santa Barbara Harbor lies just west of the terminus of the city's main street, State Street, which slopes gently out of the gracious old town to the Santa Barbara Pier. The pier forms the east edge of the south-facing main harbor, and the channel out to the sea. The fact is it's one of the few south-facing coastlines in California, and protected from most of the weather, which is why it is one of the state's oldest cities, founded two and a half centuries ago by the Spanish. On the west end of the harbor is a cluster of buildings no more than two stories high. Chandlery, Marine Museum, boat brokers, and other restaurants share the area with Brophy's.

Brophy's enjoys a second-story location, overlooking the harbor, with a narrow balcony across the front, only wide enough for the waitresses to pass and narrow tables holding only two patrons each. That balcony makes an L with another on the south side of the restaurant, which is slightly wider, and which has four tables that will accommodate up to four patrons. By not bothering to change from my sockless deck shoes, khaki shorts, and T-shirt advertising Kamchatka vodka, I get there just in time to tie up one of those four; in fact the prime one on the harbor end.

Eating there two or three times a week, and warming one of the bar stools even more often, one receives a smidgen of special consideration. First come, first serve, unless you're the guy who has the occasional party on his boat, Brophy bartenders invited.

The place is always full, good weather or bad. Santa Barbara is gifted with some of the better weather and more beautiful vistas in the world.

From the corner table, I can see across the five hundred or so slips to *Aces n' Eights,* the commercial fishing boat I've converted into home and office. With a cat named Futa, contrived from FTA, for Failure to Appear, and a boat with a name that signifies death, you'd think I was preoccupied with my business. And I am. It's not many professions that allow you to work from a converted longline boat in a beautiful harbor. I feel a little odd knowing I'm the only manhunter to operate from a boat, but not odd enough to change that fact. The good news is that crime pays, and not only for the criminal.

There are only one hundred live-aboards in this best-of-all-of-California's harbors, and I'm blessed to be one of them. Of course, the twenty-five grand I forked out under the table to get the slip was part of the blessing . . . for the prior tenant, not me. And I have to pay rent. Still, I'm not complaining.

It should be the eleventh commandment: one shall not be out of sight of surf and palm trees.

Brophy's owner is starting to look askance at me for tying up a table for four when Cynthia arrives and barely saves me—as anticipated, almost twenty minutes late. I'm into my second Jack Daniel's, neat. I am a Jack Daniel's guy in a single-malt town . . . but that's another story.

The owner's not the only one looking askance, as I must admit, for I'm staring at Cynthia. In black Lycra pants with a bright red blouse tied so her midriff is exposed, it's hard to even notice the come-fuck-me five-inch red pumps she's wearing. Cynthia's a stylish dresser, and this is just not her M.O.

Being an old-fashioned boy and an astute businessman, I rise when they approach.

"Dev . . . Mr. Devlin Shannon, meet Dr. Mohammad Hashim."

I shake hands with the man, tall, dark, gaunt, and brooding, not to speak of nervous. Then I hold Cynthia's chair for her, while wishing I could pick up a napkin and wipe my palm. Dr. Hashim has worked up a sweat for some reason. As seems to be the order of the day, I check him for telltale bulges under his suit coat. Then again, doctors are probably not high on the list of terrorist bomber candidates.

She sits with me holding her chair, giving me a great shot of the ample cleavage resulting from some wonderful push-up apparatus. I sit, next to Cynthia and across from the good doctor.

I wave the waitress over and get a perfunctory nod. She'll come when she damn well pleases. The good doctor excuses himself to the rest room, so I turn my attention to Cynthia.

"You have a new look."

She flashes me a devastating smile. "This is my Boom Boom LaBare look. I'm on a job."

"Happy hooker?"

"Exactly. Straying husband, likes 'em nasty."

"It's working." And it was. Even though I like the high-class look she usually sports, this one is wielding equal discomfort. Thank God for the lap-covering napkin and tablecloth.

"Thanks, I figured this would be more to your taste than the St. John's knits. By the way, I told the doctor I was on a special assignment for the district attorney. Sounds better than some lowly divorce thing."

"Right. I'm a little confused about something."

"I'm not surprised you're confused, Dev, but about what?"

"Why would a Muslim doctor, who probably thinks women are somewhere below camels in the descending order of importance, entrust this kind of a mission to a female? Particularly a Boom Boom Labare type of female."

"Good question. Very chauvinistic, as usual, but probably appropriate under the circumstance. Truthfully, I have no idea, other than he was a referral from one of my best clients."

The doctor cuts this line of conversation short by returning, and sitting without ceremony.

No one speaks, until Cynthia breaks the ice.

"Now, Doc, please explain to Dev what's going on with the children."

"If I may, Doctor," I interrupt. "What kind of a doc are you?"

"Psychiatrist," he says, then eyes me as if I'm about to make a smart-ass remark.

I don't, even though sorely tempted. He might be carrying some C4 under his coat, or far better yet, a wad of two hundred really big ones. I've never had any love lost for shirnks, but for a hundred grand I'll overlook this particular prejudice. I can't help wondering what he charges by the hour, if he can afford two hundred thou to bring the *bambinos* home.

"May I continue?" he asks, with some condescension in his tone.

I nod. "Please."

Dr. Hashim has only the slightest accent.

"Ten years ago, I married a woman, a woman of Arabic descent, as am I—"

*No shit, Sherlock,* I think, but don't say. Hashim is not exactly an Irish name.

"—but who was born in Spain, of Moroccan extrac-

tion. To oversimplify, we have had our marital problems—"

*Yeah, you making her walk a dozen paces behind and wear
a burka and not watch television and not drive and on and
on.*

"—and she has fled the country back to Spain, or
possibly Andorra. We share custody of the children, a
girl and boy ages six and eight respectively. I want my
children here with me, and I am legally entitled to have
them." He speaks the last sentence emphatically, a growing crescendo, his voice reverberating like Moses' on the
mountain, or better, a madman's on a box in the city
square.

I find myself wishing one could only do business with
people one likes and admires. This guy isn't one of
them.

The waitress arrives and takes his lunch order as he
settles down to a sudden calm, then proclaims being
very busy and having to leave, so please hurry. We, on
the other hand, have all afternoon, at least I hope we
do. I'm not surprised when Hashim orders the vegetar-
ian plate.

When the girl leaves, I turn my attention to Cynthia.
"You have documentation from the court regarding
custody?"

"Of course. I wouldn't have bothered you had I not.
This is legit all the way."

"And, Doctor," I ask, "you have agreed to a fee?"

He turns to Cynthia. "You have discussed this with
him?"

"He's my partner in this endeavor, Doctor. He will
know everything I know, and I will know what he knows.
That's the way we work."

"Then, yes, I have agreed to pay two hundred thousand dollars for the safe return of my children." He says
this is such an offhand manner you'd think it was two
hundred dollars he was talking about.

"Ten percent up front, to cover expenses," I say, and he nods agreement. Now for the coupe de grace as he's going my way and it's no time to back up. "And you will escrow the balance with a neutral party, an attorney, I would think, with the understanding that when the children are safely in the U.S., no matter where on U.S. soil, the money is released to Ms. Proffer and me." I have a very good reason for phrasing that sentence as I do, but am not about to expound upon it.

I can see him flinch slightly. I hope the flinch is as a result of his being offended, but I'm not sure that's the case. I hope even more his reaction is not a twitch as a result of his being exposed as a potential deadbeat. I have the distinct impression the two hundred hasn't bothered him as he never intended to pay it in the first instance.

So I reiterate, "Remember, Doc, no booty, no babies."

He clears his throat. "That seems extreme. Payment in advance, I mean." He folds his arms in front of his chest, a defensive gesture in this instance. "I have always met my obligations."

Taking a long draw on the last of the shot glass of Jack, I let him stew before I press. "You and Ms. Proffer will be here safely ensconced in Santa Barbara, enjoying the good weather, while I, on the other hand, will be risking a kidnapping charge in a foreign country."

"Kidnapping?"

"Of course, Doc. I have no standing as a bail agent in a foreign country, and your children are not bail jumpers even if I did. Your wife, and I'm sure your children, are citizens of Spain. If I'm caught leaving there with the children, without the consent of your wife, I'm kidnapping them. I only agreed to take this job because of my friendship with Ms. Proffer"—*and the small matter of a hundred grand, but that remains unsaid*—"and I have no doubt about your willingness to pay"—*another lie*—"but what happens if you get hit by a car while I'm winging my way home to Santa Barbara with your children . . . or you have a heart attack and croak from the stress of this operation? Besides, I have other specialists to employ, and maybe a bribe or two, and they'll all look to me for payment." I shrug. "No payment . . . then we're left out in the cold. Escrowed funds, or I can't risk it. Besides, it's payment on performance, not in advance."

He's silent for a long moment, and then his tone changes. "Do you always consume alcoholic beverages in the daytime, Mr. Shannon?"

The best defense is often a good offense. "Oftentimes, Doc. Mine is not a business for the fainthearted, or the weak-stomached."

"But I would think it one for the sober."

"I would think psychiatry also requires a certain amount of sobriety . . . particularly for a Muslim shrink . . . I presume you're Muslim . . . Campari is not exactly cranberry juice." The fire in his eyes is particularly noticeable as they're so sunken. All I get is a stare, and a hint of reddening in his dark cheeks, so I continue. "I'm stone sober when time for the nut cutting arrives, as I'm sure you are."

"I beg your pardon."

"A colloquialism, Doc. I do my job. In fact, I'm the best in the U.S.A. at what I do. I'm sure you know that, or you wouldn't be here, and Cynthia is the best at what she does."

"Modest also," he suggests cynically.

He is not wearing his happy face. He rises to leave, and Cynthia stands.

"It's not necessary for you to accompany me," he says, addressing her. "My office is only a few blocks, and I'd prefer to walk."

She hesitates, but then retakes her seat.

He turns cold eyes on me. "I'll have to consider it."

We both get the hint of a nod; then he throws his

napkin down in a manner that rings of disgust and walks away, just as the girl arrives with Cynthia's Dewars and soda and the good doctor's bloodred Campari and soda.

Not many people bother me, and in my business it's a good thing, but this guy puts every defensive mechanism on red alert. I put it off to his being Moslem, and looking a little like Bela Lugosi.

Cynthia sighs deeply—the sigh may be a low growl—eyeing me like a bull at a bastard calf, and takes a long pull on the drink. Then she speaks. "You know, Dev, just because you have one, doesn't mean you have to be one."

"You ready to order?" the waitress asks, pad and pencil poised. I'm temporarily saved.

"Chowder, a bowl," I say.

"Hell, you're buying," Cynthia says, "since you've probably cost us a cool hundred each. Halibut, barely cooked through, please, cottage cheese and tomatoes instead of French fries. And another drink please." She's only half finished with the first, but I can see she's decided one just won't do.

The girl leaves and Cynthia again eyes me like she'd like to bump me off the balcony. I can see that she's trying hard not to say what's on her mind, but finally pure irritation overcomes her. "You dip-shit. I had this all set up. He had a hard-on about hiring a woman P.I. in the first place. He came to me from Ogilvie and Meyers. Now they'll be pissed at me . . . and a quarter of my work comes from them. You are truly a double-dingle dip-shit."

"Cynthia, me lass, you can't trust a guy who orders Campari and soda. You ever taste that crap?" I don't get a smile, just a glare from her slightly fiery green eyes. "He'll come through if he has the two hundred. If he doesn't, then it would all be for naught anyway."

"You better hope he comes through, hotshot, or I might take one of your own filleting knives to a very personal part of your body." I can see she's only half kidding.

"Then I guess this means you're not coming back to the boat after lunch to see my collection of booking pictures. Then again, if you're only coming to borrow a filleting knife . . ."

"Platonic, remember."

"Sorry, that ho outfit of yours has made the blood rush out of my brain."

"Besides, I've got an errant husband to catch."

"Need any help with the rotten bastard?"

"So far today you're about as much help as a salted slug."

"Hang in there. That guy has alien eyes, and I don't mean the Mexican kind, the Roswell kind. . . . We'll hear from Mohammad the slippery shrink by morning. I'm surprised the rug merchant didn't start trying to deal us down."

"You giving any odds?"

"Two to one on a ten spot."

"So if I win, I'm only out ninety-nine thousand nine hundred and ninety bucks."

"Eighty bucks. It's my twenty to your ten, remember."

"Hell of a deal," she says, but her sense of humor still hasn't returned.

It wasn't one of the best lunches I've ever enjoyed, even with the great food and fabulous view. The good news is we have an extra vegetable plate to share. And no dessert to mar the waistline.

Watching her walk away in Lycra is dessert enough.

# Chapter 3

After Cynthia leaves, and I pick up the tab, I notice *Copper Glee* at the dock.

My old man's been retired from the Santa Barbara police force for over ten years, and has owned the little commercial fishing boat for most of that, since my mother passed. His, unlike mine, is truly a working boat, doing what she was built to do. Early on, when I was in high school and college, he was a partner in another boat while still on the force, but my mother hated the business and finally nagged him out. I worked on the prior boat through high school; diving for abalone and later for green sea urchins got me through the University of California at Santa Barbara. My not following my anthropology degree into teaching was one of the great disappointments of my father's life. After a stint in the Marine Corps and a visit to Desert Storm, with my diving background I got on with Commercial Marine, and was soon highly paid as an underwater welder. An accident at two hundred feet below an offshore oil rig, which resulted in my being trapped for over a half hour—a half hour's an eon that deep—and my developing an acute case of claustrophobia in addition to a slight case of the bends, sealed my fate. No more diving suits, or even diving bells. The job did buy me the right to the boat slip and most of *Aces n' Eights,* so it accomplished something other than the fact I now go crazy in tight places. Pop hated me diving in deep water on mixed gases, and hates even more the fact I'm in bail enforcement. He thinks the mixed gases, or maybe some of what was floating around the Saudi or Iraqi desert air, may have fried my brain. Who knows?

My old man, known as Pug to his friends, is directing the off-loading of at least a hundred gallons of urchins. It seems the Japanese have developed quite a taste for the caviar of the California coast variety, and they're bringing around ten dollars a pound, dockside.

"Well, if it isn't the bounty hunter," he says, giving me a glance as he works the hoist.

"Good day, looks like," I offer.

"Great day . . . Any time you cover the fuel cost, it's a great day."

On first glance at the two of us, you'd have to surmise I take after my mother. The old man's half a head shorter and built a little like a fireplug. He's got his mother's curly black Italian hair, where I'm taller, thinner, and have straight black hair. But we share the same dark brown eyes and twisted sense of humor . . . and work ethic, whether he believes it or not.

"I got an O'Douls down on the boat," I offer. The old man's been a member of AA since two years after my mom died.

"It's poker night. You want to come up and sit in?"

"Haven't made my nut yet this month. Maybe next week."

His deckhand, Iver Jefferson, waves at me, loquacious for Iver, from the tiny pilothouse of the thirty-five-foot boat. Iver's been with the old man since he bought this boat, just after they met at an AA meeting. There are not many blacks in Santa Barbara, and even if there were, Iver, at six feet six with muscles on his muscles, would stand out. Not to speak of coils of steel-gray hair on head and chest like lathe shavings in a metal shop. He's only fifteen years younger than my old man's sixty-four, but he's timeless in appearance and can outwork anyone on the harbor. He's been a good friend to both of us.

Cedric Swink bobs his balding blond head up out of the small hold. "Hey, Dev, may the force be with you." Cedric normally talks enough for himself and Iver.

I wave to both of them, and head back to *Aces n' Eights.*

Anyplace as beautiful as Santa Barbara attracts some real oddballs, and Cedric Swink is as real as they come. He scuba dives for the old man, mostly shallow water stuff less than fifty feet. Wandering onto the dock one day, from God knows where, he began regaling us with tales of diving in the South Seas for pearls, off Madagascar for diamonds, in sinkholes in Central America for Mayan antiquities, and on and on ad infinitum. At first, of course, we thought it was all b.s., as he's about my age, mid-thirties, but it all turned out to be true. That, and the fact he claims to be a Zen Buddhist monk, makes him one of the more interesting characters, even in S.B., a cornucopia of queer folk. And he's invaluable upon occasion, as he's a whiz with computers. He can hack his way through the tangled rain forest of the computer world like the proverbial knife through butter, or machete through swamp grass.

When I get back to the boat, there's a call on the machine. "Call me. It's local, but don't get excited. All I want is for you to check somebody out."

He didn't have to leave a number, even if it wasn't on my caller ID. Sol Goldman is my number-one client. Goldman Bail Bonds, in Van Nuys in the middle of the San Fernando Valley. He knows I don't do work in Santa Barbara County. It's not smart to live in the same snake pit in which you work, at least not in my business. I try to keep Santa Barbara pristine, so I'm not constantly watching my back. Sure, it pisses off some of the local bondsmen, and I lose out on a few bucks, but I went national with good purpose.

Sol answers on the first ring to his personal line. He, too, has caller ID. "Dev, my boy. You weren't answering your cell."

"Lunch date with a beautiful woman."

"I understand perfectly. I'm faxing you booking photos on Lenny Haroldstern. A very bad boy who likes to drop Ecstasy and GHB in young ladies' drinks. A bunch of young ladies, some of whom appear to be minors. A bad boy, with very rich relatives. I bailed him for a cool five hundred g's, and he cleaned out his pad and picked up his rent deposit this morning."

"He skipped?"

"No, not yet. He's not due in court till next week. But I got a sneaking hunch that since he's moved out of his Hollywood pad . . . As you know, I can arrest him if he vacates his local address without informing me, but I'm going to give him a couple of days to give me a call."

"So, why me? Not that I'm complaining. . . ."

"His auntie has a place in Montecito. Just take a look and see if he's there . . . personal favor. If he FTAs on his appearance, you'll get the call, and you'll already be on top of him."

"My pleasure. Address?"

"It's all on the fax, and I'll FedEx original booking photos tonight. Let me hear from you."

In addition to Lenny's booking photos are a few personal ones. Sometimes booking photos don't offer the best resemblance, especially when faxed. Lenny is a George Hamilton clone—in George's youth, of course—right down to the tan and dapper dress.

Why in hell would a guy that good-looking, with one of the world's great toys—he drives a Porsche Carrera—

need to dope women to get them in the sack? He must be a major asshole.

The address of his aunt, which is not on the FAX, which is typical of Sol, but is in the phone book, is in one of Montecito's more posh areas, and Montecito is one of the more posh communities in the world. Oprah Winfrey's forty-million-dollar pad, etc. A list of residents reads like the roll of presenters at the Academy Awards, plus half of the country's industrial elites, not to speak of some of the world's more wealthy. Montecito is a neighboring area to Santa Barbara, just to the south, and its border is only a mile or so from the harbor.

I have one chore before I go, feeding Futa. If the old boy's not fed regularly, I find pieces and parts of seabirds spread all over *Aces n' Eights*. He's a harbor pigeon's nightmare, and the boat earns its dead-man's-hand name.

With a touch of domesticity, I poach him an egg, cool it adequately, and spread it over his dry food. Egg, I'm told, is good for his coat. Admonishing him to leave the bird life alone and keep his urges directed at wharf rats, I mount my bicycle, which is locked to my dock box, and am off.

Having a need for a variety of vehicles is one of the curses of being a bounty hunter. The white Dodge van is necessary for transporting bail prisoners. It has strategically placed eyebolts for securing the passengers, and an expanded metal screen between the front and rear, just in case the angry work their way free. It has JOE'S PLUMBING painted on the side with a phony address.

The oatmeal-brown, slightly dented, 1990 Chevy four-door is great for surveillance and chase, if one were so inclined. It's the most nondescript vehicle I could find. The fact that it's a stick shift, now with a polished, blown, and balanced muscle V-8, is not apparent to the casual observer, but the old buggy is flat-out fast. The last, and by far the most entertaining, is my Harley Davidson Sportster. She's not the fastest out there, nor the wildest looking, but she's fast enough and reliable as hell. And I cherish her almost as much as I love Futa.

There's a huge parking lot between the harbor and Shoreline Drive, which rings the city on the seaside, but I don't like parking my vehicles where the public, particularly those who might want to do me harm, can get their hands on them. So Max Howard, for a small monthly stipend, allows me to park in his well-fenced boatyard, just to the west of the cluster of harbor buildings.

Being a high-tech kind of guy, I have looked up Ms. Melinda Grace Haroldstern's address in the Montecito phone book. Sometimes life is just too easy.

It's a beautiful day, so I think I'll treat the highbrows of Montecito to the roar of my bike. After changing to jeans and cowboy boots, and pulling on a windbreaker, I'm off to Max's. As expected, the Sportster fires up with a touch, and I'm cruising. The tourists are out in force, wandering on the waterfront walkway under the palms. I cruise past the bird refuge, then under Freeway 101, and am in Montecito. Before I come to the turn to the road where Auntie Melinda's abode resides, I see a red Porsche Carrera parked in front of a photography store. I brake and pull into a yellow zone and kill the bike. In moments I'm rewarded by Lenny Haroldstern, exiting the store and sliding his skinny ass into the Porsche. He's close enough that I can see the little alligator on his red knit shirt. He gives me a disdainful look, but little does he know how much he really disdains me.

Lenny roars off, and I fire up and follow at a discreet distance. We wind down Montecito's meandering eucalyptus-lined main street, peppered with faux-Spanish early-California architecture, but very classy faux. Everything on this lane is way overpriced for the average Joe, but most of it well worth the extra if money is of little object. When he turns on East Valley Road, I presume he's going to his auntie's.

This is not a guy, on first impression, who's going to hide out somewhere without servants and room service, so finding him near Auntie's mansion does not surprise me.

Then again he may have given up his apartment anticipating an extended stay courtesy of the state of California. But I doubt it. This guy has all the makin's of a runner, which means a pile of Franklins for me.

He wheels into a driveway so long that I can't see the house because the drive disappears into the shade of stately old oaks and underlying vegetation. Judging by the frontage I'd guess the place occupies several acres and contains the usual circa 1929 George Washington Smith–designed home, which means several million bucks in Montecito. It's surrounded by a wrought-iron fence with masonry pylons every twenty feet or so. The wrought iron is topped with spearlike spars so climbing makes one's survival a question, and the pylons are each topped by a variety of gargoyles reminding me of an English teacher I had in college—sorry, Mrs. Polkinghorn—or maybe an old girlfriend or two. I've seen enough, so I spin the bike and head back to the harbor.

One of the disadvantages of a Harley, an oatmeal beat-up Chevy, and a Dodge plumber's van, is the lack of interest by the ladies. The bike works, for women willing to wear calf-high boots adorned by chains and to get bugs between their teeth when they smile at eighty miles an hour, but that's about it. There's something about a van with tie-downs in the back that's a little disconcerting to most tasteful women.

But not to worry, I have plenty of work to do, and tonight's only invitation is to play poker with my old man's cronies, which is about as much fun as getting beaten with a rubber hose. How many times can one listen to the same old jokes and still manage a smile?

My first order of business is calling Sol Goldman. He's happy at my sighting, in fact ecstatic. At least until Lenny tries to hotfoot it out of town.

I spend the evening working the computer, finding out what cyberspace has to offer about Dr. Mohammad Hashim and about Lenny Haroldstern and his auntie Melinda. Nothing revolutionary about any of the info I gather—except the fact that Melinda's former husband, recently departed, was worth a hundred million bucks or more—but all in all it's been a good day.

Having no other opportunity to make a buck, other than my passive monitoring of Oscar, I spend most of Tuesday working on the boat. One thing about a boat, particularly one that is mostly wood, is the fact it constantly offers something to keep one out of trouble. I sand and refinish the aft taffrail until I crap out, read the latest Elmore Leonard novel for a while, then reluctantly lay it aside, don a clean T-shirt and jogging suit, jump on the mountain bike, and head for Brophy's in order to get a prime seat at the bar before the rush.

I need cheering up. The place is rocking and happy enough, but I'm not, and I bet Cynthia Proffer is mad enough to be hotfooting it over to borrow my filleting knife. I haven't heard from her, which means she hasn't heard from Dr. Mohammad Hashim. It looks like I owe her twenty bucks.

The cell phone rings just as I settle in. It's Oscar, in Paso Robles. "No sweat, Dev. I'm on him. He just turned into the parking lot. I'm going to wait until he parks and is out of his vehicle. He's got a couple of hotshots with him, but they don't look like much."

"You got some help?"

"Yeah, I got Freddy Branch with me."

"He good?"

"He's goofy, but good . . . a runner if Julio bolts. I got enough muscle, but I don't run so good anymore."

"Okay, do good. Give me a call when you get him strapped in."

"No sweat."

Some of the boys from Max's boatyard and some hands off the workboats in the harbor are comparing notes with a crew of Australians and Kiwis off an eighty-foot sailing yacht, a maxi-boat, so the talk is lively and deep enough in b.s. that I'm wishing I'd worn my rough-weather boots.

I'm about to decide to head back to the boat, as five beers is enough, when my cell phone whistles at me. I dismount the bar stool and head out on the balcony so I can hear.

"Who is this?" a businesslike voice asks.

"Who wants to know?"

There's silence for a moment, and then the voice adds, "I have your number, and I can find out who this is, so why don't you just tell me?"

"You first," I say, about half amused.

"This is Lieutenant Paul Antone, Paso Robles Police Department."

"Okay, and this is Devlin Shannon in Santa Barbara. What's up?"

"Are you a relative of Oscar Sorenson?"

# Chapter 4

The question shakes me. I take a deep breath before I comment.

"Oh, Jesus. . . . No, not related, but Oscar is an old friend, and is working for me tonight on a bail enforcement." Not only is he an old friend, but he saved my sweet young ass in sand-blown Desert Storm.

"That explains some of it. If you give a damn, you'd better come to Paso Robles General. He got cut up pretty bad."

"Damn it. . . . How bad?"

Again, there's silence for a moment. "I doubt if he'll make it. Looked like he bled out by the time they loaded him. Does he have any next of kin you know about?"

I get a catch in my throat, and can't speak for a moment. I shake it off as the adrenaline rises. "No. I think he was living with some girl, but no real next of kin that you can talk to. He's got a couple of kids by a former woman, but I have no idea where they are. I'm in Santa Barbara, it'll take me a couple of hours to get there."

"I'll be working late at the station. Drop by, Shannon. Call on your cell as you get close."

"After the hospital. . . . By the way, how did you get my number?"

"Easy, I hit the recall on Sorenson's cell phone. You were the last number he dialed."

He hangs up and I head for the Chevy, dialing the information operator in Paso Robles for the hospital's number as I jog to the car.

The hospital answers as I stop to unlock the gate to Max's, which is long closed for the day. I lie to the E.R. nurse and say I am Oscar's brother, as they aren't going to give me any info. She turns me over to a cold-voiced doc.

After the conversation, I slow to a walk. There is no longer any hurry. The ambulance came in silent and dark, without siren wailing or lights flashing.

No hurry, but now my movements become very deliberate. Things have not gone as planned for Oscar, my old friend, but they will go as now planned for Julio Sanchcz. And my plans for Julio are somewhat like McDonald's are for a beef on the hoof.

I'm looking for a killer, and I've never been real fond of how killers are treated by the California courts. Like a lot of folks who operate on the edge of the system, I've got my own ideas about justice, but fulfilling those ideas means I have to find him before the cops do.

And I damn well plan to.


I have to pull the Chevy off the highway in San Luis Obispo to gas up. I've always loved the old mission town, but in the darkness it's just another freeway gas stop. The big V-8 is fast on the highway, but even faster gulping fuel. San Luis is a college town, resting in a beautiful green vineyard-filled valley a dozen miles from the ocean. I'm wishing I could see down the emerald valley past the half dozen huge volcanic bubble domes that follow a rift and culminate with Morro Rock at the end of a sand spit in the bay of the same name. Another bubble dome, only this one has its boulder-toes in the Pacific.

Being here to go fishing or merely sight-seeing is an endeavor about which I can only wish.

Across the road from the 7-Eleven squats a small neighborhood bar with a neon beer sign punctuating every window—COORS, BUD, CORONA—and just for a fleeting moment I have the urge to wheel over there, shake loose of the highway, and belly up to the bar with the locals. Breathe some secondhand Lucky Strike smoke, lament life with a wrinkled old bar hag or a bored bartender with tobacco-stained teeth, and say to hell with it. As bad as that sounds, it sounds better than what I face.

Then an image of Oscar's blood being soaked up by the litter-strewn gravel of a county fair parking lot amid broken Coors bottles overcomes my temporary bout of reticence . . . no, cowardice. I could more easily face a charging platoon of Iraqi crazies than the cold bloodless specter of a dead friend . . . but I owe it to that friend. Even though I hadn't seen him for a couple of years, old friends are just that.

I punch it back onto the highway and watch the blip, blip, blip of the broken white line duck under my headlights. Just a little south of Atascadero I pass a large lighted sign announcing the state mental hospital for the criminally insane. I guess the community is proud of its presence. The knot in my gut resulting from the evening's insanity tells me that the nuthouse is not nearly as well populated as it should be.

The next fifteen miles up the 101 is lost in an old Whalon and Willie tape not quite repeating itself, but then I have to wheel it over to make the Paso Robles off-ramp.

Not that I'm bothered by my mission, but I can't make spit as I pull into another minimart parking lot and sit for a moment, breathing through my nose, watching the moths and june bugs madly circle a parking lot light while wondering if their endless orbits aren't a little like human existence, and wishing Oscar and I were back in an oceanside bar a few blocks from Camp Pendleton getting twenty-one-year-old testosterone-fueled urges while watching a long-legged stripper—who is far too good-looking and hard-bodied and probably softheaded for her own good. Watch her enthusiastically hump a cold brass pole on a stage above the bar.

But all that was then and this is now.

There is no longer any sense in going straight to the emergency room, so with the sour taste of bile in my mouth, but as promised, I dial Lieutenant Paul Antone at the Paso Robles Police Department and only have to wait an instant past the first ring.

"Where are you?" he asks.

"Across from the Paso Robles Inn," I tell him, checking the sign on the faux-Spanish building across the street.

He gives me directions and in less time than Willie can lament not letting your children grow up to be cowboys I am sitting across Antone's desk with a Styrofoam cup of hot coffee in my hand. Or at least it resembles coffee; it tastes moldy, like old laundry hampers smell.

He sees my wince.

"It ain't Starbucks," he says with a sad but knowing smile. Antone has jowls that would shame a bloodhound and a tie with enough spots, probably soup, that you'd think an old hound dog had been drooling on it, but he looks like a cop who might just track better than one. And he's got the Gallic nose for it, slightly red veined as if he might have long enjoyed more than his share of *vin rosé*. He's probably been on the job longer than I've been alive. He mops watery gray red-rimmed eyes with a stained hanky before he continues.

After a mucus-rattling throat clearing, Antone sighs

and asks, "Now, tell me again what your friend and employee was up to that got him shanked?"

"You first. Do you have the assholes who did this?"

He sighs deeply and seems to sink with exasperation deeper into his chair, appearing smaller but only for an instant. Then he hunkers forward, grows in stature like the neck of a bull elk in rut, drills me with the watery blues, and begins to tap a rapid pencil cadence on the desktop—a gesture of irritation, not nervousness.

"Shannon," he begins with strained patience but firm sincerity, "this is just a little old hick town and I'm a country bumpkin cop who's trying to make retirement in a couple of years . . . make it in one piece. However, you dick around with me for another nanosecond, and I'll shuck your fancy-dan Santa Barbara butt in my little ol' cold damp jail for obstructing justice. It's a short walk there and a long walk out. You and I clear?"

I smile but only with one side of my mouth. Jogging suits are usually not considered "fancy-dan." Still, humility seems in order. "So I guess I'm first?"

"I'll answer the one question. No, we don't have the assholes who cut up your buddy. Now, you're the next first, and maybe last, unless you're a whole lot of help." He again dabs at the watery eyes, but he leans back in the chair and stops the tapping.

Sometimes aggressive is the wrong ride so I climb astride cooperative, explaining what little I know about Julio and all I know about Oscar, which takes some time. When I finish, it's me who sits back in the chair and suggests, "Your turn."

"You've convinced me he was more than just a friend, but that's not enough. Do you have some paperwork?"

"No, I left in a hurry. Oscar should have had a copy of the warrant and some booking photos in his car."

"Didn't find it, and you ain't getting ka-ka from me until I know exactly who you are and that you have some authority, even though I've never been real fond of bond-enforcement types and consider you fellas way overauthoritized."

I don't bother to ask him where he got a word like authoritized, but rather suggest, "You had a sergeant here, Tom Weatherall, who retired a couple of years ago. He'll speak up for me if he's available."

"Tom retired last year and spends a lot of time fishing, but coincidentally he's fortunate enough to be my brother-in-law and I happen to know he's home." He reaches over and pokes a couple of buttons on his phone. He has old Tom on his auto-dialer, and in moments I'm a good guy again.

"So, what can I tell you?" Antone asks after poking the disconnect button.

"Where can I find the guy who was with Oscar? He had help with him, a runner in case Julio bolted, but I forget the guy's name."

"Branch. Fred A. Branch. . . . The A is for asshole as far as I'm concerned, but I've got no wants and warrants for him at the moment. Well known around town. Not exactly your basic solid citizen. He's probably still at the emergency room. He had a broken arm to set and needed a few stitches . . . a few in his head, arms, legs, and torso."

"You want to go over there with me?"

"Nope. I already wrung him out for what it was worth, and I will catch up with him tomorrow in case his memory gets any better. By the way, we have an all-points out on the Chevy this Julio and his friends fled in. We don't have a tag number . . . nothing shows up registered to Sanchez, but a yellow, lowered, and leaded Chevy shouldn't be hard to spot."

Finally, I can be of some help. "I have the details on the car back in my office. As soon as I'm back there I'll fax them up."

He nods. "I have an idea about who might have been

with him, and I'll be showing some booking pics around to the witnesses tomorrow."

"You want to enlighten me?"

"Nope, not until I have a better line on it. I don't want you hassling the wrong folks. That's my job."

I rise, dig a business card out of my wallet—having to ruffle through the many bogus ones I carry—and hand it over, leaving the hand out to shake after the card passes. He takes the hand, with a grip like a steelworker's, and says he'll try and keep me up to date, then adds, "You learn anything, and I mean anything, you let me know before the sound has time to travel from one ear through what little gray matter you might have to the other, understand?"

"Yes, sir," I reply, almost feeling like saluting, and he nods and reaches for a rumpled coat hanging on a nearby coat tree.

When he turns back, it's as if we'd been lifelong friends. He places a hand on my shoulder. "I'll walk you out. How did you get to know old Tom?"

We reminisce on the way out, mostly me filling him in on an old case I'd worked on with his brother-in-law, and then he gives me directions to the hospital, says, *"Semper fi,"* then disappears around the corner. I knew there was something about the old boy I connected with, even if the beginning of our relationship was somewhat rocky. And it was obvious he did his homework on me before I showed up across his desk.


There's something about hospitals that always gives me the willies when I first enter. I think it's mostly the smells, and maybe the colored stripes on the hallway floors so you can find your way to whatever horror awaits, and the fact the floors and walls and ceilings look and smell like the blood has just been washed away. This one is no different, and odors assail me as I follow the yellow line to emergency. I do a little mind trick and envision the vine over the swing on my mother's porch. Honeysuckle, my nose is filled with psychosomatic honeysuckle, one of life's great aromas.

I find Freddy Branch behind a pale foam-green curtain surrounding one of four cubicles in the emergency room, again after giving the nurse the b.s. that I'm his brother-in-law. He's dozing, and damn near jumps off the gurney when I shake him.

"Jesus, man, who are you?"

"Dev Shannon. Oscar was working for me."

I barely get it out before he asks, "Who gets his pay?"

# Chapter 5

This does not endear me to Branch, and it's not with a smile that I advise him, "His kids would get his pay, if he had any coming. This is a delivery game, Branch. No body, no booty."

"Yeah, I was afraid of that. I'm dying for a . . . for a drink. . . ." *Why does he say drink and I hear joint or toot or eight ball?* "But I can't leave here for a little while, the doc won't sign me out, until the smack they shot me up with wears off." A sleepy smile widens his narrow bloodless lips. "Not that I give a shit yet as it was a good hit."

I like Freddy even less. "No sweat, we can talk right here. What happened?"

He takes a deep breath, drops his bandaged head back into the pillow, rubs his cast on the left forearm with his free hand, and talks with his eyes shut as if trying to remember. As he begins to speak, I reach over and gently lift the three-quarter-length gown sleeve, and sure enough, he's got more tracks than a music CD. They're old tracks, but I'll bet he's shooting up in some less obvious place, like between the toes. *Oscar, Oscar,* I think. *Your taste in friends always was a little on the sour side.* I know this as I considered myself a close friend of Oscar's.

Amidst all the midnight-blue bruises, I notice spots on both sides of his neck, spots gone saffron. He doesn't look the type to scrap a lot, but this wasn't the first time this week, or ten days at the most, that he'd had cause to bruise.

He clears his throat. "It was all real fast, man. I was about a half dozen paces behind Oscar when he moved on the car. I was supposed to stay clear of things unless somebody ran. You got any water?"

I fill the empty glass on his gurney-side table and hand it to him. He raises his head enough to take a couple of swallows, then recloses his eyes and continues.

"Somebody in the car must have recognized Oscar, 'cause those guys piled out like strong-side tackles as he walked up, hitting Oscar with the door as the driver piled out. He had a hand on the thirty-eight police special in his belt, but he never got it out. Oscar went down and the stubby little shit-head who he was after was on him with a shiv in his hand. Before I could get to them, it was buried up to the guard in Oscar's belly. . . . Another guy had an automatic pistol stuck under my nose . . . an Uzi or Mac-Ten or some damn thing. He spun me around and used it on my head; then I remember them kicking the crap out of me. At least two of them stomping me when I was down."

"That's it?"

"Yeah, I went out for a while. Next thing I knows I'm in the ambulance heading for the docs. Doc said one or both of the assholes must have had blades in the toe of their boots, 'cause I got a dozen shallow puncture wounds they had to close up . . . chicken shits."

"You got a phone and address so I can catch up with you later?"

He fills me in as I make a note, and then I head out. But not before asking the desk nurse with whom I make arrangements for Oscar. My old buddy deserves to be buried with all the trimmings, and with the bronze star he earned. I mean to see he gets the flag-on-the-casket full show. Every one of these little burgs has a VFW and I'm sure Paso is no exception. She informs me the body won't be released until the medical examiner finishes with him tomorrow. As I head out, I feel as if I've got an anvil in my gut. Sleep is what I need and I remember passing a Budget Inn on the way to the hospital. God has ka-ka'd on my head so many times today it couldn't possibly happen again; I know they'll have a room and head that way. I want to be here tomorrow to take care of Oscar, and follow up with Antone.

The drive to a motel is not far, but far enough that I have time to analyze my conversation with Fred A. Branch. One thing you learn after a few years in bail enforcement, a few years being lied to, is how to read people who are lying, and Freddy would have choked if he said anything truthfully. He cut his eyes, fidgeted, stammered, stuttered, avoiding direct eye contact. Classic signs. Now why? I decide I'll sleep on it.

I'm cozied up stark-ass under a sheet and paper-thin blanket when my cell phone rings, and of course I've left it on the chest of drawers alongside my wallet and keys and have to get up.

It's Cynthia.

"Guess what?" she asks without preamble.

"Let me see. . . ." I feign interest. "You sound so happy it would be . . . you won the lottery . . . or more important to you ladies, you found the right shade of nail polish?"

"Close. I've got a twenty-thousand-dollar expense check in my hand."

"The good doctor?"

"Yep. And you have to be on a plane out of LAX winging your way to Barcelona day after tomorrow. The reservations are already made. Your passport current?"

"It is, but I can't do it."

"Jesus Christ, Shannon. This is a hundred grand apiece!"

"I've got a friend to bury."

"Dead friends don't really give a big rat's ass."

"They do when you were the proximate cause of the dying. Make it a week and I'll be there."

"You dumb son of a bitch—"

"A week, no matter what you think of my mother or the brains I inherited."

"Merely a figure of speech. And I was stupid enough to tell him you're the only man for the job."

"That's what you get for changing your style and spouting the cold hard truth."

"Again, you're a double-scoop dip-shit."

"Agreed. But I'm one who's going to take care of burying his old friend. Now can I get into this two-dollar bed I just paid thirty-five bucks for and be an *asleep* double dip-shit?"

"Sure, you sleep while I convince the good doctor, with a pack of lies, that you have some preparation to do before you can leave. . . . I'll call you tomorrow with the new schedule."

"You're not only incredibly beautiful, but seemingly semiintelligent."

"Fuck you."

With that I get a dial tone, before I can say I'd love to, which would be a tiny stretch of the truth at the moment. Sweet oblivious sleep beckons.


Oscar is buried up to his neck in the burning sand of the Iraqi desert, and I'm facing him three feet away. His bronze star is emblazoned on his helmet, and his eyes are only blood-and-hamburger-filled sockets in a bone-white face. The sand is green and bubbling, like the surface of a scum-covered pond with rotting vegetation littering its bottom, and the rancid scent of death is released from each assaulting sand fart. I have to dig him out, but then realize I'm buried too and can't move my arms, and my fear is palpable.

I awake with a shudder, my upper lip lined with beads of sweat, my mouth as dry as the petrified death I've been smelling, my muscles aching from straining against constraining, suffocating, confining sand. I kick the cheap blanket and sheet off. Anything, even the room itself, even the dank air of the room pressing in on my lungs, is far too confining.

In seconds my mouth is under the lav faucet and I'm gulping water.

I stand at the window and, almost in a panic, slide it open, breathe deep, and eye the open sky and stars for a long time before I try the bed again, then close my eyes praying I won't dream. Dead sleep . . . pardon the pun, no dreaming. Buried in the sand or trapped under a rock slide is not new to the middle of my night, but facing an eyeless friend is . . . not a pleasant addition to my old demon, claustro-fucking-phobia.

Conscience, and the night, and old haunts, are strange taskmasters.

My ringing cell phone awakens me just as the shades are being bathed with light. The clock says six-thirty, and the cell phone caller ID says Cynthia again.

"Nice to be nudged by you in the morning," I say, without other preliminaries.

"You got a pencil?"

"And a good morning to you," I chide.

"Pencil?"

"Okay," I say, after I put my feet on the floor and grab the pad and pen provided on the bedside table. Budget Inns are not all bad.

"Your tickets are bought. You leave a week from today."

"Much better," I compliment her, then realize what she said. "Tickets? I presume the good doctor is accompanying me?"

"No."

"What do you mean, no? How the devil am I supposed to get back here with two kids . . . kids who may not want to come . . . without a legal guardian along?"

"His au pair is going with you."

"Au pair?"

"Nanny, with the children's passports in hand, and with some legal documentation authorizing her to accompany the children as temporary guardian."

"So, just who is the nanny?" I ask, wondering what I've gotten myself into.

"A two-hundred-fifty-pound Norwegian girl who eats bail enforcement types for a snack. She was an Olympic shot-putter."

# Chapter 6

As usual, Cynthia is giving me a rash of ka-ka on the phone. "Good, she can help me fight off the *guardia.*"

"Maybe, but actually she's about a hundred twenty pounds, so she won't be much help . . . other than as a distraction."

Now my interest is piqued. "A looker?"

"Actually, Lothario, I think she's a little more than just a nanny to the good doctor, or so I surmise, so it's hands off or maybe watch your hundred grand fly away . . . and yes, she makes Miss America look like a boy."

"Ah-so, so Mrs. Hashim may have had other motivations to head out to beautiful *España?*"

"Maybe, but that's not our concern. Actually, my concern is you keeping your mind on your task, while spending a few days with this lady. Don't let your mind wander, it's too small to be out by itself."

I ignore her sarcasm and doubts and hesitate a moment before getting serious, as it takes a little extra effort for me to do so. "Cynthia, actually I couldn't have left for at least a week, even if I didn't have to bury this friend."

"Oh."

"Oh. I do need to do a little preparation, you know. I need to find a driver over there who is vouched for by someone I trust, and who knows the territory like he knows his girlfriend's netherparts. I need to read up on the place."

"I know, I know. I just didn't want our bird to fly any further. You can pass for a Spaniard, but I don't know about a Moroccan . . . and she's got family on the south side of the Med."

"Good, so long as you know I'm not schlepping off a piece of biz as important as this."

"Schlepping . . . you've been spending too much time with Sol Goldman. Get your friend taken care of, and get back here. Actually, I have a pile of information on Spain and Andorra that I've put together for you; plus the good doctor has some pictures of her family's place, and maps, and other stuff."

"And what if the kids are uncooperative?"

"He's a psychiatrist, remember."

"So?"

"A psychiatrist is a medical doctor, and writes prescriptions."

"Jesus, I hate more than you know to drop dope on some helpless kids . . . that's against my better judgment and what morals I have left."

"Sleeping pills, children size. Hardly dope."

"Call it what you want to . . . dope's dope. I'll be home tonight, and will call."

"Funeral will be over?"

"No. But it will be arranged. I'll have to come back here in a couple of days. Hey, by the way, did you get your man?"

"Man?"

"The errant hubby?"

"Was he in my sights? Of course I got him."

"So the divorce is imminent?"

"Actually, no, given the fact his libido stays in neutral when not in his own garage . . . so to speak. My client is a very intelligent woman who values her family and the ten-year investment in her marriage. My role was only to expedite his facing up to what she perceived as, and he would not admit having, his problems."

"And how did you accomplish that?"

"About six o'clock last night, after a couple of drinks at Harry's, with my invitation he trotted along to the Peppertree with his bloodhound nose tracking the Lycra, right into the room I'd rented. To his great consternation and astonishment, his loving wife came in right behind him . . . even before he could get his mitts on me, and I had to lay my sap on him."

"And?"

"And as of tomorrow he's off to his first appointment with the shrink, which was her whole motivation. To get him some help."

"Getting him to the shrink?" I guess the incredulousness rings in my voice.

"Yes, Shannon. She realized that, like a great majority of you of the weaker sex, her husband would not discuss his wants and needs and fears with her, and had a phobia for some kind of feminine reinforcement of his masculinity. Fears that could only be temporarily assuaged by copulating with the nearest available female . . . strange stuff, I believe you Neanderthals call it."

"Oh," I say, deciding that I've probably heard enough.

"Oh, and she knew that his indiscretions were not only damaging to his marriage, but the jerk manages the office at an insurance company and has two dozen young, vulnerable, and probably equally insecure ladies working for him. A sexual harassment lawsuit in the making. Believe it or not, his boss in L.A., another insightful female, is fully aware of our plot to bring the gentleman, kicking and screaming, into the twenty-first century, and hopefully into maturation in a marriage to a loving woman whom he doesn't deserve. . . . I guess he's good at his job, or the boss wouldn't bother."

"Thank you, Dr. Freud. You know, you talk more like a therapist than a down-and-dirty private dick."

"You're welcome. By the way, Shannon, the shrink has a few slots open."

"Thanks, but I've already had my session, the last ten minutes, and I don't expect a bill."

"You just get to Andorra and bring back the goods and I'll call it even."

"Yes, ma'am. Hey, Cynthia, seriously . . . I'm glad for you and the wife who's trying to keep her family together . . . a worthy endeavor . . . and I have high hopes for the hound dog."

"Me too."

I get a dial tone.

She's gone like the will-o'-the-wisp she often is, so I jump up to shower, brush my teeth with the edge of a finger greased with a tiny motel bar soap, use the forked-finger comb, put back on my day-old underwear, T-shirt, and jogging outfit, and prepare to see what the good lieutenant has turned up.

And Freddy. I need to see if Fred A-for-asshole Branch has detoxed and maybe can remember a little more, maybe even something truthful. I also have to call on Oscar's live-in lady, and see if I can find his children and the mother thereof. Conscience dictates that I make sure the living are living as well as can be expected.

A fun day. Looking forward to it about like I would a root canal performed with a posthole auger.

Antone is out somewhere flashing booking pictures at witnesses, but is due back for a meeting before lunch.

Freddy has been released from the house of horrors early . . . probably has no insurance and they kicked him out. But, like a good manhunter, I have his address.

Patti McAfee, who answers the door at the address, had

been girl-next-door pretty at one time, but of late she's
been cozying up to Big Mac and his buddies. The corners
of her eyes are fairly well tracked by crows and they aren't
all smile lines. The flesh has gone as gray as the flat eyes.
She smiles at me as she introduces herself, a slightly desperate smile I suspect given to every person who rings her
bell, even vacuum cleaner salesmen, but the smile doesn't
carry up to the eyes. Dead surrender in the peepers and
far too cold for the rather round and jolly face.

"It's nice to meet you. Is Fred here?"

The smile goes as flat as the eyes. "Haven't seen him
in a couple of weeks."

There goes the good manhunter bit. "No kidding.
He gave me this address as his residence just yesterday."

The lips draw tight, the eyes narrow, and the plump
cheeks redden. "He stole my television, right in the
middle of *Survivor* . . . carried it right out of the house
and by now has shot it up his arm. No, this ain't the asshole's residence. I haven't seen him in over a week, and
hope I never do again."

She starts to close the door in my face but I put a
palm against it. "Hey, wait a minute." The door opens
again. "I need to get hold of him. You have any idea—"

"He's got a brother that he hides out with when he's
in deep shit. You a cop?"

"No, a friend of a friend."

"Drive west on Pine until you come to a dead end.
It's the place with the cars on blocks, the six mangy
dogs, and the yard full of garbage. . . ."

I turn to go, but she yells after me, "I doubt if there's
one there, but just in case, bring me a TV if you see one
lying amongst all that junk."

"Sure, a TV, so you can catch up on *Survivor.*" I wave
over my shoulder.

The wail of a small child rings over the sound of what
I thought was the TV, but now presume is a radio. She
shuts the door with more fervor than necessary.

So yes, Fred A. Branch is a liar, verified by the fact he's given me a phony address. And he's supposed to be one of the good guys.

Now it's find Oscar's lady, then his family, which is the only thing taking precedence over finding Julio Sanchez. I have Oscar's business address, and find it's a shabby two-story stucco apartment building. The door to number 7—suite 7 on his card—is standing open, and a gaggle of neighbors have gathered to give condolences. There are a couple of casseroles on the kitchen counter, which adjoins the living room, as well as a pie and cake. The half dozen folks there stop and stare at me as I stand in the open doorway and survey the living room.

"Can I help you?" a young Hispanic girl in the middle of the group asks from her perch on a gold furry sofa. She doesn't try to rise, as she has a baby in her lap.

"Hi, I'm Dev Shannon, an old friend of Oscar's."

She hands the baby to another girl on the sofa and rises, standing with her hands folded in front of her. "Oscar told me a lot about you, Mr. Shannon. Would you like a cup of coffee, or tea?"

"Just stopped by to pay my respects, and to see if I can help you with anything. But coffee would be great." I follow her the few steps to the kitchen as the others go back to their reminiscing.

She has those incredible dark eyes and long lashes that seem to go with Hispanic. A beautiful girl, if a little thick in the middle. I suddenly feel bad about Oscar all over again, and the anvil in my stomach seems to get heavier.

She pours the coffee and hands me a cup. "Thanks. . . . I'm sorry, but my mind's not working today. Oscar told me a thousand times but I've forgotten your name."

"Lawanda . . . Lopez still. We were going to get married at Christmastime. My friends call me Lalo, kinda like Jennifer Lopez. Jalo, you know."

"Sure. Lalo, I like that. And the little one?"

"He's Oscar too. Oscar and I have been together . . . were together . . ." She dabs a dish towel at eyes that seem suddenly honestly wet. "Almost three years."

"I hate to ask you now, but I really want to find the guys that took Oscar away from you two. You know anything about this guy he was picking up? A Hispanic guy, Julio Sanchez."

She turns away and pours herself a cup, then turns back and is a little too definite with her response. "I don't know hardly any Latinos up here. I came up from Monterey Park and met Oscar right off. I only know friends of his, and some guys where I work."

"And that is?"

"Valpredo Valley Winery. I run the tasting room there as of a couple of months ago."

The coffee is surprisingly good. "So you just started?"

"No, I got a job there right off, three years ago, doing cleanup and cooking a little, but then I got promoted to tasting room manager."

"How about Fred Branch . . . you know him?"

"I've met him a couple of times . . . when we'd run into him at the market or something. Oscar didn't bring him around the apartment hardly at all. Said he wanted to keep his work away from us at home."

"He a user?"

"Oscar? Hell, no." The black eyes flare and this I take as gospel truth.

"I didn't mean Oscar. I meant Branch."

"I have no idea. I don't think Oscar would hire him to shovel dog crap if he thought he was a user."

I sigh deeply and drain the coffee as one of the gaggle sticks his head in the tiny kitchen.

"You okay, Lalo?" The guy looks at me as if I were a buzzard circling the remains.

I take two steps to the sink and wash out the cup and place it on the counter. "I've got to get moving. Thanks for the coffee."

As we go to the door she and I talk about Oscar's funeral. As I surmise by the surroundings, there's not a lot of dough lying around for funerals and she's made no arrangements, and has no idea how to even get in touch with Oscar's first wife and kids. I tell her that I'll take care of things, and she agrees, informing me that she and Oscar have no church affiliation, while following me out to the car. I suggest the VFW thing, and she thinks that a fine idea, as Oscar was very proud of his service record. I tell her that all she has to do is show up . . . and accept the flag . . . and grieve, but I don't add that part. Even though I think she may not be telling the whole truth, I do think she's sincerely grieving. It's Tuesday, and we settle on Friday, which is as good a day for a funeral as any, providing I can get the body released. And I excuse myself, dropping the Chevy into low and easing away.

Now it's back to the P.D. and Antone, then to find Fred A. Branch. Why do I have this feeling that Branch will lead me to Julio Sanchez? It's something that niggles at me, the reason for which I can't put my finger on, but it's there.

Antone is in, and I'm sent to his desk.

I give him a perfunctory salute and he clears that rattling out of his throat while motioning me into a chair. "You've been a good boy, haven't you, Shannon?"

"Why do you ask?"

"Your eyes are a little on the red side. You been drinking already this morning?"

I laugh, then study him in return. "Your eyes are a little glazed. You been overdosing on doughnuts?"

I get that same old tired hound-dog smile. "God, I'll be glad when I retire and don't have to hear any more cop-doughnut jokes." He removes and begins to shine his glasses. "Now, answer the question. Have you been a good boy?"

# Chapter 7

Antone gives me a hard look over gold-rim glasses, a watery-eyed but still piercing, inquiring look; a look that suggests I'd better answer the question about being good in the affirmative.

"You'd be proud of me, Sarge," I say, remembering his *semper fi.* "It was Sarge, I'll bet?"

"Does it still show? It's only been thirty years."

"And I didn't have a computer to pull up your background."

"Yeah, yeah. But I did to pull up yours, and you were a sarge also, but I was made master and you were busted back. Now, what have you found out?" He sits forward in the chair, but it's a less aggressive pose than the last time—his neck doesn't swell this time.

"Not much. Went looking for Freddy, but he's been released and the address he gave me is an old one, one at which he's no longer welcome—"

"Patti McAfee's place." He gives me a wry grin. "I dropped by there myself after I found he'd been released. I was right behind you. She said, 'Some cute guy, Dev or Dick-head or something, had just left.'"

I ignore the crinkle in his eye. "I told you I'd called

on Branch. . . . Then I headed to Oscar's place to pay my respects. Other than that nothing, *nada* . . . but I'm just starting."

"So, even though I told you to butt out . . . where's butt-breath Freddy?"

"Don't know." It's maybe the truth but probably a small lie. The fact is I want to find Freddy before the brass-badges do, so I change the subject. "You get anything with the mug shots?"

"A lot, actually. I think I've made the guys with your Julio. I'm adding them to the all-points soon, but not yet."

I smile back, but it's not sincere. "He's not my Julio, at least not yet. So, you gonna share?"

"Nope. In a while maybe. But not yet. I'm not sure enough yet to pull a warrant on the other two. You've been running on adrenaline and I think I'll wait till it wears thin. You headed back to Santa Barbara, like a smart guy would? Like I strongly suggest you do?"

"After I make arrangements for Oscar's funeral. You got any suggestions as to a bargain-basement undertaker?"

"All of them are overpriced, but try McGafferty's. Tell him I sent you and that I'll fine him big time the next time he double-parks the hearse if he treats you wrong. He's in Rotary with me, and I'm the *presidente* this year."

"McGafferty's it is. Then I'm heading back. I'll give you a call tomorrow if that's okay?"

"Sure, you do that. You know, Shannon, if you were on the force we'd take you off this case because you're too emotionally involved."

I give a mock salute again, then rise to leave.

"Shannon," he says, stopping me.

"Yes, sir?"

"I'm serious. Do me a big favor and stay out of this until I give you the word."

"Sure, Sarge."

"That's an order. And I'm a lieutenant now, so don't be demoting me."

"Yes, sir." I give him a real salute this time.

"How come I'm not convinced?"

I just smile, about-face, and head out.

Now it's a shot at Fred A-for-asshole Branch.

As Patti McAfee has instructed, I drive west on Pine until I run out of road, and there, in its glory, squats a single-story clapboard house painted a stunning baby-do brown surrounded by a yard full of junk. The Fred A. Branch brother abode, no less. I nose into the five-foot-high cyclone fence, its diagonals alternating with white and green plastic fillers, and head for the gate.

Having had some experience with dopers, and dope dealers, I respect the sign on the gate, MAD DOGS: TRES-PASSERS WILL BECOME DOG CRAP.

As I stand in deference looking over the gate, a troop of five pit bulls round the corner from the backyard at a dead run, slavering, barking, and leaping over junk as well as a fairly reasonable Harley, on their way to inter-cept the friendly bail enforcement agent.

It's all I can do not to climb on top of the Chevy, but I maintain my tough-guy cool and dignity, and trust the gate and five feet of cyclone.

They raise hell on their side of the gate until one of them takes umbrage at the other and a real brawl breaks out among the dogs. Only then does the front door open and a bearded Goth appears, his stringy shoulder-length hair askew, baseball bat in hand. If this is a Branch, he's heavy boned and thick, a lot bigger than brother Fred. He runs from the house directly into the melee. I admire his gonads almost as much as his tattoos, as I wouldn't have entered the fray with an AK-47. In two sec-onds the dogs are sent howling to the rear of the house.

Then he looks over at me and growls, "You got busi-ness here?"

With a day's growth of beard, fork-finger-combed hair, and a well-rumpled jogging suit, I don't exactly look like a representation of any of the phony business cards I carry—insurance agent, appraiser, gas company public relations man, etc.—so I decide to come on as a friend, as if Freddy might actually have one. "Freddy Branch asked me to stop by."

"That ain't the password."

I give him a wry grin. "I'm not a member of the club. I got business with Fred."

"You a cop?"

I glance down at the jogging suit, and spread my arms for his inspection. "Do I look like a cop?"

"That ain't an answer."

"No, I'm not a cop, not even a private cop, I got personal business with Fred, money business."

He stands and stares, slapping the bat into the palm of a meaty hand.

"Is he here?" I press.

"I got a beer getting warm in the house. But since it's my bro you're asking about, I'll give it one more try. What business?"

"He was working for me . . . actually for Oscar Sorenson, but Oscar was working for me, so I guess—"

"I hear Oscar took a hit in the gut and painted the parking lot sticky crimson. You don't look like no bounty hunter or bail bond pussy. So, what do you want?"

"I still need somebody to do some work."

This puffs him up. "Butch Branch is the name, ass kickin' is the game." This makes him laugh a little crazily, a laugh that might echo down the halls of Atascadero while the inmate was finger-painting the walls with his own feces; then the look hardens, and he appropriately adds, "Fred ain't shit. I been knottin' his melon for thirty years, when I could catch the slippery prick. You want somebody to bust some beaners, I'm your man!" He drops the bat, expands his chest, pulls up the sleeve of the Corona-emblazoned, soiled, and holed T-shirt he wears; then flexes his left biceps into a knot while patting it with his right hand, making the tattoo of the leopard stretched across it dance as he flexes and relaxes. The tattoo's solid black except for streaks of red where its claws are supposedly opening gashes and its glaring red eyes. Then he smiles like a cat after a canary. "This one is wanted for murder," he says, his voice down a full octave, and then he repeats the process, flexing the right and patting it with the left while a swastika-over-crossed daggers dances, "and I'm afraid of this one myself." He guffaws proudly and I smile politely. It is an impressive biceps and chest, even if the beer gut below protrudes from the too short T, detracting from the image.

"Might work," I say, shaking my head, giving a low whistle, feigning admiration that I sure as hell don't feel, while judging if he's not too tall to put a brogan up beside his head even though I haven't done my stretches this morning. But being a master of deceit, I smile as I suggest, "Let's talk about it."

"I'll go get us a couple of beers."

"Not inviting me in?" I'd like to see for myself if Fred's in residence.

"Dogs ain't et yet. Better we talk outside the fence." He laughs that crazy howl as he retreats to the house.

As soon as he's gone, the hounds of hell round the house again, blood in their eyes. When he returns, the dogs have to be booted away from the gate in order for him to get out and keep them from getting at me.

We settle back with the camaraderie of man-with-money-meets-man-wanting-money, and lean against the oatmeal Chevy.

"You know this Julio Sanchez?" I ask.

"Did you see the biggest of them pit bulls?"

"I guess."

"The black and white one with the ragged ear. If he was on two or three pads of acid, that would be Julio; but I can take him, need be and the money right." He's downed the can of Pabst Blue Ribbon in two gulps, and crushes the container, which is not the least bit impressive until he takes the flattened can and twists it into a figure eight. That takes some finger and hand strength, I determine, but decide not to try it until I know damn well I can do it.

I shoot the bull with him for another fifteen minutes, then finally come to the real point of my being there. "I need to talk with Fred, even if you're taking over for him."

He leans over and presses one nostril shut with a finger while he blows a stream out of the other onto the ground, then backhands his nose. "He headed out of here this morning. I wouldn't give him no dough and he was strung out, so he's probably on his way back to Bakersfield."

"What's there?"

"Our ma. How much you gonna pay for Julio?"

Actually, I no longer want someone else to find him. I want that pleasure for myself. "Busting Julio is gonna be my pleasure, but I'll pay five hundred cash money to someone who puts me onto him, providing I don't pay until I'm looking the acid-dropping pit bull in the eye."

"Hell, you probably won't be around to pay up after you get face-to-face with the Julio dog. You gonna pay some kind of advance?"

"I don't do advances."

"Oscar paid Freddy forty bucks in advance."

"That's Oscar's business. Call me if you got a line on him." I hand him a card with nothing but a phone number, then move back from leaning on the hood and open the door and fire up the Chevy.

He hears the roar of the engine, and yells as I back out. "What you got in there?"

I give him a thumbs-up, ignoring the question, back up, then peel out just in the off chance I might throw a rock that beans him or at least give him a face full of gravel. No such luck.

The Branch boys are a pair to draw to.

Interestingly enough, one of the pieces of junk I noticed in the yard was an old refrigerator, one with the old-style handle that latched shut. I file that piece of information in the old gray matter. It's sometimes strange the things one can be cited for, and Butch is just the boy not to take care of a misdemeanor citation, which will result in a bench warrant, resulting in Paul Antone or even Dev Shannon being able to put the bum's rush on his happy home.

The next hour is spent at McGafferty's arranging for the funeral. Mr. McGafferty himself—slick hair, black suit, black tie, black military shine on wing tips—waits on me, managing to maintain that funeral director's chronic constipated look, which sours even more as I select the cheapest service. We go from service to storage and I actually find a coffin done in blue-jean denim; and it's no surprise it's one of the more affordable. The first hint of a smile, and relief, comes to his constipated continence when my Visa card clears.

Oscar would have approved of the blue denim.

Then I visit the local VFW and, thanks to the fact one of the members is a pastor and is available to do a service for a fellow vet, the arrangements are complete for three days hence, Saturday. I leave Lawanda's address and phone number with the VFW so they can finalize the arrangements, then call the now never-to-be Mrs. Sorenson myself as I wheel out of town to tell her the only thing left for her to do is to put the obit in the paper.

I'm not surprised to hear that Freddy Branch has dropped by on his way out of town, claiming Oscar owed him a hundred bucks, then when she didn't buy the bullshit, that he needed to borrow a hundred. He got a little ugly when she informed him she needed what little money she had, but fortunately she still had a gaggle of friends around who didn't hesitate to run Freddy off, who probably didn't look too imposing covered with bruises and wearing a cast.

The good news is that Lawanda Lopez's friends got his license number and a description of the little Toyota truck he was driving. Bingo, he's mine!

I told her I'd see her at the funeral home on Saturday, figuring that the best way for me to get a line on both Fred and Julio was to get back to *Aces n' Eights* and get into my Rolodex and Google.

The setting sun is doing a van Gogh on the western sky as I board the boat, and, after I dish up some Kibbles n' Bits for Futa, I take a little extra time on the bow enjoying God's nightly ever-changing painting. The evening air seems a little extra clean after a day spent in Oscar's world. My cell phone rings and it jerks me back into mine.

Cynthia asks, "Can I come over? I've got a lot of material for you."

"Come on, but bring a six-pack, anything but Corona."

I love Corona, but Butch Branch, Freddy's brother, seems to favor it, and that's enough to put me off.

"I will, if you've got a bottle of Chardonnay to trade."

"You're on."

I begin to scheme, as there's something about being close to the death of a friend or loved one that stimulates the procreation juices in humans. Maybe I'll get lucky, but this is one woman who requires a man with a fine hand, easy touch, and smooth convincing line to get next to.

Of course, she's well worth the extra effort.

But first I have to make a quick trip to Brophy's.

I notice that *Copper Glee* is dark as I pass her berth, and am disappointed to find Cedric missing from his normal stool at the bar and not answering his cell phone. I leave word for him to call me, hustle back to *Aces n' Eights,* and call the old man, asking him to find Cedric and have him hunt me down. Then, having put the word out as widely as possible in order to find my computer guru, I hit the shower and get next to the razor.

By the time I'm slicked up and am patting on the aftershave, I'm being hailed with a sweet "permission to board."

Impeccable timing.

# Chapter 8

I love the reincarnated hip-hugger style and it looks particularly fetching in form-fitting black on a long-legged, sleek-muscled redhead. The long auburn hair is pulled back into a ponytail, and with four inches of perfectly tanned midriff showing just over the hip-huggers, she could pass for a senior at the nearby University of Santa Barbara even though the laugh lines at the corners of her eyes say she's far more knowing than any sorority girl. She looks incredibly fresh, particularly with the soft lighting in the main salon of *Aces n' Eights*.

What I don't like is the fact a briefcase is hanging from one hand and a book and sheaf of papers are tucked under the other arm.

"You look great," I say, taking the six-pack and popping out a can of Heineken while taking the rest to the half-pint boat-size refrigerator.

"Thanks. The Chardonnay?"

I pour her a generous glass of Kendal Jackson, hand it to her, then clink beer can to wineglass. "To beautiful redheads," I say.

"No . . . to successfully recovering the Hashim children," she replies, obviously more in tune with business than with my shamelessly obvious low lighting. To emphasize that fact, she drops the briefcase and papers on my chart table, which doubles as a desk, and switches on the over-desk light. "Let's go over this stuff."

"I'll do it later. It appears you've brought me several *hours* of homework. More importantly, there is the remnant of a beautiful sunset outside, a clear night with the promise of a blanket of stars, and I'm about to put some great tunes on the stereo. I can go over that pile of stuff in the morning, when I'm fresh of mind and body."

She smiles a little too knowingly. "Low lights, Chardonnay? I thought you were going with some billion-dollar Montecito baby on a regular basis?"

"Two or three dates. And I didn't check her financial statement."

"But I bet you pulled a D-and-B?"

"She was a nice girl—"

"You did, you pulled a D-and-B," she says, then laughs aloud.

In fact I did pull a D&B, an abbreviated version off the computer. Cynthia knows me a little too well. But I didn't really give a damn about how much she was worth, as it was more than obvious she was worth a heck of a lot more than me. Old habits, when dealing with new people . . . "Okay, so I did. I wanted to know to whom I was baring my soul, and as I suspected, she turned out to be far too blue-blooded for me. She's cognac; I'm beer."

"At least you're honest," she says, still smiling broadly.

"Nice girl, but too stiff, and I never would have passed family muster," I add, hoping the subject is dropped. Then I confess, "I had dinner at the family estate up near Lake Cachuma and they had more knives and forks and assorted accoutrements at my place setting than I have on this whole boat."

"And did you use the right utensil?"

"I used, in my infinite wisdom, the same one everyone else was using. I did get some strange looks from her old man when I smeared the beluga caviar on my steak, thinking it was some *frijol* concoction."

"Bull. I've seen you smear beluga on a cracker with the best of them."

"Doesn't necessarily mean I like it."

"So, she was blue-blooded, and," she adds knowingly, "she was lousy in bed."

I clear my throat. "Even if I knew that to be a fact, I would never share that information."

"Just as I thought." She laughs again; then we're both quiet for a long spell. "You say she was too classy for you, and too stiff. So you've invited me over, which must mean that I'm not classy, and I'm loose, not stiff."

I roll my eyes. "Women! One, you invited yourself over on the guise of working. Two, it means I much prefer your company. The company of a real down-home all-American girl."

"Who's great in the sack!"

"Well, there is that."

She glares at me as if trying to make up her mind, then moves toward the ladder and I follow her up on deck. She still has the glass in hand, so I presume she's not beating a retreat up the dock. I'm right, as she settles on a deck box. Just the hint of red is glittering on the western horizon, and the stars are, as predicted, coming on strong overhead.

"You're right," she says softly. "It is going to be a beautiful night."

I take her new attitude as some sort of affirmation. And I take a seat next to her; the box is barely big enough for the both of us, which is a good thing in my intimate hip-to-hip estimation.

She turns and looks up into my eyes, her beautiful browns only six inches from mine, then again bursts into laughter. She rises and crosses to the lifelines and leans against them. "You're doing it again, aren't you, Shannon?"

"Doing what?" I ask innocently.

"Circling."

"Circling?"

"Yep, you're coming back around after another unsuccessful attempt at a relationship with some other woman. Two or three dates . . . Bull! I personally saw you with little Miss Taffy Grogan of Grogan Chemical fame and fortune at least a half dozen times. You went with her for at least four months."

"So, maybe it was four or five . . . dates I mean, not months. It didn't come to anything—"

"So you're circling back to good old Cynthia."

I take umbrage. "Bull! I don't circle back. I've tried to have a meaningful relationship with you for five years."

This makes her laugh way too loudly. Then she collects herself. "You've been watching too much daytime television, Shannon."

"What's wrong with Oprah, our neighbor, or Dr. Phil?"

She ignores that. "Meaningful relationship to you is an occasional roll in the hay."

"Not true, I love meaningful relationships. I've had dozens of them. Some as long as a weekend." This silences me for a long moment, and then I smile at her. "So, as a distant number two, what the hell is the matter with a little roll in the hay? You know, get the old juices flowing, good aerobic exercise, all that . . ."

"Not a thing, even though it is a distant second. Of course, as the Navy SEALs are quick to point out, being second is actually being first loser." Her eyes seem to warm and she glances away. "It's just hard, Shannon. The hell of it is, I'm sort of a one-man kind of girl."

"If you'll recall, Miss Proffer, it was you who said you wanted to date other men, the last time . . ."

Again she laughs. "Being a one-man kind of girl who is afraid of commitment is a quandary, even for a great intuitive, deeply intellectual investigator like myself."

I rise and cross the three feet between us, leaving the beer behind, take the wineglass out of her hand, set it aside, rest a hand on each of her hips, then give her my most convincing and sincere look. And the hell of it is, I do mean what I'm saying. "So, you want to give it another try?"

She doesn't answer, just looks up, tender and inviting, so I take the invitation and bend to kiss her, deeply, thoroughly, folding her into my arms. Cynthia Proffer is the best kisser I know, with the absolute world's softest and most inviting lips. Not only the kiss, but her perfume is intoxicating. I move ever so slightly to the side, dip, and scoop her up into my arms, then head for the ladder—when a raspy voice echoes across the deck.

"Devlin, you are seeking me?"

I stop dead in my tracks. The lousy luck of the Irish.

"Put me down, please," Cynthia says with a giggle, but I swear there's a remorseful tone to her voice.

I carefully place her back on the deck and she brushes the rumples out of the short blouse and hip-huggers, and smiles at me with an enticing twinkle in her eye. I'm trying hard to figure if her smile is sad, pensive, or happy to be out of the situation.

I can't help sighing as I finally answer Cedric, who's standing at the rail, his arms folded in front of him, watery pale blue eyes taking it all in as if he's disgusted with me, when in fact . . .

I frown at him.

"Yeah," I admit, "I *was* looking for you."

"I'm here."

Cynthia has regained her composure. "You got a paper cup? I want to take this very good wine with me."

"I won't be but a minute," I say, desperately trying to

regain just a smidgen of the moment, trying to convince her to stay.

"In one minute I'll be back at my car. Fate has spoken, saving me from a fate worse than mere death. Paper cup?"

"In the net hanging over the sink." Space is at a premium on board a boat, so hanging nets abound outside stuffed cabinets.

"Am I coming aboard?" Cedric asks.

"Might as well." My tone indicates he's as welcome as a wharf rat carrying the bubonic.

"You don't seem overly jocose?"

"Jocose?"

"Happy to see me, cheerful."

I shrug. Cedric has many shortcomings but one of them is not his vocabulary, which he loves to exercise on me knowing my propensity for plain, straightforward talk. Maybe it comes from the class of folks I deal with on a regular basis, but then again, I do try and refrain from swearing, believing deep in my heart that swearing is a cheap excuse for any true appreciation of the language. I try not to mistreat the King's English to the extent of resorting to expletives, though I do occasionally swear, but only under my breath, and only with good reason. Right now, backed up with a mouthful of expletives, I feel like swearing the proverbial blue streak.

In a mental, physical, and libido-adjusting moment Cynthia is gone with a casual wave over her shoulder and I'm faced with a tall, lanky, wispy-haired blond ex-Buddhist monk in cutoff jeans and a T-shirt. An out-of-shape T-shirt emblazoned with *Life is a Bitch, Probably Because You've Married One*, who already has my computer fired up. At the moment the Cynthia-Cedric thing seems a very bad trade.

What's past is prologue.

One luxury I've allowed myself is a state-of-the-art computer and we're fortunate to have high-speed Internet access via cable TV here on the dock. As soon as the computer boots up, my e-mail alert sounds.

"You want to clear this stuff off before I begin?" Cedric asks.

"Should I?"

"Extricate it from the confines of your hard disk while you enlighten me as to my quest."

I take his place in front of the computer and begin summarily deleting, without opening, the dozens of messages with telltale subject lines: Add inches to your manhood, Money from Nigeria, Get a $7,500 unsecured credit card, Free software, Delivery Address Required for Free Shipment, You've won!, etc., etc. I'm deluged with digital drivel. Delugitized, if you will.

It takes several minutes but I need the time to explain that I want him to break into—maybe peek into is better terminology—the Paso Robles Police server and tell me who is newly wanted by Paul Antone, and has possibly been added to an all-points along with Julio Sanchez, and to find out who is the poor soul who is Freddy Branch's mother and where she's located in Bakersfield. I could get the wanted stuff anyway, but not until it's public information. More importantly, I want Cedric to see what's going on with the interoffice e-mail between Lt. Paul Antone and his cohorts, and between Antone and other P.D.s around the state. If he's getting leads from other parts of the state, I want to know about it. This is definitely not public information.

I also want him to send a mass e-mail to the other members of the National Institute of Bail Enforcement. I need to hire someone in Spain, someone I can trust, and some of my peers, brother enforcement agents, will know exactly who that someone might be. I only have a couple of days to make an arrangement for a driver, interpreter, and backup man. With luck they'll be one and the same.

Cedric may be the world's first Buddha-monk-computer-nerd. He retakes the chair and in moments the computer is humming. When Cedric is at the computer he slips into some kind of Buddhist trance and does not respond to questions unless you place a hand on his shoulder, connecting him back to the real flesh-and-blood world. Occasionally, he emits a grunt, or joyful cry, or some exclamation, such as the "Dummies," he's just muttered, or just after a "Ha, serve and protect, obvious." Then the printer is pounding away and I have two wanted bulletins in hand—Charley "Chucho" Rodriquez and Cesar "Raton" Reyes, also known as "Mouse." I know enough Spanish to know that *raton* means mouse. Reyes is as disproportionately large as Rodriquez is small. The former, Mouse, going three hundred pounds the last time he was booked, and the latter, Chucho, one twenty-five. It's always confounded me that people who are going to live outside the law decorate their bodies with identifying marks. Each of them sports a half dozen tattoos. They're walking billboards screaming "Arrest me, arrest me!" The good news is they're both wanted for failure to appear, Rodriquez skipped on a ten-thousand-dollar bail posted on a court case for possession, and Mouse Reyes on a twenty-five-thousand-dollar possession with intent to sell. I know the Santa Ana bondsman and can deal with him, and hope to make a deal with the Burbank guy who's written the other bond. They both have rap sheets as long as Bill Clinton's.

FTAs. The boys are worth seven grand to me. And Julio's worth ten. Jump bail, I'm on your tail. I might get my expenses back for running these lowlifes down, and even make some money while having the pleasure of sending them all to never-never land, hopefully somewhere where Oscar Sorenson can piss down their tattooed backs from high above, somewhere hot enough that they'll welcome it.

No rest, until the arrest.

Just as I've finished reading, Cedric descends to planet Earth and looks up from the keyboard. Then he pushes one more key and the printer is chattering again. He looks up, yawns, as if what he's just performed is as rote as breathing, and pops his knuckles by entwining his fingers, extending his arms, and bending his digits backward. To me his keyboard dance is digital magic. He offers, "Mr. and Mrs. Harold Branch live on Woodrow Avenue in Bakersfield."

"What was 'serve and protect'?" I ask, as always, fascinated by Cedric at the keyboard.

"Passwords for the Paso Robles Police Department server. Not too original. The human psyche is so predictable. The departments are all filled with bureaucops."

But I'm again lost in the information. "These guys have been bad, bad boys," I say, handing him the rap sheets.

He studies the papers for a moment. "And sanguineous."

"Okay, what's san . . . san whatever you said."

"Sanguineous. Bloodthirsty."

"Sure, I knew that one."

"A congeries of culpability with the devil, if you will."

"Sure, a congeries. What do I owe you?"

"Dinner and a couple of beers?" he says, eyeballing me with those watery blues.

"Might as well. Night seems shot to hell."

"To quote the infamous Steve Martin, do you know that look women get when they want sex?"

"No."

"Me neither. Let's go eat."

I laugh, regaining my squelched sense of humor. I head below. "Grabbing my coat." And say over my shoulder, "And I thought this was going to be my night."

"Ah, fate," Cedric says as I head into my stateroom.

"Confucius say, 'Some days you're the dog, some days you're the hydrant.' Best we commiserate over a plate of some unfortunate creature of the deep . . . a halibut perhaps . . . at Brophy's."

"Confucius didn't say that," I mumble.

"Still, it seems fitting."

Cedric is considerably better than no company at all.

# Chapter 9

Cynthia is nothing if not thorough. I'm still running on libido when I return from Brophy's, at least it's now idling, but sleep is not in the offing. So I dig into the prodigious amount of material she's provided. First there's the legal documentation, court records and birth certificates, photos and detailed descriptions of mother and children, right down to fingerprints of the kids, thanks to some program of children ID in which their mother had participated. Nice-looking kids. The mother must have been born in Spain, as she has a Spanish first name, Paloma, a middle name that is probably gained from her maiden name, Aziz, and of course the last name Hashim. The oldest child, Ardishir, nickname Arty, is now eight, a bright-looking kid with an inquisitive and rather mischievous look; the youngest, little Gigi, a nickname for an unpronounceable Arabic girl's handle, is six, looking in every picture extremely self-satisfied, confident, with a serenity belying her years. Both are endowed with impish smiles, long lashes, and beautiful large so-brown-they-are-almost-black doe eyes, windows to innocent souls.

The FTA is accused of committing a crime, but all

the bond enforcement agent has to know is that he did not appear in court. It's best not to even consider guilt or innocence beyond that. Best to consider the court as omnipresent, omni-powerful as we're instructed by civil society. We track those who have violated the bail-bond contract by not appearing in court as promised. That's the crime that initiates the pursuit; of course the level of pursuit is governed by the crime. You don't hunt a DUI with a twelve-gauge, unless he's a DUI who has a rap sheet with a long list of felonies.

These children haven't failed to appear, but rather are the subject of a court order; there's no question of their innocence in all of this. I've often been disturbed by the thought that the legal system, as well as the average estranged parent, treats children as little more than chattel. And this mother? She's fled with her children. Going against the court order means it's fairly cut-and-dry so far as I'm concerned. But God knows what truly motivated her flight, probably the good doctor getting his flute waxed by the blond Norwegian au pair . . . but who truly knows? All I have to know—judging by the legal documents I now have in front of me—is that Dr. Mohammad Hashim is their father and shares legal custody. So, in the eyes of the law, Mom is outside the law by taking them out of the country without the good doctor's express written consent.

So, morally right or wrong, I'm bringing them back.

Thank the good Lord I don't have to be an inquisitor in regards to the morals of each situation I confront. God willing and the *guardia* being asleep at the proverbial switch, and Spain having no Amber law, I can get the children safely back under the auspices and protection of the American judicial system.

The second packet includes a number of pictures of the wife, her family, and their two regal residences—a villa overlooking the sea on Costa Brava just north of Barcelona, Spain, and a country house nestled in a velvet-green valley below the snow-covered peaks of Andorra. Andorra, I learn, is a small principality, with a very large economy, perched high in the Pyrenees Mountains sandwiched between France and Spain.

Both areas look like places I'd like to visit under more recreational circumstances.

The third packet deals with Spanish and Andorran legalities, small print that I have no intention of digesting. Number one, I won't understand most of it, and number two, if same becomes necessary I'll have astute and very highly paid counsel at my side consuming anything I might stand to make in the way of income from this adventure. I have to operate on the presumption that my knowledge of Spanish and Andorran laws will be unnecessary.

Ignorance is bliss, if no excuse.

I plan to be winging my way over the Atlantic with the children napping at my side long before the Iberian Peninsula is aware of their absence.

Cynthia has also provided a guidebook to Catalonia; an English-Spanish dictionary; an English-Catalonian dictionary (the regional dialect spoken in northeast Spain); and an English-French dictionary. As well as detailed maps of the region.

I finally hit the sack, my head swimming with factoids, but my loins still lamenting the dead and concerned with procreation. After a half hour of tossing and turning I resort to counting sheep, but keep seeing them grazing on the slopes of the Pyrenees while Arty and Gigi skip and run among them.

I wish it were this gentle scene that graces my dreams when I finally fade away, but in fact it's the bloody sockets of Oscar Sorenson's cadaverous skull that confront me while I'm trapped in the sand and cannot reach him. I awaken in a cold sweat. Realizing where I am, I exclaim aloud, "Oscar, we're going to have to stop meeting like this," and get up to rinse my mouth. When I return to bed I arrange one of my two pillows cuddled against me lengthways so I can embrace it, where Cynthia should have been, silently promise Oscar that he will be avenged, and with Futa my only bed- and soul-mate, sleep the rest of the night undisturbed, ghosts of both living and dead seemingly assuaged.

I spend the morning answering e-mails from fellow bail enforcement agents, and find myself particularly interested in one from Tubby Stokes, an old friend in Miami whom I've worked with a few times and whose skills and judgment I admire. Tubby puts me onto a pair of brothers, the Lizaola boys. Fredrico and Antonio Lizaola are reputed to be in the know in Catalonia, good with their hands, with Fredrico a skilled driver and Antonio a bull who's not above using whatever's at hand for a weapon. In the e-mail Tubby regales me with a story of Antonio taking out three very bad boys using a high heel he's plucked from the foot of one of their girlfriends. Creative under fire is a good thing. Both the boys have a sheet, but it's always been connected with work—disturbing the peace, assault, etc. I call Tubby after reading his rundown on the Lizaolas and thank him, call a local liquor store in Miami, and have a half gallon of Dewers, Tubby's drink of preference, sent to my co-hort, then send the Lizaolas an e-mail, telling them I can guarantee them three or four days' work at five hundred Euros a day if they provide the vehicle and gas.

As the funeral is Saturday and the flight Sunday, and as the good doctor wants one more meeting before I depart, we decide on this afternoon. It seems he takes Friday afternoon off. He selects the meeting place this time, and it's the Wine Cask downtown. It's an upscale place in the Paseo Building, and the meeting is at cocktail hour in the busy bar. The bar is separated from the restaurant by a patio, and it's there I find them. He and Cynthia are seated when I arrive.

The meeting goes without a hitch. To my surprise, he's pleasant and upbeat, despite his macabre and Machiavellian manner.

Cynthia was to take care of the escrowing of the money and the agreement. She hands it to me, signed by her and Hashim, in triplicate. I read, cross out *children delivered to Santa Barbara,* write *to U.S. soil,* initial the change, sign, and give her back all three copies.

"Initial the changes," I request, and fold my hands in my lap like a good deal closer.

Hashim reads the change and starts to complain, but I stop him with a raised hand. "If you recall, Dr. Hashim, I originally said on U.S. soil. Safely in U.S. hands should satisfy you."

He eyes me as if I'm trying to pull a fast one, which I am, but he can't figure it out, so he initials the change and hands one copy back to me.

"The money's in escrow?" I ask, and Cynthia nods.

"All except for this," she says, handing me twenty thousand in American Express traveler's checks, in Euros, in my name.

I ask about the au pair before I leave, and he informs me that Sonya Johanson is shopping in Los Angeles and will join me in the international terminal at LAX. We will be flying British Air business class, leaving at two-thirty Sunday afternoon with a direct flight to Barcelona.

Then he gives me a zinger. "By the way, I have not informed Sonya of the nature of your trip. She is under the impression you are a social worker, appointed by the court, but paid by myself. But don't worry, she really doesn't understand these things."

I can feel my teeth grit. Then I manage, "You're telling me that that lady you have entrusted with your children is not aware that we may be taking them under false pretenses?"

He shrugs. "She thinks you are a social worker. I thought it best."

"Jesus. You're not trying to make this hard or anything."

"It makes no difference. She has the legal right to act as guardian. All you have to do is get them in her hands, and she has the legal right—"

"Sounds good when you say it fast," I say, obviously pissed. "She has the legal right in the U.S. What her rights are in Spain or Andorra is a question for an international lawyer. Not a bail enforcement agent, a private investigator, or a shrink." I turn to Cynthia. "Did you know about this?"

She shrugs. This meeting is becoming a shrug-fest.

I shake my head and rise. "I've got to get back at it. I've got to rethink this thing."

"But," he snaps, "you are still going?"

"I'm going," I say, stuffing the twenty thousand in my back pocket, "but I'm not real happy."

"You will be happy," he says, dabbing at his mouth with a cocktail napkin, "when you have one hundred thousand dollars in your bank account."

"I'll be somewhat happier," I say, then turn again to Cynthia. "I'll call you after I'm settled in, be it near the beach house or the mountain one. Try and stay available in case I need something."

"I'll do my best," she says.

"Do better than that." With that, I turn to leave with her knowing I'm more than merely miffed.

He calls me back. "There is something else." He hands me a prescription, made out in my name, for what he assures me are child-strength sleeping pills.

I cringe, but take it.

After getting back to the boat, I take the opportunity

to push some weights and work off the anger, then take a five-mile run on the beach. It's just the ticket, and for a change, I sleep the sleep of the innocent. Somebody's fooled.

The funeral is better attended than I anticipate, seeming to have the better part of a hundred assorted folks in the chapel and at graveside. I'm surprised not only to see Lalo, Oscar's current lady, but to meet his ex-wife and children. The ex-wife, Linda, seems to be a nice lady and wonderful mother. His children are impish pug-nosed twin girls, eight or so, who seem a bit bewildered by the whole thing. And I'm even more surprised to see Patti McAfee, Freddy's ex-girlfriend, and Freddy's brother, Butch, together. As I recall, Patti told me she barely knew Oscar, or didn't know him at all. But Butch acted as if he'd known Oscar, so maybe she's here as Butch's date. Fred A. Branch is nowhere to be seen.

I'm not surprised to see Paul Antone fifty yards from the service parked under a wide spreading oak in an unmarked car, taking long-lens photos. There's another guy with a military haircut and a bulge under his coat, and I make him surreptitiously taking pics with a digital camera that fits comfortably in his palm. It's nice to see the boys in blue at work, even if they are in plainclothes.

The VFW does their normal fine job, even bringing tears to my hardened eyes when the color guard does its thing. The three-gun, three-shot salute is sharply executed, and the bugler follows with a fine rendition of Taps. With the concluding note, I again swear in silence to Oscar that vengeance will be his. The Lord works in strange ways, and I intend to be one of those strange ways.

I pass the opportunity to attend a feed and impromptu wake at Lalo's and promise I'll be in touch soon. I do go away from the funeral with Linda Sorenson's address, just in case there's something I can do for the girls at some point. She informs me she's about to remarry, proudly pointing to a parked Acura.

"My fiancé is a dentist in Huntington Beach."

It seems the girls will be well cared for.

Other than that, all of consequence I take from the funeral is a Visa card with almost three thousand bucks added to its balance, and a hollow heart.

I'll be back at the boat in time to pack.

As much as I hate to take the time away from pursuing Julio and the boys, I have to keep the phone bill paid so I can function.

Speaking of phones, I call my cell phone company and make sure they've overnighted me a European phone. I'll have the same number, which is a bit of a problem as casual callers will be eating up my wallet at a buck fifty a minute. But I am pleased, first, to get through to a real human, then, second, to verify that, yes, I'm now international. The phone should be waiting on the boat.

I call Cedric and make arrangements for him to feed Futa and take care of his sandbox. He agrees, then gives me one of his bits of wisdom. "Be careful over there, Shannon. Don't get scared half to death twice." I thank him for his sage advice.

As a last-minute bit of preparation, I've purchased a small spiral notebook that fits in my back pocket. I call this my mission book, and it's been a longtime habit of mine. I reduce all the written materials I have to this small book, and fill half of it. The other half will be for notes as the mission progresses.

And my preparations are complete.

Tomorrow, *España*.

# Chapter 10

I know from a hundred yards away that this has to be Sonya Johanson, the au pair, and, *au*, what a pair she has.

There's something about Swedish women that shines. They're health personified, with rosy cheeks and eyes with whites so clear and sharp they gleam. She's in comfortable black slacks, with a tailored sky-blue blouse. No jewelry other than tiny pearl earrings, and no makeup that's obvious. Her hair's straight and short, bobbed off at the neck, and blond as a two-year-old towhead. Sky-blue eyes are taking it all in. She looks to be in her early twenties, but I've been fooled by healthy Scandinavians more than once. By the time she's within hailing distance, I've admired her other very healthy attributes several times. She's athletically trim, but fully endowed.

And probably highly intelligent.

Having been fortunate enough to have dated *Svenska flickas*, Swedish women, I view them as a dictionary while most California girls are a coloring book.

I wave and call out, "Miss Johanson?"

She smiles, and in heavily accented English, answers, "Mr. Shannon."

"My friends call me Dev."

She walks over with an extended hand. Nice nails, but not overly long. All in all she's a very trim, efficient, and workmanlike package. I'm surprised that she has no carry-on, only a beach-bag-size purse.

We shake, her grip firm and warm, and without further ceremony find adjoining seats in the waiting area.

"You travel light," I offer.

"Too much trouble going through security. I have more den enough." Her smile is radiant. Teeth as white and straight as tiny just-shined piano keys.

"There will be four of us in a small car. I hope you didn't bring too much?"

"I've traveled a great deal, Mr. Shannon. I have just the right amount, and if not, we can store some things in Barcelona."

"Dev, please. We may not be returning to Barcelona," I say, then regret offering more information than she needs to know.

"Really, den where?"

"Don't worry, we'll see your things are taken care of."

As we move to the line, and make our way forward, I'm pleased and a little bothered to find she's a touchy-feely type—unlike the other Scandinavian girls I've known. She has her hands on me most of the way. Light brushes, taking my arm as I carry her beach bag, touching my cheek one time when I say something clever about a dark-skinned gentleman being chosen for a "random" search.

What little I know about this woman, she's a real off-the-cuff charmer. Since she's been told I'm a social worker, I doubt if she's impressed with my occupation, so it must be my boyish charm.

We don't talk any more until we're in the air. We're seated next to each other, business class, with me on the outside near the aisle and her at the window, in seats that fully recline. To say she makes me a little nervous is an understatement of the first order.

It's going to be a long trip, and it may be hard to keep concentrating on the objective, when senses are assailed by a female of astronomical attraction. It's clear to me what tempted the doctor to stray.

Thank God for Elmore Leonard. I'm glad I'm only halfway through the novel, knowing he will take my mind off the luscious lady at my side, who's to be at my side for days. When I begin reading, a Tangueray martini at seat side, I'm surprised to see her pick a paperback out of the beach bag—not surprised that she reads, but that she reads English. I smile inwardly when I note it's Janet Evanovich she's selected, who writes hilariously about a female bond enforcement agent. I've read all of her stuff except this one. It's all I can do not to inform Sonya that I'm a by-God real in-the-flesh manhunter, not a fictional one. But I manage to refrain . . . having been told by my mother that modesty is a most attractive quality in a man.

I'm pleased to see my travel chum has good taste in fiction, and hope she finishes this one on the trip over, so I can read it on the way back. I may need a good laugh by the time this trip is complete.

Finally, supper service interrupts our reading.

Over some beef dish in a burgundy sauce over rice, and the second martini we're both enjoying, we continue the conversation. By the time we're into the lemon bar dessert, I get up the courage to inquire about something that's been niggling at me. "Dr. Hashim has been separated from his wife for some time."

"Ya."

"Did you . . . were you somehow involved in the divorce?"

"What do you mean?"

"Involved."

"Involved?"

I'm not getting anywhere, so I ask straight out, "Did he leave his wife because of you?"

She laughs demurely, then laughs louder.

The steward comes by and empathetically laughs also. "I'm glad everyone's in a good mood," he says. "Another drink?"

I wave him off. "What's so funny?" I ask, a little miffed as it doesn't seem nearly so far-fetched to me as it obviously does to her.

"He is not inclined dat way," she says, smiling broadly, and this time it's my turn to look incredulous.

"What do you mean?"

"You do not know Mohammad well?"

"No, not well. We've only met twice."

"I am sure he is gay."

I am incredulous. I'm not a homophobe, in fact I have gay friends. It's hard to live in a beach town and not have, as gays in good economic circumstance seem to have great taste in where and how to live. Of course, I've learned in my chosen profession that lowlifes and scum balls are not immune to the swishy life. I've even had my suspicions about Cedric, but then he'll come up with some offhand comment like, "She kicked and scratched and screwed like a rabid Siamese Simian," when relating a ribald story. But I'm astounded, not only because I didn't read it in the good doctor's demeanor, and reading people is a good part of my business, but also because I'm on a very dangerous trip in order to recover children for the gay half of a marriage.

I really don't know how I feel about that. It's going to take a great deal of introspection. Hell, maybe I am a homophobe, if it's going to take so much thought? But I'm not; I'm a live-and-let-live kind of guy. I'm a little frustrated with the thought that this is bothering me so much. I set it totally aside, as she's smiling at me, enjoying the moment far too much. This is the second zinger of this assignment. I'm really hoping it's the last.

"So," I ask, "are they really his children?"

"Of course, many gay men have relationships with a

wife, or haf had with a former wife." She's still smiling. "Did not the court tell you?"

She thinks I've been appointed by the court to go with her to bring the kids back. I sigh deeply, and let her misunderstand. "So, I'm bringing these kids back to a gay man." I shake my head and go on with my dinner, eating in contemplative silence for a while. By the time I'm finished the lemon bar I've decided that it's not my business, it's the court's. So I ask, "Did the subject come up in the divorce?"

"In a fashion, and the judge would not allow any testimony. He said the only thing mattered was if Mohammad was a good father and good provider. And he vas . . . is." She occasionally drops her Ws and replaces them with a V, but normally corrects herself.

"Is he a good father?"

"A very good one, I tink."

"You tink? You think." Hell, she's got me doing it.

"Yes. I *tink* he's a very good father."

I shrug, slug down the last of my martini, and wave the steward over for another. Somehow I think I'm going to need my rest, and three or four martinis might be just the ticket to outsville. As soon as the dinner platters are cleared, Sonya excuses herself to the ladies' room, taking her beach bag along. She has to step over me, and even to momentarily be between those tan legs . . . I have to admit I enjoyed it, and the thought of staying there for most of a night flashed through my mind as I stared at that perfectly rounded and toned backside disappearing down the aisle.

Looking up from my book a few pages later, I see her returning down the aisle, barefoot, wearing a lace-trimmed flannel very pink nightgown, obviously covering nothing but skin as no bra would allow that amount of nipple peak. The nighty's cut six inches above the knee. The sight gives me a weak and breathless moment. She smiles indulgently, steps over me again—patting me on the cheek as she passes, this time causing my heart to skip a beat—retakes her seat, thank God covers herself with a thin blanket, fluffs up a pillow, drops the seat to its full reclining position, and gives me her back.

I wave the steward over again. "I need a headset and another martini. What's the movie?"

"A thriller," he says, gives me the title, and I again thank God as I haven't seen it. "What time is it in Barcelona?"

He thinks for a moment, checks his watch. "Two-thirty P.M. here, ten hours later in Barcelona. It's four-thirty A.M. there."

"So, ten hours' flying time, it'll be two-thirty P.M. when we arrive?"

"Sounds right."

I set my watch, forward so the date will change also, then follow Sonya's example and recline my seat. Out of self-preservation I totally ignore my traveling companion, and by the time the movie's half over, the martinis have done their work.

I awake, realizing I haven't dreamed of or thought much about Oscar. Renewing my promise to him, and silently thanking him for not visiting me in my dreams, I go on to the next most important matter at hand. Coffee.

Barcelona from the air is like any other big port city by the sea, a large port with a lot of streets leading away through commercial and residential areas to industrial ones. I've read all the material Cynthia has provided, but you don't know a city until you've lived there a year, and some are so mysterious you don't know them even then. Barcelona has been ruled by the Spanish, of course, but also the Romans and Moslems and a half dozen others. All those cultures are reflected in its architecture and monuments. I have to believe it's a very mysterious place. It's in the province of Barcelona, on what's known as the coastal area of Costa Dorada, just south of the province of Girona and the coastal area known as Costa Brava, where the Aziz family has one of their homes near a village called Tossa. Girona is a border province with both tiny principality Andorra de Vella and France. Which leaves me the option, escape south through Spain or north through France.

Barcelona is the largest city in either province with a two-million population. And the airport, Barcelona-Prat, is south of the city, and I'll at least get to drive through the old city on the way north. I will not have time to taste its mystery.

Per our e-mail arrangement, Fredrico and Antonio Lizaola meet us at the baggage belt. They recognize me by the black and silver Raiders' cap I'm wearing. Fredrico is as tall as me, but thinner. He sports a proud, if somewhat crooked, Gallic nose, full head of dark hair, and rather a sallow look, but he seems fit. His brother, Antonio, who communicates mostly in guttural grunts, is a little shorter than I am and his nose more pugged than his brother's, but he probably outweighs me by fifty pounds and it doesn't look like fat. He's got the hands of a longshoreman, and scarred knuckles that seem to testify that he's done his share of heavy work, and I don't mean on the docks. His hair is dark but thinning, and he's got a scar from eye to chin on the left side of a slightly pockmarked face. He's no pretty boy. At least once those hands and corncob-size fingers didn't fend off a weapon of some sort . . . probably a broken bottle by the ragged and puckered looks of the scar-line. His most noticeable feature is a lazy eye with sagging eyelid. It makes him look as if he's always questioning what you say.

Both of them seem to speak passable English. With my barely passable California Spanglish, we should get along just fine.

I introduce them to Sonya—now outclassing even the abundance of beautiful women in the sleek modern air terminal in a well-fitted but otherwise modest blue pantsuit and white silk blouse—and she gives me a quizzical look, but keeps it to herself. The boys can't help staring, as even though she's had a very tough trip, she's still stunning, having gotten up well before me to rejuvenate herself in the ladies' room. They should have seen her in the revealing nightgown. I, on the other hand, look as if I've been dragged to Spain behind the 747, flapping in the frigid air all the way. I can tell by Sonya's confused look that she's wondering what an au pair and social worker on a peaceful mission to escort children across the sea need with a couple of obvious toughs, and I don't blame her under the circumstances, considering what she's been told.

I'm going to have to tell her the truth, and soon, but I'm going to wait until just the right time.

The good news is she has only one suitcase; the bad is it's half the size of a Volkswagen Beetle. It's standard black, but with the astuteness of a well-traveled soul, she's plastered a stick-on daisy on each side—easy identification. The hard-shell bag has wheels and a retractable handle, but Antonio doesn't bother, he swings it along beside him as if it were filled with Styrofoam—and I'm damn sure, knowing women, it's not. It's always puzzled me how lace and makeup can weigh like lead.

The boys manage to get her monster-size suitcase and my duffel bag stuffed in the rear of their stubby Spanish, dented and scuffed, hatchback car. Like them, it has more than its share of character lines. They secure the hatch by tying it down with twine.

And, as soon as I tell them where, we're off. Destination, Tossa de Mar on the Costa Brava, only fifty or sixty kilometers north of Barcelona. Before we left Santa Barbara I made a decision, thanks to the travel guide, to use the central Catalan town of Girona as our base of operations, as it's relatively close, and equidistant, to both the mountain house in Andorra and the beach house at

Tossa de Mar. It's the largest city in the area, has plenty of facilities, and more importantly, is only eighty or ninety kilometers from the French border, with Andorra to its northwest and Tossa its southeast.

The first objective is to locate the kids, and the obvious place is either of the two family residences.

As we leave the airport, located south of the city, and move north on a modern four-lane highway, I'm astounded by how much the country looks like the California coast. As we pass through Barcelona, I'm surprised by the amount of graffiti on the walls and buildings. It is a city of intricate old buildings and architecture, but none of them seem immune to the testosterone-driven egos of Barcelona's youth—now I can see where the gangs of east L.A. get their talent. But then we're out of the big city, and the country's even more like California—long river-bottom valleys; rich chaparral-covered hillsides; cliff sides that meet the sea. With the exception that there are stone walls and buildings that look as if the Romans might have constructed them—this countryside was well developed when California was nothing but mud huts. On every hilltop there seems to be a cathedral or castle, or at least a walled village. The meadows are in bloom, and some sort of big red wildflower spots the verdant hillsides.

I can't help getting the impression that it's a nice place for children . . . but so's Santa Barbara.

I'm in the front with Fredrico, who seems the more eloquent and better English speaker of the two. Sonya is stuffed in the backseat with Antonio. As soon as we're well out of the city, safely on A19, Fredrico begins to question me about the mission. "So, who is it you are after, Señor Shannon?"

"Call me Dev. Children. A young boy and girl."

"And what have they done?"

"Nothing. Their father has custody . . . partial custody. Their mother took them out of the U.S., he wants them back, and is legally entitled to have them."

"So, who is the mother, and what brings them to Spain?"

"Paloma Aziz Hashim, she was born here, and her family still lives here." Sometimes it's not wise to tell your associates too much. I should have remembered that. Fredrico stares at me as if I've just turned my head around three hundred sixty degrees, mimicking the lovely wild-eyed child in *The Exorcist*. Then he slowly recoils against the door as if I'm about to spray him with a stream of green vomit.

"Aziz?" he asks.

"So, what about it?"

"Aziz is a very dangerous name in *Catoluna*. In fact, from Barcelona to Marseille." He feigns spitting in disgust, then adds, "Moroccan scum."

I shrug, feigning disinterest, when in fact I'm more than a little fascinated. A "big name" can mean big trouble. "So, big how?"

"Big trouble," he says, parroting my thoughts as if he could read my mind.

"How so?"

"They are the most powerful Moslem family in *Catoluna*. Drugs, how do you say . . . hijacking, even murder. High up in Moslem Mafia."

Zinger number three.

# Chapter 11

Without instruction from me, Fredrico zooms across the right lane without looking back, takes the next off-ramp without bothering to slow down. The high-centered car leans dangerously and I'm white-knuckled, grabbing the armrest.

"I didn't see a sign for Tossa," I say.

"I have talk with brother."

He whips the car off the narrow crossroad and slides to a stop, is out long before the dust settles, waving at his brother to follow.

Antonio unstuffs himself and meets his brother at the rear of the car. I adjust the rearview mirror so I can see what's going on. They argue back and forth for a few moments in machine-gun Spanish, and then Fredrico stomps forward and leans down. "We need talk," he says.

"What is going on?" Sonya asks, but I ignore her and unlimber from the little car, following Fredrico. Antonio stands leaning against the back-hatch with his arms folded in front of his broad chest, making his biceps look even larger than the eighteen inches I've estimated. His saggy eye is studying me quizzically.

But, as usual, he's not talking. It's Fredrico who speaks. "Not enough money."

"We made a deal," I complain.

"Not a deal for going against Aziz family."

"What's such a big deal?"

"Five hundred day, U.S.—"

"That's too much."

"Each."

Now *I feel* like spinning my head three sixty and slimming him with the green stuff. "Bull. We have a deal!"

He shrugs. "We take you to Tossa, you fill up car with petrol; then we leave you. That all you owe."

I study that proposal for a while. I can rent a car, but I can't speak the language well enough to get along, and I sure as hell won't know anyone to hire for the kind of work we may have to do. I sigh deeply, and slightly up the ante by using U.S. dollars. "Three hundred *U.S.* each, bandito."

Antonio and Fredrico chatter back and forth so fast I only catch a couple of words, but one of them is *muerta.* I know enough Spanish to know that means dead. If they're convinced dead is one of the options of this deal, then I'm beginning to understand their reluctance.

Finally, Fredrico turns back to me. "Four hundred a day Euro each. But is final offer."

I again shrug. I don't have much choice. "Don't expect to do much sleeping," I say, my tone obviously disgusted.

"We go," he says, and we pile back in the car.

Even bail enforcement agents can't fly internationally with weapons, so I've come on this trip as clean as a baby's backside—except for a few select items I was positive the home security boys would miss. Now I'm beginning to wonder if I should have made arrangements for something heavy.

As we barrel on down the highway toward Tossa—it's a little disconcerting to look over and see the speedometer reading over one hundred forty and you're in a sardine can, not an SUV or a Porsche; then you remember it's kilometers—I ask, "Will the Aziz family have guards?"

"Yes."

"Armed guards?"

*"Sí."*

I stare out at the passing countryside for a while. Kidnapping will get me a lengthy enough term in a Spanish jail, but armed assault would add a few years. Then again, kidnapping is probably a long enough term that it wouldn't matter if a few years were added, so I ask, "How about us?"

"What do you mean?" Fredrico asks.

Obviously, Sonya has overheard this exchange. Her voice is shrill. "Yes, just what do you mean, Shannon?"

I turn and eye her. This is not the "right time" as I anticipated, but it seems it's the time nonetheless. "Sonya, your employer did not exactly tell you the whole truth. I'm actually a bond enforcement agent—"

"Like Stephanie Plum?" she asks, eyes wide.

That's Janet Evanovich's heroine in the novel Sonya's reading.

"Yes, like Stephanie, only not nearly as pretty."

"And you're not a social worker?"

"Hardly."

The light comes on. "And Mrs. Mohammad does not know we're taking the children."

"Correct . . . this is a quiet project, until she does find out, and then all hell will break loose." The backseat goes silent.

"So," I ask Fredrico, "how about us?"

"I get anything you like, Señor Shannon . . . it only take money. Antonio and I, we will be armed."

I sigh again, seeing more of this deal's profits flying

away. I picture Ben Franklins with little wings, flapping away over the Spanish landscape. What could be worse? Then Sonya again speaks up.

"I am not being paid enough." She's getting right into the swing of things.

"We'll talk about it later, in private," I say, with enough adamancy that she shuts up, but I can hear her hyper-ventilating. She's not happy, I'm not happy, the Lizaola brothers are not happy. I hope somebody, somewhere, is happy. I hope Dr. Mohammad Hashim is happy, the prick.

As we near Tossa, I glance at my watch, see it's cock-tail time, and suggest, "Let's find a tapa bar, and get a *cerveza frío?*"

"That is good," Antonio says from the rear seat. I've finally found his hot button.

"Fredrico, is Aziz more powerful in Spain or France?"

He thinks a minute. "He is very powerful in this part of the Mediterranean, but I would say Spain. In France he has to deal with interests in Marseille."

Then France it is, I think but don't say. I won't again make the mistake of telling my cohorts too much.

We come out of the countryside down a hillside into one of the most charming villages I've ever seen. As we get into the little town, the sea is its backdrop, as is a cliff, a high point with sheer rock walls extending into the azure Mediterranean on the south extreme of a horseshoe bay on which the village rests. A breakwater shelters the harbor and a half mile of white-sand beach. The village's primary industry is fishing—casual fishing by the looks of the boats in the harbor—and wine corks, thanks to the cork oaks covering the verdant hills over-looking an azure bay with hints of turquoise.

What could be better than wine corks as an industry?

The rocky point is wildflower covered and crowned by a walled part of the town, and a stone structure the brochures have informed me is a hermitage, San Teimo, or something like that. Walls with ramparts and towers, the ramparts entwined with bright blooming wisteria and bougainvillea. A pair of cannons peek out from the ramparts, probably a later addition unless the hermitage monks were the kind to take an active part in defending their abode.

Fredrico, with skill only a local could possess, winds through streets hardly wider than the car.

Pedestrians have to flatten themselves against stone walled buildings to let us pass, but do so with a smile. They're happy, even though it appears we're about to squash them into the wall's mortared crevices.

We pop out of a deep ravine darkened by afternoon shadows between two multistoried buildings onto the bay front—and have to squint, as the sky's brilliant and the sand incredibly bright. Across from our bayside road rests a wide beach, covered with sunbathers, and, even though it's late in the afternoon, more of them walk in scanty attire down the narrow boulevard. Across the bay is a lighthouse, built in a time well before electric lights and giant lenses, when they hauled firewood to the top. Part of the beach, unfortunately, has been converted into city parking, and that's where we head.

In moments, each of us is reclining in a webbed chair with a cold beer in hand, sitting on a patio in perfect weather, looking out at a view that may even surpass that of Santa Barbara's and enjoying the spectacle of passing sun-worshipers that's at least as tasty as my hometown's.

Life is good, only occasionally tempered with bad.

"Did you bring a swimsuit?" I ask Sonya.

"I did, but bikini bottoms," she says with a smile, "is all I need on most Costa Brava beaches."

I nod sagely, and say a silent prayer that we'll find time for a little sunbathing. I will be more than happy to take my pocketknife to my jeans and produce the

Oklahoma version of swim trunks. I do have an extra pair of jeans in the duffel.

In order to get my mind off that scene, I glance at my watch. It's four-thirty P.M., which would make it six-thirty A.M. in Santa Barbara, and I decide to call Cynthia, just to check in. It'll serve her right, as she's normally a late riser. I excuse myself and wander across the boulevard to the beach. I call, but Cynthia's not home. In her business, she could actually be working. As soon as the digital wonder of the cell phone system knows where I am, my message indicator shows up on the screen and the phone gives me a little beep. I dial my messages and am surprised to hear Lawanda Lopez, Oscar's lady, her voice panic-laced. "Mr. Shannon, this is Lawanda . . . Lalo. I . . . I've found something that Oscar had. I have to talk to you. I don't know what to do. Please, please call me. No matter what time it is."

So I do. She said anytime. She answers the phone, sleepily, obviously she's in the sack.

"Lalo. Dev Shannon here. What's up?"

"I'm so glad you called. Thank you. I need to talk to you. Can you meet me somewhere later?"

"Lalo, I'm thousands of miles away, on a trip . . . a job. I'll be home inside of a week—"

"Oh, God. This can't wait a week."

"So, what did you find?" There's a long silence. "Lalo?"

"I can't talk over the phone."

"Can the police help—"

"God, no. Don't tell them, don't tell anyone."

"Lalo, I don't know anything to tell anyone. If you can't talk on the phone, then it's got to wait."

Again, there's a long silence. "I thought you were Oscar's friend?"

That twists my gut. "I am, Lalo. I'm also in Europe. I can't just run over even if I want to . . . which I do . . . but I can't. You sure you don't want to tell me—"

"I can't. Call me when you get back." I can hear her begin to cry.

"I will, I promise. As soon as my plane touches down." Then I have another thought. "Lalo. My father sometimes works with me. Can I have him come see you?"

"Is he . . . okay? Can I talk to him."

"He's better than okay. You can tell him anything you can tell me, and he'll help you out, okay?"

"Okay. What's his name?"

"Patrick Shannon. His friends call him Pug."

"Okay, I'll wait for his call."

I ask for her work number, jot it down, and call the old man on his cell. "Pop."

He's been up for hours, knowing Pop as I do.

"I thought you were in Spain?" he asks.

"I am, the wonders of cell phones."

"What's up?"

"Are you out on the *Copper Glee?*"

"Nope, took a day off."

"Good. I need you to do me a favor." I explain the situation, then ring off, knowing Lalo is in good hands.

Wondering what the devil she found, and why it's got her so upset, I return to my table and the fact all the beers are drained, and the tapas eaten.

"Let's go find out what the Aziz family is up to," I suggest.

"Is it far?" Fredrico asks.

"A couple of miles, back the way we came, but on the coast road. I'd like to get there before dark."

"Should the woman go?"

"It's fine this time," I say, "in fact probably better. We're just going to take a look."

"Maybe I should wait," Sonya says, apprehensively.

"No. You'd like to see the seaside, and this place is supposed to be right on the sea."

She rises without further argument.

We drive south along the sea, a small two-lane road right above the ocean. When it cuts inland, I know we're at the spot. There's a point that the road cuts off, and that's the location of the Aziz place, a fenced compound of one large house and two smaller ones, and some outbuildings. The large house is right on the point and none of the buildings can be seen from the road.

Soon we come upon a stone wall, taller than a man, with broken shards of glass implanted in its top, then a wrought-iron double gate protecting a paved lane. No one seems to be at the gate, but then again if he was back in the twisted small oaks that cover the property, he couldn't be seen from the road.

"You're sure this place is guarded?" I ask Fredrico.

"Yes, sure. All the Aziz will be guarded. He has many on his, how do you say . . . payroll."

"Then how do you suggest we check out the place?"

"I have binoculars under seat. The next point, as far into the sea as this one, only a half kilometer across the small bay. We see more of property from there."

After the long plane ride and the cramped car ride, I'm ready to stretch my legs. Sonya elects to wait in the car, and in ten minutes we've hiked through the woods out onto a point just south of the Aziz place, but across a small inlet.

The main house is impressive, perched on a cliff side a hundred feet above the sea. The waves crash below. The smaller houses and outbuildings are scattered among the oaks behind the main house. I borrow the binocs and study the place. You can't see what's going on around the small houses or outbuildings, but the main house has large windows to take in the view, and a patio the size of a tennis court.

A lone woman, an older woman is my guess, is seated on the patio, under a large green umbrella, and seems to be enjoying a snack. This wouldn't be unusual at this

hour in Spain, as the supper meal is usually taken at ten
P.M. or later. A servant checks with her, but returns to
the house. We watch for a half hour, until it grows dark
and the woman goes inside. Then the place seems as
silent and placid as the sea is roiling and wild.

"I have a phone number," I say, but don't want to call
and ask for Paloma. I think it would be better if a
woman's voice was on the line. "Let's go back to the
car."

When we reach it, Sonya is outside the car, leaning
up against it.

I decide the direct approach is best. "I need you to
make a phone call."

"To whom?"

"Paloma, but I don't want you to talk to her, just find
out if she's there."

"No."

"No?"

"No."

I sigh. "I know, it's not in your job description."

"You said we would talk."

"So we will. How about now?"

"Now is fine."

We walk down the road, I glance at my watch and see
it's May 3. It's beginning to get chilly, with the sun
down. We get away from Fredrico and Antonio.

"So," I ask, "what do you want to talk about?" knowing damn well what she wants to talk about.

"I am only paid as an au pair. I am not James Bond,
or even one of the Bond girls. If what I overhear is correct, this could be very dangerous. I love the children
and want them to be wherever is best for them, but if I
am to be in danger . . ."

"So, what's right?"

"Ten thousand dollars."

I manage to look dumbfounded. But in fact, she's

got me over a barrel. All the paperwork shows Sonya as the guardian. I'm screwed without her. I see many, many more Franklins flying away into the clear blue Spanish sky.

"One thousand," I say.

"Take me back to Barcelona," she replies.

Damned Swede must have gone to negotiating school. "Okay, okay, twenty-five hundred, if we get the children."

"Take me back."

"Look, I don't get paid if we don't get the kids. How about five hundred now, and two thousand if we get the kids?"

"Twenty-five hundred now, twenty-five hundred when we get the children."

I sigh as if she were taking the gold out of my fillings. "A thousand now, two thousand if we get the kids."

"Take me back."

"Okay, okay. A thousand now, four thousand if we get the kids." She's not a Swede, she's a bloody Arab rug merchant. She must have learned to negotiate from Paloma Aziz Hashim.

"Two thousand now, three thousand when we get the children."

At least she's thinking positive. "Done. I've got some traveler's checks in my bag. Now will you make the phone call?"

She reaches for the phone. I dial after referring to my notes in my small mission book that fits in my back pocket, and hand her the cell phone.

"Paloma, *por favor?*" she asks in perfect Spanish. I didn't know she spoke the damned language. She's more than just a magnificent butt and beautiful accoutrements.

"No, Señora. *Amiga. Apolonia Alverez.*"

She waits a moment, then smiles and says, *"Gracias,"* and hands me back the phone.

"So?" I ask.

"Traveler's checks?" she asks in return.

"You're a hard case, Apolonia," I say, but head back to the car.

"Dev, what is a 'hard case'?" she asks, tripping along behind.

This time Sonya and I take the backseat, after I've dug the checks out of my duffel bag. As we head back to town, without the Lizaola brothers seeing what's going on in the backseat, I endorse twenty nice fresh American Express traveler's checks over to Sonya Johanson. More Franklins winging away. After she's carefully counted them, she offers, "Paloma and the children are on holiday."

"Not Morocco?"

"No, I don't think so . . . in the mountains."

"Where?"

"That is all the woman said. The mountains."

"I should get my checks back," I threaten.

She smiles, and stuffs them into her ample cleavage.

"Now I really should," I say, but only sigh, then turn my attention to Fredrico, who's driving. "Andorra, Fredrico."

"Andorra?" he asks.

"Andorra," I repeat. "But stop at the Girona Reál Hotel in Girona on the way, so we can check in and clean up."

"One hour, *mas y menos,* to Girona Hotel," he says.

So I lean back to catch up on some sleep, as much as I'd like to enjoy the scenery. But sleep won't come. The heck of it is, I just slept a solid five on the plane.

I've fought this jet lag thing a few times, and it really screws you up. If you fly at night as we did, not long after you arrive it's time to go to bed again.

The bad news is the sun has set and that precludes my enjoying the scenery. So instead, I sit back with my eyes shut and try to figure out all the ways that dealing with the well-connected Aziz family will limit my options.

Severely, I'd guess.

# Chapter 12

Girona, the capital of the province of Girona, is another relic of Roman times. Lying at the foot of the Pyrenees with the coast not far, it's an important crossroads, a meeting place for peoples of different cultures. Sol Goldman would be at home here, as the Jewish community thrives and the town is rife with Jewish tradition. The Romans, Peter the Great, the French, the War of Spanish Succession, and, of course, the Moslems, all left their mark on Girona. I'd love to spend a week here, parked in a café on the banks of the Onyar River, in the shadow of centuries-old cathedrals, watching the folks stroll by while sipping a good red wine.

My guidebook has explained that the Catalonians are a proud people who have fought Spain for their independence more than once, and laments of FREE CATOLAN, written in Catolan of course, still decorate walls from Barcelona north. Four rivers converge here, with Andorra to the northwest, France just kilometers to the north, and Castilian Spain to the south. It's a place that resonates apathy with the rest of Spain now, the country that many Catalonians still feel is their captor. The language is even different from Castilian Spain's.

The Girona Reál is a medium-priced hotel, on Rambla de la Llibertat inside ancient sixty-foot-high stone walls. I would guess the hotel was built just after World War Two. It's a little worn, but will do nicely for our purposes—clean, if not fancy. I hate to have an attendant take the car, as I like to know where it is and how to get to it quickly, but I relent and give the valet the keys. I take two rooms, one with a queen-size bed for the Swede, and one across the hall with two queens. I doubt if the men in this operation will have time to do more than shower, but if sleep becomes an option, then there's room.

The Lizaola boys turn on the TV and zero in on an old *Law and Order* rerun, in Spanish, while I shower and shave. As this is a night op, I don a black turtleneck and black Levis, black lace-up combat boots, pack a small duffel bag with a few specialized items I've managed to get through airline security, carry my light black leather jacket, and am ready to go. I carry the rest of my things in the bag, as I have no idea if we're coming back here. We're ready, except for a couple of items. Fredrico and Sonya have cell phones, and we both take a moment to program each other's number, and Sonya's, into the speed-dial. Then I teach both the boys how to use the pair of Motorola handhelds I've brought. The little radios travel well and without notice, as people now use them to find each other on the beach or in the shopping mall, and mine are the good ones, range over five miles in ideal conditions, earphones if you need privacy, and you can set them to vibrate rather than squeal so you know to listen up.

I knock on Sonya's door, knock again, and again, and she finally answers, dripping, her body wrapped in a towel she has to hold together, her hair wrapped in another. I've written down my cell number and Fredrico's, and hand them to her. "Hang on to these numbers. Can you keep busy here for a while?" I ask, trying to keep my eyes discreet.

"A while?"

"As much as forty-eight hours . . . maybe more. I don't want you to leave the hotel, Sonya."

"Two days? I am in a city . . . a beautiful city . . . and cannot shop?"

"Not outside the hotel, not unless I call and tell you that you can leave."

"That's not fair."

"Fair is not part of the deal." I lower my voice so the Lizaolas, standing down the hall, can't overhear. "If you want the next three thousand, you have to earn it. You may have to leave in a hurry, and I won't have time to sit around here and wait for you to wander in, understand?"

"You'll call, and tell me if I can leave?"

"I'll tell you what, it'll take two hours' driving time to get to Andorra, and we probably won't spot the kids, if they're even there, until morning. I'd rather you had room service, but you can go where you like tonight. But be back here by ten P.M. Wait for my call in the morning before leaving the room, understand?"

"Okay. I saw there's a spa and beauty shop downstairs. My fingernails, and toes." She giggles. "How about if I am there in the morning . . . maybe?"

"The room or the spa, nowhere else. If you go to the spa, tell the desk so they can redirect your calls there."

"Thank you, Dev." She flashes me a devastating smile, reaches up and pats my cheek, and the towel drifts low enough that I know her traveler's checks are somewhere else, but my mind is now on business. I know myself going into an operation, and no matter what earthly charms tempt, I'll be lost in the deal until the kids are safely on American soil. Not necessarily with a Kmart in sight, but at least technically on American soil.

This time I take the backseat, Antonio drives, and Fredrico takes the suicide seat. We work our way out of the city and are soon in the Pyrenees, climbing through a long canyon in the black of night. The road is only two lanes, and should be four, it's plenty busy. Andorra de Vella is the capital of Andorra, and the Aziz Andorran compound is twenty or so miles past the capital city higher in the mountains.

"We need eat," Antonio says.

"In Andorra de Vella," I say, and he grunts in return. "Can we rent another car there?" I ask.

"Of course," Fredrico answers. "It's city. Many cars."

I manage a catnap, as the wheels occasionally squeal and the car is swung out into the passing lane and back. Antonio is a fast driver but a competent one. And it's a good thing, as the road is now not only winding, but high above a river with a deep crevice below. I can tell by the occasional light along the river, that in some places we're at least five hundred feet above the bottom. We only make one stop on the long trip after we've left the valley floor, and that's at the Andorran border. Even with heightened border security all over the world, the Spanish Andorra border is very casual. The guard waves us through.

I'm a little astounded by the traffic as we near Andorra de Vella. It's stop-and-go, the roads jammed with cars, some with Andorran license plates, but many French and Spanish. Andorra is tax free, so the Spanish and French flock there to shop. The stores stay open until ten P.M., but I didn't anticipate this kind of traffic. This could severely impede any kind of fast escape as there is only one main road south to Spain and one north to France.

The trip takes an hour longer than I'd planned.

"Eat," Antonio says in his loquacious manner, as if it's a promise I made written in blood.

"Okay, the first joint that looks good to you," I say.

He finds a place, a one-acre mini version of a U.S. highway truck stop complete with fuel, surrounded not by eighteen-wheelers but by smaller Volvo and Mercedes flatbeds, panel trucks, and vans, and in moments we're at a Formica table with COKE and BEER signs adorning the walls, being waited on by a gum-gnawing brunette with ample hips and well-reddened lips. Had she not been speaking Spanish, I'd have sworn we were in Ohio. I tell Fredrico I'll have whatever he's having, with the exception that I hear him order *cerveza* and call the waitress off on that one with "No, *café negro.*"

But I'm glad I let him order.

The food is straightforward, but laced with little niceties that brings it well above most U.S. truck stop fare. The salad has marinated black olives the size of my thumb, and is topped with a thin slice of ham, like Italian prosciutto. The bread is hard crusted and fresh as Cedric's smart mouth. Second course is a chicken dish, in a sauce heavy with cheese and the same olives, only hot this time, with chunks of boneless chicken served over rice . . . a generous plate full. Dessert is sliced cheese and fruit. If I couldn't sleep before, I probably can now as I leave stuffed, even after a cup of coffee so strong it would float a spoon.

We find Andorra N3 northwest, and I have Fredrico, who's now driving, push the button on the odometer to tell us how far we've traveled, and we're soon climbing again. I've read that one of the main attractions of Andorra, other than the tax-free shopping, is the skiing, and now we're ascending deep into mountains seemingly as formidable, and intimidating, as the Rockies.

A wave of fatigue hits me, but I'm forced to ignore it as I'm particularly interested in this section of road, the last thirty or so kilometers to the Aziz compound. If we snatch the kids at or near the Aziz home place, we'll be forced to come back down this road, as the road west peters out in the mountains a few kilometers beyond the turnoff to the Aziz place . . . and that's a tough one. One way out, down a dangerous road, with two little precious packages in the car.

I've not only got to get the kids out, but I've got to get them *safely* out. I couldn't forgive myself if anything happened to them. The execution of this mission has to be perfect.

I try and note every side road and turnout as we proceed, but it's truly dark as the moon is not up yet. This will only be a recon mission, so I'll make it a point to come back down the mountain in the light.

To my surprise, my cell phone rings. I check my watch as I answer, and note it's ten P.M., but only noon California time.

To my additional surprise, it's Sol Goldman, my biggest client before Dr. Hashim came along.

"Dev, my boy."

"Sol, what's shaking?"

"Actually, my lad, I am."

"Lenny's on the lamb?"

"Exactly. He didn't show up in court this morning. It's a five-hundred-thousand hit for me, so, my lad, you have to make this one happen."

"Sol, I'm in Andorra."

"Andorra? Where the devil is Andorra?"

"Between Spain and France. A child recovery."

"My God! That Andorra! Oy vey! How soon will you return?"

"Hopefully by the end of the week."

"I am forced to call upon others?"

"Sol, we can get my father and his crew to work on it. You remember we used them on the Prescott matter.

We had him snagged in three days, remember? I'd be using them if I was there, and I can keep in touch by phone until I return. If they find him before I get back, they are perfectly capable of picking him up."

"I don't know—"

"Trust me, Sol. Pug was thirty years a dick with the Santa Barbara P.D. and a real bloodhound; Cedric is my computer guru and can digitally find anyone anywhere; and Iver is enough muscle to take down a dozen Lenny Haroldsterns and all his cousins . . . and the brains to know when to use it."

"You are sure you can handle this from there . . . bet-your-mother's-good-name-on-it sure?" Sol's voice gets a little maudlin, and somewhat strained, a tone I've never heard from him. He's always the apex of positive. "Dev, my boy, I cannot stand a half-million-dollar hit."

"Didn't you cover it with collateral?" I ask, astounded that he'd risk that amount.

"Not all. He put up a condo, even brought me a recent appraisal, which should have covered three hundred thousand of my exposure, but it appears the young man altered the report and the property is worth only two hundred. It's amazing what you young people can do with computers these days. I guess I am getting too old for this business, and maybe a little greedy this near to retirement."

"I can recommend some other guys, Sol, but I trust my team more than anyone I can refer you to."

"That is good enough for me, my boy. I'll send the contract to your address?"

"Cedric is getting my mail, but you know we won't wait. I'll get on the phone to them as soon as I hang up."

"Don't let me down, Dev, my boy. If you do, old Uncle Sol will be moving on board your boat and you will be caring for him in his old age."

"That's all I need, a live-in kosher cook."

As soon as I hit the kill button, I'm dialing my old man again. But the damn phone craps on me.

"Turn around," I command Fredrico.

"We have only gone twenty kilometers. You said thirty."

"The phone's out of range, and I have to make a call."

"It will not wait?"

"Turn around, Fredrico. We'll only have to retrace a mile or so. Poke the button again and clear it, and remember where we are, so we can pick up where we're leaving off."

It is four miles back down the road before I'm able to get through. If I ever see that guy on TV who harps, "Can you hear me now?" I'm going to clock him one. I'll never understand the magical wrath of cell phones. I don't find the old man at home, but do get through to him on his cell phone, and quickly get Pug lined out, telling him there's a hundred-grand fee at stake, as much as I stand to make from the Hashim deal, and that there's a quarter of it for him that he can split with Iver and Cedric any way he likes.

As soon as he can get a word in, he stops me cold.

"I visited with Lawanda Lopez . . . just left there."

"And, the mystery is?"

"Mexican brown, two kilos, nicely wrapped as if it just landed from Tijuana or Thailand. I have it in the rear seat. You know, I have to turn this over to the Paso P.D."

"Lieutenant Paul Antone. Why didn't the lady call the cops?"

"I worked with Antone one time . . . good guy. Lawanda was worried about Oscar's memory. Just wanted to protect him, and knew you'd know what to do. I didn't disillusion her on that one."

I let that slide, and he continues. "I'm on my way there now. I told her the P.D. would have a few questions for her, for her to tell the truth and that she had absolutely no knowledge of the drugs."

"Okay. Thanks, Pop. I can't tell you how much this surprises me."

"You can't second-guess people, son. Cedric told me only yesterday, 'Support bacteria, it's the only culture most people have.' "

# Chapter 13

Sons and fathers. I guess it's the same with everyone. "I think you've given me about that same advice a time or two, Pop. But not Oscar. He wasn't the sharpest knife in the silverware drawer, but he was a straight arrow."

"Yeah, and a friend of yours, an old marine buddy. Your judgment may be clouded by green fatigue. You need to shine up your rose-colored glasses. That advice I've been giving you for more than thirty years, it's still good."

I don't want to argue at a buck fifty a minute, or hear another metaphor with a color in it. "Keep me up to speed on this," I say.

My mind must be an easy read.

"How the hell much does it cost me to call you in Spain?"

"It's a local call for you, Pop, remember, you dialed 805. But it costs me like hell, so let's get off this money-muncher."

"Bye."

And we're turned around and back up the road to recon the midgets.

It's another half hour before I find the turnoff.

There's a small but elegant sign, a brass plaque set in stone, it reads NIDO DEL ÁGUILAS. Eagle's Nest. The road to Eagle's Nest is little more than one lane.

We turn up the road, travel a winding mile in a narrow canyon, and are stopped by another set of tall wrought-iron gates flanked by a stone wall not unlike the one at Tossa. This set has a tiny stone house just beyond. A few sparks drift up out of the chimney so someone must be home, and the lights come on as we stop. There must be some kind of alarm, probably a pad in the road or a laser beam across it, because the Lizaola car is quiet, if less than elegant, and we've made little sound.

A man appears in a few seconds, carrying a double-barreled shotgun as if he's very comfortable with it. I've always admired Spanish doubles, but not when they're aimed my way, even if casually so.

Fredrico is out of the car in a heartbeat, his hands plainly at his sides. He chatters with the man, shrugging his shoulders more than once, and then both of them are pointing on up the main highway and Fredrico is nodding. Then he returns and slides in.

"Learn anything?" I ask.

"The way to Merenges, on up the road."

"Okay, so we go back down the road, find a place to park, and proceed on foot."

"Antonio bad leg. You and I on foot. Antonio stays with car."

I shrug. It's a job I could do alone. I don't plan to tangle with the Aziz guards, so it doesn't matter. But then things don't always go as planned, so it might matter. I think for a moment, then instruct Fredrico to leave his phone with Antonio, as we may need him to pick us up somewhere else along the road. But of course the phone doesn't work this far out of town, so I set the Motorola radios to channel 6.1, listen for a moment to make sure no one's chattering on that airway, and hand the radio to Antonio.

We find a flat spot not a half mile back down the road and are able to pull the car into the woods. It's dark, but we think it can stay there unseen from the road. Antonio is snoring before we're out of the car.

I'm a little shocked by the cold, and now wish I'd brought something stuffed with goose down to wear, but Fredrico is dressed light, so I'll have to tough it with my leather jacket.

He reaches under the seat, retrieves and shoves a Spanish automatic into his belt, nicely blued and better in the dark than something stainless. I'm feeling a little naked in that department. He has a carry light, but I'm better prepared there, as I fish my headlamp out of the duffel and fit it over my black fisherman's knit cap. My belt comes off and I detach the buckle, which allows me to slip thirty inches of piano wire out of the belt's length. As I always remove the belt with its heavy buckle before going through the metal detector at the airport, this one's never been challenged. It's a garrote, a restraining device, although I always try and carry plastic cable ties—or even better duct tape, which works as well as handcuffs—and anything else for which you need a short piece of wire. It has fittings on each end that screw on and off, giving you some purchase when handling it, and the ends also screw together, making a fine restraint. Godzilla couldn't break the thing.

Fredrico looks a little surprised when I fish a travel-size can of Gillette Foamy—a very special can made just for me by some friends in the movie special-effects biz—out of the duffel and fit it into a loop and attach it to the belt.

"You plan shave?" he asks.

"Nope, I might have to pepper-spray a bear, however."

"Aw, very good. Aziz hires men the size of bears."

Also I clip my folding knife onto the belt. Its blade is only three and a half inches, which I used to be able to carry on board a flight, but now it has to ride in the checked luggage. It's an SOG of the finest German steel with one side of the blade serrated—it'll cut through a half-inch iron bolt—and with a cast-aluminum-machined handle that sports a small compass and a spot for an eighth-inch-diameter magnesium rod that can be removed and scraped with the knife to get a pile of highly flammable shavings to quickly start a fire. The knife has an assisted opener, and with a touch of the thumb, one-handed, the blade snaps and locks in place in a millisecond. A small but powerful uniscope goes into my pocket. It's variable from 2 power to 10, and much less bulky than binocs.

Had this been closer to home, I would have had my night-vision equipment, but it can be hard to explain to the customs people entering some countries, and I'd decided to get along without its help.

Fredrico, his heavy binocs around his neck, leads the way until he finds he has to use both hands to climb, and my hands-free headlamp works better than his carry light, so I take the lead. We move up well above the road, and it's a half mile through the underbrush before we come face-to-face with the stone wall. Only a few yards above where we find it, I discover by focusing the beam to spotlight mode, the wall disappears into a vertical cliff face. We move up higher against the cliff and are able to easily scale the wall at that point.

I'm silently singing the praises of Browning boots as the rock is sharp and steep. Lesser boots would be history after a couple of miles of this, and I figure that's about what we'll have to travel before getting in sight of the compound.

We top a rise and see it in the distance, still higher above us, a single strong mercury yard light illuminating stone structures. As we get closer, we come upon the road again, and it's a good thing as it's cut into a cliff side that climbs almost vertically above, and drops away below to what I can now hear is a tumbling creek.

As we begin to move up the road, and it appears we're only about three hundred yards from the compound, I stop and bend close to Fredrico's ear. "Remember the alarm in the road below. There are probably more devices. We need to get off the road as soon as possible."

He looks up at the cliff, and shrugs. "Where?"

"As soon as possible," I say, and continue up the road.

I find a small ravine, and begin to climb, jamming my hands into cracks and fissures as I learned in a couple of rock climbing classes I've attended. It's only fifty feet or so to the top of the cliff, and we manage it smartly. Now we're horizontally even with the compound. A few feet higher and we're in the chaparral and cover, and can see into the lighted courtyard.

"What now?" he asks.

I'm not about to try and penetrate the compound when I don't even know if the kids are there. "We wait for dawn."

"That's three or four hours," he says.

"So?"

"So, I sleep," he says, moving deeper into the undergrowth.

"So, sleep. I'll keep watch."

I doze, but don't really sleep. Most of the time, I'm moving about, uncomfortable in the cold. I spend a good while cursing my chosen profession, which seems exciting to the uninitiated, when in fact it's months of boredom peppered only lightly with moments of sheer terror. Still, my motto is no rest until the arrest.

Finally, I see the sky begin to lighten. Noting that I can see my breath in the cold, I shake Fredrico awake. "We need to make sure we're out of sight."

We move higher on the hillside, to a spot where we're completely hidden by the undergrowth, and wait for full light.

Why does predawn always have to be the coldest time of the night? We're now forced to remain stone still, as it's no time to be seen from the compound, only a hundred yards from our roost. And of course, when the sun finally does touch on the buildings, we're in the shade of the cliff side above and it'll be another two hours before we warm up.

I'm not so cold I don't take time to admire Henri Aziz's taste. The location of his house is nothing less than magnificent, at the top of a deep pass with views to the north and south—fabulous views of mountains that I now realize are snowcapped. A three-foot-wide waterfall comes off the mountain to the west, across from our perch, and forms a pond that's inside the compound; then its resulting creek turns in a steep ninety just before it reaches the house and tumbles out and under the wall, crashing down the ravine below the road. Pines line the mountains above the house and oaks grace the hillside. There are probably few places in the world prettier than this.

But we don't have to wait long in the cold. In less than an hour, seven-thirty by my watch, the courtyard comes to life. An automatic garage door opens in one of the outbuildings and a long black limo emerges. I fish out and snap open my little telescope, focusing on the courtyard.

About the same time the front door of the main house opens, and an older man escorts two small children out onto the portico. Another man, a no-neck type in a suit and porkpie hat, rounds the building and is spoken to by the older man. No-neck nods obediently, opens the door for the children, who are kissed and hugged by the older man before they enter the car, and then No-neck closes the door and joins the driver, a thin sallow-faced type in standard chauffeur's uniform, in the front.

"Henri Aziz," Fredrico says quietly in my ear, "the old man, boss of bosses."

We cannot move, as the courtyard has a clear view of our perch, and the children, Arty and Gigi, are disappearing down the driveway. Again I get a glimpse of Franklins winging their way into the stratosphere . . . as there's no telling where the children are off to. Maybe an airport and Morocco, although I didn't see any luggage.

We wait until the courtyard is clear of life, then break for the ridge forty yards away, which will put us out of sight of the courtyard. We reach it and scramble over some rocks, but I turn and see the same old man out of the house, and looking our way. Then he spreads his arms wide, yawns, and heads for an outbuilding.

"He see?" Fredrico asks.

"Don't think so."

We're out of sight of the compound, but will have to go in and out of sight a couple of times before we have to climb the mountain to clear the guard station. As soon as I think we've got a chance, I get on the radio. "Antonio." Nothing. We move farther down toward the car, with me calling every ten steps. Finally, my radio crackles, and Antonio's voice comes through loud and clear.

"*Sí.*"

"Where the hell you been?" I ask, then regret doing so as the only thing that's important is that he follow the limo.

"You got to push this little ting," he says, rather sheepishly.

"Yeah, you got to push the thing. Did the limo pass?"

"Limo?"

"The big black auto? *Auto negro?*"

"*Sí.*"

"Follow it." I hand the radio to Fredrico. "Tell him."
He looks at me inquisitively. "Without us?"

"Yes. We have to know where the kids are going."

He chatters at Fredrico, then hands me the radio. "So. What about us?" he asks.

"We walk, or hitchhike, until we can make phone contact with Fredrico or call a cab or some damn thing."

Antonio shrugs, then talks to himself as we move out. *"Loco Americano,"* he says, then what I presume are a string of Spanish expletives. I'm just as happy that I don't understand the rest.

We clear the guard station with no problem and make the main road. Fredrico manages to conceal the automatic in his coat, and I hide my paraphernalia, using my knit cap as a haversack. We only have to walk a mile before a farmer in a flatbed truck, with sideboards four feet tall, stops and offers us a ride—in the rear with two pigs, a half dozen sheep, and a sheepdog who seems to question our intent. Most of the trip down the mountain she has her lips curled and is growling like a wronged woman.

It's fifteen or sixteen miles down the road before our benefactor puts us out, having to make a turn. I've managed to reach Antonio, but decide we'll go ahead and take advantage of the farmer's kindness rather than call Antonio off his vigilance.

The kids are at school, a private school on the outskirts of Andorra de Vella, Escuela del Reyes. School of the Royals, which figures. The limo has dropped them off, very carefully seeing that a school employee has taken them safely in hand, waiting to pull away until the children were inside, then disappeared up the road. Antonio, I'm happy to say, has not been made as a tail, and stayed close by where he can observe the school. This is too good to be true, as every school day the limo will be bringing them down the mountain, then picking them up and taking them home, if logic prevails. Of course, logic is the result of conclusion, and conclusion, if Cedric's logic is correct, is merely the place where you stop thinking.

Antonio and I walk another quarter mile, both of us smelling a little like pig dung, a sharp and particularly sour and unpleasant odor. We find an inn with several rooms, and make our way across the parking lot to the office, borrow a phone book, and I have Fredrico call us a cab. It takes thirty minutes, but then we're off to Avis.

I get my first real look at the city of Andorra de Vella. It's an amazing place, with at least a dozen high-rise construction cranes in sight from any given location. I've never seen so much activity in a city, new building everywhere, remodeling everywhere, and in the midst of all this activity, a grand old city with regal buildings of stone. And people. The place is a virtual beehive. And most of them are carrying shopping bags.

I remember in my reading that Andorra was a region fought over by a pair of medieval lords, until they got together and wondered what they were fighting over. It was a rocky high clime with very little productivity, basically a pile of rocks. Goats were about the only thing that proliferated. So, with the encouragement of the locals, they each proclaimed the place free—neither of them would have it, because in fact neither of them really wanted it. The place was more trouble than it was worth. The locals, being no fools, had an agreement drawn between the warlords, and as soon at they had a copy in hand hurried off to the ultimate power of Europe at the time, the pope. With the pope's endorsement, the agreement was steadfast, and neither of the feuding lords would dare violate it. Warring with each other was one thing, warring with the pope completely another. The kicker was, taxes were deemed the privilege of the royals, and the lords had put in a provision that the locals could never levy taxes. What was a bane in medieval times became a boom in modern ones. No taxes. People flocked to the place. And still do.

In another thirty minutes, my Amex cleared, and in record time I'm behind the wheel of a shiny black four-door Mercedes S340 sedan. It's fast, and good in the turns, can easily hold four, and the backseat is child-proof. When the doors are locked, they can't be opened from the rear, and the windows have a child switch and can't be lowered, unless the driver wishes it so.

While we're waiting, I take the time to call Sonya, find her in the beauty shop getting those toes prettied up, and give her a three-hour reprieve. She's happy as a woman with two thousand dollars to spend and a beautiful European city in which to spend it can be.

I ask her to get a pad and pencil, and give her instructions regarding the next twenty-four hours, then ask her to read them back to me. This operation will get very tight from now on, and timing will be of the essence.

I chastise her before I hang up. "Remember, only three hours, then be back in the room."

Then I set out on another quest. It takes almost an hour, but I find the Andorran equivalent of Ryder Rent-a-Truck, and we leave with me driving the Mercedes and Fredrico behind the wheel of another Mercedes, only this one is a twenty-eight-foot, fully enclosed, eight-foot-wide, and nine-high, furniture van . . . big enough to park the S340 in its rear.

We find a place to park the truck, and Antonio climbs into the black Mercedes to give me a hand with translation, although I've been told that English is a second or third language for many Andorrans.

A few more shopping chores, and I'm ready. The first, a change of clothes for the children, is easy enough, except for a bachelor guessing the size of a six-year-old girl and an eight-year-old boy. I end up with sweatsuits, or jogging suits, or whatever one calls them for children.

Spider-Man is the mode of Arty's, and some teddy bear motif for Gigi. I buy two each, exactly the same.

We make a stop at a hardware store and a minimarket.

Now for the tough one.

This one takes us two and a half hours, and some real talent on the part of Fredrico, and almost five hundred dollars U.S. on my part, and most of our time is spent in alleys behind stores and shops, but finally, thanks to a dishonest store employee, we're ready.

To Fredrico's credit, he doesn't ask me if I'm crazy when I buy what I buy, but finally does ask, "What are they for?"

"My secret weapon," I tell him.

# Chapter 14

Now, it's Escuela del Reyes with only one more chore to perform on the way. It's more difficult than I imagined, but we finally find an abandoned gravel pit with a ramp that will serve.

We find the school after a little back road searching, and it's impressive. Two stories of stone, probably a two-hundred-year-old building. Even though that's a teenager by European standards, it's impressive to me. Centered on the building's facade is a pair of stone lions guarding the entrance, which is a twenty-pace-wide set of marble stairs leading ten risers up to a pair of doors emblazoned with gold and silver, all under a portico with Corinthian columns. A fountain graces the portico, half under and half out of the covered area, with a pair of dolphins spouting water. Below the fountain and lining the circular driveway are a profusion of flowers, even though it's early at this altitude.

The building is well over a hundred yards long, with a soccer field on one end and a swimming pool on the other. Both devoid of children at the moment. Twenty tall windows in the lower story and twenty matching in the upper penetrate the stone walls on each side of the entry. Over the portico is a stone relief of a battle of some kind, knights on horseback.

There are no other buildings for a quarter mile in any direction, and the ones beyond are much smaller, seeming to be residences.

Escuela del Reyes is very, very impressive. More impressive than the security man who wanders around under the portico, in uniform, unarmed, occasionally yawning.

We pick Antonio up, surprised to see us in the black Mercedes.

"You steal?" he asks.

"No, I rent," I answer, with equal succinctness.

We park down the block, not so far away that we still can't see the front of the school.

I lay out the plan for them. And repeat it, and repeat it again, until they're mouthing their individual parts in the scheme of things.

We go fetch the truck.

It seems there's only one way up to the school, a narrow lane, winding through the woods. There are several houses around, but they're sparse, and interspersed with meadows and groves of trees. We find a track of a road that's seemingly unused, leading back into a copse that is thick right down to the road's edge, and Antonio takes the wheel of the truck and backs it into place.

Glancing at my watch, I figure we have at least an hour's wait, if the private Escuela del Reyes keeps the same hours as Spanish public schools. I make sure the radios are set on the proper channel, listen to them for a while to again make sure no one is clogging up 6.1, then take Fredrico with me and drive another half mile down the lane away from the school.

We don't have long to wait, as the black limo passes, No-neck again in the passenger seat, and the same hollow-cheeked driver.

"Count ten, and pull out," I say into the radio.

Dead silence.

"Antonio."

"*Sí*, have to push to talk," he says.

"Count to five now."

I wheel the Mercedes out onto the lane and follow the limo at a discreet distance.

It's good when a plan comes together, particularly when working with a guy who has to give some thought to "push to talk."

The big furniture truck wheels out directly in front of the limo, completely blocking the narrow lane. Before Antonio can get the truck stopped the limo driver is blowing the horn. He's stopped only a few feet from the truck. We pull up behind the limo, pinning the big car between us, and act as if we're waiting patiently.

Antonio gets out and moves to lift the hood on the truck, shrugging his shoulders at the limo as he heads that way, feigning engine problems.

The limo driver remains behind the wheel, but No-neck unloads, obviously miffed, rounds the hood of the big limo, and heads for Antonio. He makes a fatal mistake, leaving the limo door open. A good security man would never have left his driver vulnerable.

Seeing this, Fredrico steps out of the Mercedes and closes on the open door, just as No-neck reaches Antonio, and, being a fiery Spainard, gives him a shove. I, too, open the door and put one foot out, ready to move. Fredrico and No-neck are equally matched under normal circumstances, both Goths from a former time, but No-neck suddenly goes reeling backward, stumbling and falling to the ground, withering in pain and screaming like a grizzly as Antonio gives him the full force of the pepper spray, directly in the face.

Antonio is standing there with a stupid grin on his face, Gillette Foamy in hand, enjoying the ease with which he's dispatched No-neck, when the driver's door flies open and Sallow-face jumps out dragging a shotgun behind him before Fredrico can get in the passenger side and put the automatic in his ear.

I move quickly, round the door, and just as Sallowface raises the weapon—the grin is gone from Antonio's mug and even his saggy eye is open wide—am able to kick his knees out from under him and give him a couple of chops to the neck as he goes down.

He's let go with both barrels of the shotgun and the report echoes through the canyon.

But the shots have gone high.

I kick the shotgun away, spinning into the ditch by the road. He's still trying to get on his feet, so I save my hands, having broken them once too often, and give him a combat boot to the side of the head, bouncing his noggin off the limo side panel. This seems to do the job, as he slumps, unmoving.

I look up to see Antonio, white as the truck he's standing beside, patting his face to see if he's received a face full of buckshot. Then he picks something off his forehead, walks over, and hands it to me. "What this?"

I laugh. "The wad, out of the shotgun shell. You got off cheap."

The three of us gather them up and load them in the back of the truck, No-neck still screaming and rubbing his eyes. Then I roll the door down and lock it.

They're secure for the moment, and we've gained a shotgun. The only damage is a good-sized dent in the limo door, where Sallow-face's head bounced off the side panel.

Another car, a white BMW four-door, has come along behind, but when the action starts, it almost runs off the road trying to execute a speeding reverse turn. It careens out of sight by the time Antonio has backed the truck off the road, and Fredrico and I have donned No-neck's and Sallow-face's chapeaus. Mine, as driver, the standard military bill cap in basic black, and Fredrico's a porkpie in plaid. We're stylin'.

In a flash Antonio is wheeling the truck back down the road, and Fredrico and I are in chauffeur and guard mode, heading for school. When we arrive, kids are pouring off the soccer field, heading for the building. As planned, I park directly in front of the school, under the portico. Fredrico unloads, opens the passenger door casually, then heads up to chat with the security man, still standing under the portico, still yawning.

We're operating under the presumption that the security man does not know all the men employed by Aziz, and there's a tense moment when Fredrico engages him in conversation, but he seems unperturbed.

Our wait is short, and it's a good thing, as I can hear a faint siren in the distance. A few other cars are already there, waiting, and one of those small twenty-passenger buses, like hotels use to pick up patrons at the airport—except this one is painted bright yellow and bedecked with enough lights that it resembles a fire engine—ESCUELA DEL REYES painted on its side in black lettering.

Kids begin pouring out of the double doors, now propped open. A matronly lady with well-coifed gray hair exits the building, Arty holding one hand, Gigi the other. She walks gracefully down the wide staircase, circles the fountain, and heads straight for the limo. To my chagrin, she lets go of the children just before reaching the car, and looks about, I presume searching for No-neck.

But Fredrico is close behind them, and when he sees her look inside the limo, see me, and straighten as if she's been goosed, he gathers up a child under each arm, sweeps her aside using the kids to do so, and throws them into the back, following them in, slamming and locking the door behind them.

Little Arty yells something in Spanish, then starts swinging at Fredrico, who grabs his wrists, only to have the boy begin kicking him.

"Go," he yells as he's subduing the child, and I spin

the wheels. I'm at the first turn, and take it, then come to the road we'd backed the truck into, which now shelters the black Mercedes rental, and swing the limo in, having to take a couple of small trees out in order to pass the Mercedes and get the limo well enough inside the copse so it's not seen from the road. It's a good thing I do so, as I can see a police car fly up the school road behind me, siren blaring, lights flaring.

In moments, we've unloaded the kids, Arty still kicking and screaming, and are in the Mercedes, turning back down the lane the way the cop car came up. All this time, Arty's fighting and Gigi is yelling at the top of her little lungs.

This is not exactly how I'd envisioned it, but it'll have to do.

We wheel the Mercedes down the lane and inside of five minutes are back in the traffic of Andorra de Vella, and in ten we're at the assigned place just outside of town, the unused gravel pit that has a timber-rimmed dirt loading ramp. Antonio has the truck backed up to the ramp.

With Gillette Foamy in hand, and Fredrico backing me up with the automatic, I open the truck door. Sallowface is a little angry, and charges me, only to get a shot of the pepper spray and go to his knees. No-neck is a little more subdued, having already had a taste of the Foamy. I tell him to turn around and get on his knees, and Fredrico repeats the order. He does so and I bind his wrists behind him with plastic cable ties that are standard fare for my kit, but these I picked up at an Andorra de Vella hardware store. When both of them are wrist bound, we blindfold them, lead them out of the truck, and shelter them behind the ramp so they can't be seen from the road. We bind their ankles, then tie them together at the ankles. There's no way they can get to their feet, unless one of them drags the other along. And there's no way they can get the license of the Mercedes, even if they may remember from earlier that it's a black one.

With the kids in the car, I drive up the handy ramp and easily load it into the truck, with Fredrico to drive the big van and leaving Antonio with having to make his own way back to town, only a mile or so, to call a cab and go pick up their hatchback, which is still parked not far from the school. It's the most dicey part of the op, but I can't imagine the bad guys already making the hatchback as hostile.

The truck fires up and rumbles away.

I've not had a chance to say a word to the kids, and Gigi is still wimpering. So I try and console her.

"Hi, Gigi. I'm Dev. We're going to see your dad."

"Papa," she manages between sobs.

"My father is in California," Arty says adamantly.

"Yes, Arty, he is. You remember Sonya—"

"Where is Sonya?" he demands.

"She's going to meet us, down the road a ways. Then we're all going to get on the airplane and go meet your father."

"It's too dark," Gigi says, the only light in the back of the truck coming in from vent holes over the cab. She's right, it's too dark, something I hadn't planned on. It's damned hard to think of everything on short notice.

"You stink," Arty says.

"I took a walk in the barnyard," I offer. The fact is, pig dung is tough stuff.

I decide to be magnanimous and ignore the insult. "Do you want a Coke, or some candy?"

She sobs again. "I want my *abuelo.*"

"Your grandpa?" I ask, trying to remember my Spanish.

"Yes," Arty says. "My grandfather is a very important man, and you're in very much trouble."

"Seems to be my lot in life," I say. "Now, how about that Coke?"

Arty relents. "I will have a Coke." Seeing it must be okay, Gigi does likewise and I pop the top on two of the canned Cokes out of the six-pack I bought at the mini-market, and hand them into the backseat. Then I realize that Gigi has only said she wants her grandpa. So I ask, "So, where's your mother?"

"In Morocco," Arty says, "seeing her uncle, and seeing if we want to live there," then burps after taking a long draw on the Coke. "How long do we have to be held prisoner in this truck?" he asks. He's a smart kid for eight.

"We'll be in here about two hours, and then we can come out."

"I want to be out now."

This kid knows his own mind and is not bashful about stating it. We continue to chat, him accusing, me making excuses, as the truck heads north, swinging and swaying on the curvy road. After a while, I check the phone to see if we're in range, but we're not. I need to make sure Sonya is at the hotel, and knows Antonio is on his way, if he made it back to the hatchback, and if he was able to slip away from the school.

It's the better part of an hour before we stop. Fredrico has warned me that we'll stop, or at least be considerably slowed down at the border crossing into France.

"Where are we?" Arty asks.

"Just stopped for a minute," I say, keeping my voice low.

"Help! Help!" Arty yells.

He thinks he knows why I've lowered my voice, and screams at the top of his lungs. I spring over the seat and get a hand over his mouth as he's into the third "help." A real smart kid.

Gigi picks up on it, and she too begins to scream. Now I'm astraddle the console, wedged between the bucket seats, a hand covering each of their mouths, trying not to hurt them, but having to keep them quiet.

We edge forward a car length, and I realize that we're in a line coming up to the border crossing. I let them go long enough to climb over the seat and get between them.

"Arty," I explain, "we are maybe a quarter mile from the guard shack, and your yelling is doing you no good, only making me mad, and I don't want to have to clock you one." I shake my fist at him. Not that I would, but he doesn't know that. "So you keep your mouth shut, understand?"

He folds his arms in front of his chest and stares straight ahead. "When are you gonna let us go?"

"When I get you to your father."

"My grandfather will send people to come and get us. People who are bigger and tougher than you are."

"That's your father's problem. They can deal with him. My job is to get you back to your father."

"You'll be sorry," he says.

I decide to change the subject. "I bought you something."

"What? A Gameboy, I hope."

"No, not a Gameboy. Some clothes. Check them out in the sacks on the floor."

I can hear the sacks rattle, then, "I hate Spider-Man."

"Figures," I mumble. "Change anyway."

"I don't have to."

"Yes, you do. And help your sister change."

"Pretty," I hear Gigi say as Arty helps her. At least I've made one of them happy with my choice. Batting .500 is good enough for the major leagues.

In a few minutes, the truck speeds up again, and I presume we're through the border station.

I return to the front seat and pick up the Motorola. "You're clear of the border?"

"*Sí,*" Fredrico replies. "As soon as we are down off the mountain, I will stop where we can unload the car."

I picked the black Mercedes at Avis only because

they didn't have a white one, as white ones are even more common in Andorra than black. Common is what I wanted. Even most of the taxis are Mercedeses. It seems every fifth car in Andorra is a Mercedes, so I hope we'll be hard to spot. I glance at my watch. It's four-thirty, an hour and a half has passed since we snatched the kids. Now, if we can just get rid of the truck.

The truck came with ramps, which are hanging on brackets on the truck's side, but I wonder if they're not at too steep an angle to unload a vehicle. If we don't find a ramp, which is unlikely, then we'll just have to dump the damn thing. Hopefully, without injury to the vehicle, as I have plans for it.

I feel the truck leaving the road, bouncing across a field. When it stops, I'm at the roll-up door by the time Fredrico reaches it.

He rolls up the door, and I squint in the sunlight; then I realize my mistake. I left the keys. The Mercedes roars to life.

My jaw drops, and then with a call to action I leap out of the truck before I get run over, pulling the door down as I do so, just as I hear tires squeal. I'm barely clear of the rear end of the truck when the Mercedes slams into the rear door, bending it six inches outward. Closed doors don't seem to concern Arty. Then the tires squeal again, and it slams into the front of the truck body, then again, and slams into the back. It's now ballooning a foot out. The damned little brat's been watching too many action-adventure movies.

Wham! He hits the front again, then the back. The smart little twerp, he's pretty damned worldly for eight years old.

I look at Fredrico, wondering if he's got any ideas, but get his normal shrug.

"I guess you should have take keys," he says.

"No shit, Sherlock," I say, as the Mercedes hits the front, then the back again. This time, the roll-up door flies away, but the car doesn't have enough momentum to make it all the way out of the truck, and with a crash and boil of dust, it's high-ended with its front end up on the truck bed and its rear bumper on the ground. The back wheels barely touch the dirt because of the angle, and no matter how hard little Arty tries, the wheels only spin. I walk over to the driver's window, and realize he's on the floor, working the shifting lever in the center console with one hand, and the gas pedal with the other.

Little Gigi is in the backseat, screaming in a good banshee imitation. Both of these kids, as well as their captor, are going to need the services of their psychiatrist father by the time this is over. And I had high hopes not to even frighten them.

"Arty," I call out over the racing engine and spinning wheels. Of course the door is locked. He can't hear me, so I knock on the window, bruising my knuckles almost as much as my black-and-blue ego.

Finally I get his attention and the car engine stops racing. He climbs up awkwardly into the driver's seat, now an upward-pointing V.

"What?" he asks, his nose almost against the window.

"You're stuck, Andretti."

He shrugs, and I have to presume he has no idea who Andretti is. Shrugging must be a national pastime.

"Open the door," I command.

The kid actually gives me the finger. An eight-year-old has flipped me off. Only one who's been raised in California . . .

I reach down and find a rock the size of a softball. Then show it to him through the window. "If you don't open the door, Arty, I'll have to break the window, and you'll get splattered with glass; then maybe your little hard head will get knotted with this rock. And all of this will make your sister cry again. Understand?"

He nods his head, sighs, then reaches over and hits

the power locks. The kid knows as much about this Mercedes as I do. Maybe more.

I reach past him and snatch up the key. I turn around to show it to Fredrico, but he's staring off into space. "What?" I ask.

"I think we got company," he says.

# Chapter 15

I look back down the road, wondering what he's worrying about, then realize he's looking up. A Jet Ranger helicopter is a half mile away, and coming straight at us.

"Get in the truck, and pull it out from under this thing," I yell. He breaks for the cab at a run, and I yell at Arty, "Get in the backseat with your sister." He jumps over the seat, and I climb up and in so I can hold the brake on, for whatever good it might do. By the time the truck is fired up, the chopper is circling the truck and car, and I can see four faces peering down at us. No-neck and Sallow-face are free.

The chopper has no markings, other than its call number, so I presume it's private. It appears that Henri Aziz is keeping the cops out of it, which probably means he wants to do some very bad things to the people who snatched his grandchildren, and doesn't want to worry about legalities.

Fredrico slams the truck into a forward gear and pops the clutch, but the damned car is hung up, and merely slides forward with the truck.

He does it again, and again.

Gigi is screaming at the top of her lungs, and Arty is

jumping up and down in the seat. "It's Grampa. Grampa. Boy, are you in trouble!"

The chopper is setting up for a landing in a clearing not fifty yards from us. The rotor wash is already kicking up a cloud of dust, and the *whomp, whomp, whomp* of the big rotors makes it impossible to hear anything else.

Again Fredrico pops the clutch, and this time the car jerks free of the truck bed and bounces on its front wheels like one of those California low-riders with the gizmo that makes it jump up and down.

I slam it into reverse just as the chopper settles, the rotors start to wind down, and its door flies open.

Thank God the Mercedes is still operating, even though crunched both front and rear, thanks to my eight-going-on-eighteen-year-old passenger.

I spin the wheels and pull up even with the truck cab, just as Fredrico leaps out. I unlock the door so he can get in, and of course Arty takes the opportunity to pop his back door and jump out. But I'm on him before he gets ten feet.

The boys in the distance are armed, but one of them, the old man, I think, is making sure they don't fire. I hold Arty up so they can see what he's wearing. They think I'm using a human shield but I have a method to my madness other than fashion approval, then throw him back into the backseat. Fredrico's in the passenger seat and reaches back and gets a paw on Arty to keep him down while I get in and finally get the doors locked. We're bouncing back to the highway before the chopper occupants can get to us and feed us to the rotor blades like carrots to a Cuisinart.

I check the rearview mirror and see they're piling back in as the rotors race back up to speed.

As we race down the French back road, I ask Fredrico, "You got any bright ideas?"

"You ready to use secret weapon?" he asks.

"Yeah, but they're in the trunk."

"There is a tunnel up ahead. Somewhere near by. Stop in there, if we get there, and I get them out."

"We'll get there. They're not going to try anything fancy, so long as the kids are in the car."

"Then maybe we should not use secret weapon?" he asks.

"The grandfather is in the car, and the river is up ahead. We'll shake the chopper, with the weapon. Mind over matter, Fredrico. Mind over matter."

"What is mind over matter?" he asks.

But I'm concentrating on my driving.

I drop down to the speed limit. No sense getting stopped by a highway cop, and the Jet Ranger is a lot faster than this Mercedes and I'm not going to outrun him no matter how fast I go.

But, with luck, I can outsmart him.

I've studied the map for this route at length. The highway crosses the river several times in the next few miles, and it's a river crossing I'm looking for. Just the ticket for what I have in mind.

Fredrico was right about the tunnel, and we've only gone another five miles before I see it coming up.

"You've got to move quickly," I say, "or they'll know something's fishy."

"Quick, like the snake," he says.

I slow down to let a car pass, satisfied that there's not another car for well over a mile behind us. As soon as we enter the tunnel, only a little over a hundred yards long, I slide to a stop. Before the car settles, Fredrico is out of the passenger door, around the back, has the trunk open, and is back, stuffing the two child-size mannequins I've bought into the backseat.

"I got something for you to play with," I tell the kids, who are now sharing the seat with a pair of store dummies.

"These aren't dolls," Gigi says.

"Nope, but we're going to dress them up," I say. "Hand up the bags," I say.

"No!" Arty says, putting his hands into his armpits in defiance. "I won't help you. No!"

"I will," Gigi says, getting into the swing of things. She grabs the bags and hands them to Fredrico, who dresses the mannequins, rather clumsily in the tight quarters, but manages to get the identical sweat suits on them.

"That doesn't look like me," Arty says. But the mannequin's not a bad replica, not from five hundred feet in the air.

"So, where's the best crossing?" I ask Fredrico.

Again, he shrugs. "Any of the ones coming up. The first one is close to the water, but there's one just before the village of Mont-Louis that is very high off the water. Maybe fifty meters."

"Good, we'll head for that one. That should get the old man's attention, if he's any kind of grandpa."

Now, just so this helicopter is the only one to join this chase . . .

We pass the first river crossing, and it's only twenty meters or so above the river.

"Only a kilometer or two," Fredrico says.

Again I let a car pass, wanting to have an easy stop on the bridge. There's an oncoming car, but none behind us as we near it.

"Get down on the floorboard," I command the kids.

"No," Arty says.

But Fredrico turns and grabs him by the knee. A little pressure and in seconds he's down. "You hurt me," he screams at Fredrico.

"He is a foul child," Fredrico says.

"Foul or not, we're stuck with him for a while, so you might want to get along."

Through clenched teeth, he manages an apology, "*Arrepentido*, Arty."

*"Da nada,"* Arty answers politely.

I slam on the brakes, reach between the seats, where the plastic Arty is propped, throw open the door, and round the car to the railing, high above the river. I hold the mannequin above my head with both hands, like it has some weight, waiting for the chopper to catch up, then arch it out into the void. It makes a few sickening turns in the air, and even gives my backbone a chill—I can't imagine what it's doing to the old man. Before it hits, I'm back and get Gigi's replica, and repeat the process. The chopper is in very close now, and I can see panic on the old man's face, pure agony, so pure it even makes my heart ache, as the little body arches out over the river and plunges below. Even I think it's a despicable trick.

Then I'm back in the car, and driving like hell, and it's a good thing, as the chopper is catching up, only this time the cargo or rear door has been opened, and it's a gun barrel sticking out.

"Did not work," Fredrico says.

"They'll go back. No one would leave their kids . . ."

I hope I'm not wrong, as I sure as hell don't want AK-47 bullets flying around while the kids are actually still in the car.

Then we're in the village, slowing, surrounded by traffic and buildings. I wheel it quickly into a tight alley. The chopper passes just overhead, and then in a moment, banks back toward the river crossing. I gun the car, come out of the alley on a side street, and in seconds am out of the little village and burning up the highway, with the chopper nowhere in sight.

"We need to get off this highway." I'm not what you'd call desperate, but my voice is an octave high.

"In a few kilometers, at the village of Prades, there is a road to the left. It's many kilometers more to Perpignan that way, but it's through some very heavy forest, and deep canyons. It will be very hard to spot a car from the air . . ."

"Next left it is."

Fredrico and I are silent for a long while. Then I give him a smile. "The cream always comes to the top," I say.

"I do not know what that means, Señor Shannon, but I know Henri Aziz, and know he will kill you, slowly, for making him the fool."

"Not for a while, Fredrico, my lad. Not for a good long while." I hope I'm right. In order to prevent it, I need to get out of his sphere of influence, Costa Brava in Spain, and the Camarge in France. And I mean to do so as quickly and surreptitiously as possible.

But I can't get on a plane with the children without Sonya and her legal documentation.

It's sixty kilometers to Perpignan, the first decent-sized city, and more importantly, the city where we're to meet Sonya and Antonio. And the good news is it will probably be good and dark by the time we get there. Darkness is my greatest ally when being sought from the air.

We reach the outskirts of a city with small strip malls and modern buildings that reminds me of any hundred towns in central California, just as it gets dark. Every few minutes I check the cell phone to see if it's found a tower, and finally it shows that it's in service. I call Sonya, but she's obviously somewhere where she can't get service. I leave word, then hang up, hoping for the best.

Now if only Sonya and Antonio are here as they are supposed to be; and if they've done what I requested.

My phone beeps with a message as we get deeper into the old city. Finally, we're confronted with a stone wall and ancient Perpignan. The center city. I check the message and see that Cynthia has called, as has Pug. I decide to try them back after I solve the immediate problem.

"How's your French?" I ask Fredrico. My tongue ties up when I try to get beyond *merci* and *toilette*.

"Petit," he says, holding his thumb and forefinger a couple of inches apart in international language.

"We need to find the main police station, the gendarmes."

He looks at me a little oddly, but does not ask why I'm looking for the police when I've just kidnapped two kids, and says in a civil tone, "I think you mean commissariat."

"There." He points at a uniformed gentlemen standing on a street corner. He's obviously a cop, in any language.

I can feel Arty sitting forward behind me, and know he's about to sing out, probably in perfect French. So I pull up a hundred feet down the road from the cop.

"Get out and walk back," I tell Fredrico, motioning at Arty, who's already waving at the cop and trying to keep me from seeing what he's up to. I give him a hard look, but he ignores me. Although Arty's wide-eyed and alert, Gigi, I'm glad to see, is asleep.

In moments, Fredrico is back in the car and directs me through narrow streets until we come out of the old city, and on its edge find a modern two-story building surrounded by cop cars. I drive around its perimeter, but don't see the car I'm looking for anywhere.

"You hungry?" I ask Fredrico.

"Can eat," he says.

I continue down the road until I find a café, park on the street, hand him a couple of U.S. twenties, and trusting his judgment, send him inside with only one instruction, "Get Cokes for the kids."

He returns with a sack full of sandwiches, two Cokes, and a bottle of wine, sans label, but corked, and a wad of francs. The cork's been loosened. When I eye the wine, I suddenly realize how beat I am. If I drink it, my eyelids will be sagging as much as Antonio's lazy one.

I've been operating on adrenaline, but now there's no chopper circling overhead in the darkness.

The sandwich is white chicken on a hard roll, with olives and tomatoes and red onions. I wish I had time to eat and drink my way through Spain and France. Another time, when half the underworld of two or three countries is not looking to tack my hide to the toilette wall, or use it for butt wipe.

I have a few bites, take one swig of the wine, then step out of the car into the cool night, cautioning Fredrico to lock the doors as soon as I exit, and make my first call. Sonya is still not answering. That worries me. I glance at my watch and see it's seven-thirty P.M., nine-thirty A.M. in California. It's a polite time to call.

"Can't you get a job in Nevada?" Cynthia asks sleepily.

"What, you still in the sack?"

"How's it going?"

"Well, the good doctor threw us a few curves."

"Such as?"

"Such as his father-in-law being high up in gangster land. Maybe the Cyrano de Bergerac of the local arm of bent noses."

There's silence for a moment. "No wonder he thought this job was worth two hundred big ones."

"And such as the good doctor being light in his loafers."

"No. Who told you that?"

"Sonya."

"Well, that's a surprise."

"Do you have any reason to believe he's not?"

"Do you mean has he made a pass at me? No, but that doesn't mean—"

"Anyway, the good news is the eagle has landed—"

"Outstanding—"

"I am north of objective two, have a few bad boys hot on my tail, and am about to head out a few hundred kilometers to the first alternative. *If* I can tie up with Sonya." Cynthia and I have discussed my basic strategy for this operation, and there's no reason to go into detail over a cell phone. The damned Aziz family probably owns the cell phone company.

"Where's Sonya?"

"Long story, but one I hope is going to end quickly. I'll call you if there's anything you can do."

"Make sure," she says. Now that she knows I have the kids, she's wide-awake.

I hang up and call Pug, who answers on the first ring. At nine-thirty he's been up for many hours. I'm sure he has his tenth cup of coffee in hand.

"What's up?" I ask.

"Lenny Haroldstern. Cedric spent most of the night in hyperspace and Iver in the real world . . . in the weeds."

"And?"

"And, we're making headway. How smart is this guy?"

"Probably pretty smart. Probably very connected. I wouldn't be surprised if Rio is his next stop. His family has a chest full of gold. As I mentioned, he was staying with his aunt in Montecito, and I'd start there."

"We already cased the place. Iver spent half of yesterday and last night in the bushes and brambles with binocs. He's not hiding at Auntie's, or if he is he's living in the wine cellar."

"Not a bad place to hide out," I suggest, but am not serious. "I just think she might be helping him out. This punk is used to living high and I'll bet he's still on the tit. He hasn't worked a day in his worthless life."

"We're following up on the auntie, checking her credit card charges, et cetera. Cedric will know every mole she's got on her inner thighs before long."

"Okay—"

"By the way, Aunt Melinda's a looker."

"Really, that's a surprise."

"Yeah, young widow of Lenny's uncle. Old Unc had great taste. Not the normal aunt thing for young Lenny the lech, or leach as the case may be."

"Interesting."

"How's the wife-and-rug-rats-on-the-lam thing going?"

I fill him in, with the same basic double talk I'd given Cynthia, so anyone listening wouldn't have a clue, then ring off after he cautions me to be careful, which goes without saying.

As I reach for the door handle, the cell phone rings.

"I am at the police station," Sonya says without bothering with hello.

"Good. Be there in one minute."

Not knowing the city of Perpignan, I'd suggested to her that we meet outside the main police station. It's usually an easy place to find in any city as almost everyone can give you directions, the law-abiding, and the not so sanctimonious.

In moments I locate the white Mercedes. Sonya has followed instructions to a tee, or so it seems, renting another car. This time it's a 500. The girl has style, particularly when I've told her I'm paying her back. I'm happy to see that Sonya and the children have a joyous reunion, complete with hugs and kisses. That should make my life easier.

I pay the Lizaola boys off, and give them a five-hundred-dollar bonus. I may, some day, need them again, if they live long enough, having made enemies with the likes of Henri Aziz. Fredrico offers to sell me the automatic for two fifty American, and I'm tempted, but pass. I don't even want to be enticed into a shoot-out with the kids in the car. Even with the bonus, the Lizaolas seem glad to be shed of me, like snakes being rid of a confining skin that makes them vulnerable to predators . . . or maybe as happy as a nice family whose crazy aunt has just left after spending a week embarrassing them with the neighbors. They exit with the proclamation that they're off to visit relatives on the Costa del Sol, far from Barcelona and the Aziz family. At a brisk walk they head for a bus station.

I hope I don't regret not buying the automatic. It was a nice little nine-millimeter.

The map says A75, and it only takes me a few minutes to find it. I could find an airport to fly out of a lot closer than Paris, but I have my own reasons for wanting to get to the capital. And I figure all the smaller airports in Southern France will be under the surveillance of the Aziz boys, if they're half so well connected as the Lizaolas think. And someone who has a Jet Ranger at his disposal is probably damn well connected.

"Have you slept?" I ask Sonya.

"Yes, I had a good night's rest last night, and napped in front of the TV this afternoon." Her tone goes chilly. "I *had* to stay in the hotel, except to find this white Mercedes, which was no small task, remember."

I give her my most heartwarming smile. "You did good. Your toenails are beautiful. Can you drive?"

"Of course. You smell bad. Where have you been?"

"Around Robin Hood's barn and back," I say. And she looks a little confused.

I whip off the freeway. Walk around to the passenger side and let her out.

In moments, after I've cautioned her not to attract the attention of the highway patrol, I've got the seat laid back, and I'm in never-never land, serenaded to sleep by Sonya leading the kids in a chorus of "The Itsy-Bitsy Spider."


After trading off driving and sleeping a couple of times, stopping to eat, and at least three pee-pee stops for the kids, we roll into the outskirts of the City of Lights in the early afternoon.

Now that I'm in the big city, a city with which I'm not

familiar, I want one piece of insurance. I call my good buddy Cedric.

"How's Futa?" is my first question.

"Full of wharf rats and happy as a clam. Where are you?"

"Paris, and I may need some digital help."

"Aw, Paris. Confucious say, in Paris a fool and his money are soon partying."

"Right, right. I'll pay you for a day, a Franklin, notwithstanding what you might make from the Haroldstern deal, if you stay home doing what you do so well, keeping your fingers on the keyboard. Until you hear from me, check out the sites for Paris as I may need directions or addresses or God knows what . . . and won't have time to stop in a service station. First is Orly Airport, but be ready to help me around the rest of the city just in case." It's always good to have a contingency plan.

"For a day's pay, you'll have my complete alacrity."

"Right. How's the Haroldstern thing coming?"

"There will be no respite for the miscreant. Interestingly enough, I've discovered other credit cards being billed to the same address as that of the aunt, one Melinda Grace Haroldstern. Only these bills are in the name of one M.G. Greenbaugh, and on further investigation, the computer reveals that Mrs. Melinda was formerly Miss M.G. A runner-up for Miss Texas a few years ago, by the by."

"So, she had a maiden name. Most married women do."

"So, might a young man travel as M.G.? Of course he might. In pursuing that reasoning, I find there are charges on the card from the Pacific Northwest, as late as this morning. And Miss M.G., which we must presume is one and the same Mrs. Melinda, is still in residence in her palatial abode in Montecito. So one must wonder who is using M.G.'s ten-thousand-dollar-limit Visa card. Perchance our errant FTA? Using it with some intelligence, however, as it's only been swiped at ATM locations. No telltale hotel charges. Three hundred cash in Tacoma only this morn."

"Perchance is right. A damn good chance! Good work. I may have to fly to Seattle."

"Coincidentally, Devlin, not to be mundane but this is garbage day in Mrs. Haroldstern's part of Montecito, so Pug and Iver will soon be refuse rummaging the ravages of the household, presuming her hired help remembers to put it out. It's nice to have a technical job."

"Please get on-line and find out the schedule for the next few direct flights to LAX from Orly. Flights with availability for four. The cattle car, please, as it's going to be expensive enough."

"That's a snap. Do you want me to call you back?"

"No, I'll call you when we get to the airport entrance. Stay on top of Lenny. Feed Futa, even if you think he's ravaging the wharf."

"Of course, to ease your concern, he has meowed for you often and fondly, and with great remorse at your absence. We are fast friends, and I will fill his bowl with a cornucopia of kitty cat delights."

"Stand by for my call, and stay off your cell phone."

"I'll sit, but I'll be here."

There has been no sign of the Aziz bunch, thank God, but I haven't written them off yet. I figure it won't take them long to find out where we stayed in Girona, and that Sonya was with us, and that she rented a white Mercedes. But all that has bought us a lot of time.

Precious time. And I'm now hundreds of kilometers from the Aziz center of power. I hope that's far enough, but doubt it.

I only need a few more hours.

# Chapter 16

The good news is that A20 takes me almost to the entrance to Orly. The bad news is the traffic is terrible, even in the early afternoon. We are stop-and-go, and still several kilometers from the airport.

It takes us the better part of an hour to make the last twenty kilometers, but the airport access is plainly marked from the freeway. And the traffic is much lighter as I wheel off A20 and onto the Orly access road.

My fatigue is assuaged by the fact I can see airplanes winging overhead.

I dial Cedric back, and to his credit, he picks up on the first ring.

"There are a half dozen flights leaving for the U.S. in the next four hours, but only two direct flights. One to Miami and on to Mexico City, one to LAX."

"It'll take us two hours at least to clear customs."

"Then it's Air France 1420, leaving at four-fourteen P.M. That gives you two hours and ten minutes. And it's the one to LAX."

"And there's room for the four of us?"

"Just happens to be. There are two sets of two seats. So each of you can accompany a child. Terminal One,

Gate C46. I'd dump the car on the departing passenger level and let the gendarmes tow it. You'll never make it if you screw around with the rental return."

"Book it," I say, without even asking how much. I know it's too damn much, but after wrecking a Mercedes sedan and a Mercedes truck, what's a few thou more?

I'm only a kilometer from the terminal buildings, and madly watching for a turnoff to the Terminal One building, when I approach an overpass.

I sigh deeply. There's a gentlemen standing on the overpass, binocs in one hand, radio in the other. And he takes great interest in us as we approach, then runs across two lanes and glasses the car as we pass under and move away, then slams the radio up to his face.

It would seem we've been made. I doubt if anyone's enthralled by just any white Mercedes.

Watching carefully in the rearview mirror, I see two identical black four-door Renaults enter the terminal approach road from the overpass. I hope if it's them, only one of the cars will be our pursurers, not both.

Good old Shell, the international oil company, has a station just before the terminals, located in sort of an island between the main terminal access road and a service road that passes the rear of the service station and is an access to rental car return. The best of both worlds.

I decide not to waste any time, but to go ahead and test the Renaults. They're only a couple hundred yards behind, with two cars between them and us. I take the first curb cut into the Shell, and pull up to the fuel island, but remain behind the wheel with the engine idling.

Sonya's been sleeping, at least dozing, and the kids are asleep in the back. She sits up, yawns, and stretches, as I stop.

"We there?" she asks, then realizes we're at the fuel island. "A lot cheaper here than if you wait for the rental company to it fill up," she says, offering her traveler's wisdom.

"I wish I had a full tank," I say, more to myself than her, as I've checked the fuel level when I turned off the freeway and I'm sorry to note that I only have a quarter tank. Not stopping back down the road could suddenly get very expensive.

One of the Renaults speeds past the first Shell entrance, but the other swings in. Then I notice that the first has stopped, blocking the second curb cut, the exit back onto the terminal access road.

I'm up against them both, and it appears each has a full complement of four men.

I hit the redial while slipping the Mercedes into reverse, waiting for the first black Renault to ease up behind me. He stops a car and a half length back, nowhere near any fuel hose. When all four doors open, and four bent-nose boys begin unloading—and I catch a glimpse of an automatic shoved into the driver's belt when his coat blows aside—I decide he who hesitates is lost, and with the shifter set to R, floorboard the big Mercedes.

The wheels spin on the slick concrete, and the four boys, realizing I'm coming their way, scatter. The Mercedes finally catches traction, smokes the tires, and slams into the Renault, driving it backward. I have the doors locked, and even though at least two of them make the side of the car and grasp the door handles, they can do nothing but yell French expletives.

As soon as I push the Renault all the way back against a concrete block wall, I slam my white tank into drive, and they really begin to scatter as I'm coming back at them. Two of the no-necks in the other Renault have exited it and are stalking across the tarmac toward the fuel islands.

I get their attention as I clip one of the first four, sending him reeling, then head for the second bunch.

The nearest of them has a stainless revolver in hand, looks like a police special, but doesn't have time to level it as the Mercedes is about to make a hood ornament out of him. Bearing down on you, that little three-pointed star in the circle must look a lot like a gunsight.

Getting close enough that one dives for the tarmac and the other has to dive across the hood of that Renault, I cut the wheel and head around the Shell to the service road, hang a left toward the terminal; then, as Sonya has come fully awake and is screaming in my ear, I realize I'm going the wrong way on a one-way road.

Oh, well, even a sophisticated, certified bail enforcement agent can't be expected to do everything right.

That's the bad news, and the worse news is that the two Renaults are not far behind, already pacing me and only tailing me fifty yards on the terminal access road, which is only twenty-five yards away and running parallel to the rental return road.

With my right hand on the wheel, my thumb on the horn, dodging oncoming traffic, which seems to be working even harder to dodge the madman in the Mercedes, I put the phone to my ear with my left hand and see if my redial has worked. "Cedric?"

"Yeah, I was just waiting for the excitement to die down."

"That may take a while. I need to know my alternatives to get to Paris Central, and to the American embassy."

"A moment."

"Let me have that," Sonya demands, her hand extended.

"Take notes," I tell her, happy to get both hands on the wheel. She finds a pen and picks up a white sack off the floor that's had food in it, but is now being used as a garbage bag. It'll do for notes.

"Is that my grandpa?" I hear Arty's voice in my ear.

"Sit back and get your belt on, and make sure your sister's tightly belted in."

"You're in trouble," he says, as if I don't know it.

"Belt up, Arty!" I raise my voice at the little lamb for the first time.

Meanwhile, Sonya is scribbling away.

"Okay," she says, and starts to hang up.

"God, don't hang up!" I yell at her also. "Keep him on the line."

There is far less traffic on my rental return road than there is on the terminal access road, so even as I'm fighting against the oncoming, I manage to get to the turn in for the rental return road a hundred yards in front of the Renaults. I have to swing hard left, then a hard right across three lanes of traffic, causing a half dozen cars to hit their brakes and slide to a stop, forcing the Renaults to brake to a standstill.

Then I'm with the traffic, in the far left lane, and only doubling or maybe tripling the speed limit.

"So?" I ask her.

"So, I have the address of the American embassy, and we can drive there, or we can take the underground. RER B is the one to take."

"If I can lose these guys, we'll drive. If I can't, I'm sure they'll cut us off at some point in time. Maybe we'd be better off to ditch the car at an underground station and get lost amidst the commuters."

She shrugs. She's picked up Fredrico's habits.

"If you lose them," she suggests, "then we can come back to the airport, go to Charles DeGaulle, or take the train to England. I know where the station is for the chunnel train."

I think for a minute. "No, the underground is too risky, and so's some train station. It's the embassy. The kids will be safe there, and so will you."

"That's sweet," she says. "That is the first time—"

"You have to take care of the kids, remember."

"Of course I remember, but still—"

"Directions to the embassy?"

"Two, avenue Gabriel."

"That's an address! I need directions."

"Of course you do, if you'll calm down."

I'm driving a hundred miles an hour, being pursued by eight toughs in very fast little cars, having to dodge slower traffic, with ten kilometers of city to cross, and she wants me to be calm. Okay, I'm calm. "Directions!" I yell.

"It's two blocks north of the Seine, in the center of Paris, near Rue Royale. Near Jardin Des Tulleries . . . the park."

"Okay, but where do I go from here? Let's take this a few blocks at a time. You navigate, I'll drive."

"I'm not sure this is worth three thousand dollars."

"Don't start negotiating!" I yell again.

"I am not. I just said—"

"Directions!"

"Get on A6 north, you should see the signs just coming out of the airport, just follow it until it becomes a four-lane city street, cross the Seine, then bear left along the river. Follow the signs to the Louvre, it's near there. You know, the art museum?"

"I know the Louvre is a major Paris art museum. Thank you, finally."

Now I know where I'm going, but the Renaults have been gaining, slowly, picking their way through the traffic.

I pray that the traffic will allow us to keep moving, at least faster than a man can run. If we get below fifteen miles an hour for any distance, the bastards can leave their vehicle and catch up to us on foot, break out the windows, stick a gun in my ear, and it'll be hell to pay.

For some reason, even though the traffic has lessened as accesses to other freeways have taken cars off of

A6, the two Renaults have hung back. They have something in mind?

What?

I can see one of them in the passenger seat talking on a cell phone, and that makes me nervous.

I see ahead, by a lane converging sign, that our freeway is soon to become a city street, if a wide one. Maybe that's what the plan is. Get us on a city street where they can force us off the road without traffic flying by at eighty to one hundred kilometers an hour.

I realize they are positioning themselves so one's on each side of me. When they accelerate alongside, they'll have me bracketed in between them.

Only a few hundred yards after the freeway ends I can see the first of what I presume will be many stoplights. Stoplights are not part of my plan. But I've only got a couple of kilometers to go. If I falter, they'll be on me like stink on that pig truck we caught the ride in. I can see the Eiffel Tower in the distance, and wonder if I have an alternative route.

"Is the embassy near the Eiffel?"

"Across the river. The tower is on this side. Go like I told you."

"Yes, ma'am. You might want to hang on."

"What?"

"Just hang on."

# Chapter 17

There's only one car in front of me as I see the light turn yellow fifty yards or so ahead. The Renaults are two cars behind, one on each side.

I find a narrow slot and gun the Mercedes, slipping over a lane until I have a clear shot at the light. It's red twenty yards before I reach the intersection, but there's no turning back now.

I clear the traffic from the left with no problem, but have to swing way over into the oncoming lane to miss the traffic coming from the right. Horns are blaring, French men and women are shaking their fists at me. If they knew I was an "ugly American" they'd probably be running me down to hang me from the Arc de Triomphe. But the two Renaults are locked in traffic at a long light.

"Nicely done, Dev," she says.

An actual compliment.

"Thank you. I'm sorry I yelled at you."

"That was neat," I finally hear from the backseat.

"I want my mom," Gigi says.

"Is your belt on tight?" I ask.

There's one cross street without lights, then another intersection with a stoplight.

I can see I'm not going to make this one; in fact there will be at least two cars between me and the intersection, and the Renaults have worked their way free and are only three and four cars behind, one in the left lane, one in the right, leaving the middle lane for me. Slipping over into the left lane, I look for my alternatives. Now there's a divider between the opposing lanes, but it's only curb high and six or eight feet wide. The divider is full of blooming flowers.

We're slowing.

Suddenly the Renault in the left lane jumps the curb, and is charging forward on the center divider, flowers flying everywhere. Before he can reach me, I follow suit, cutting him off, but not keeping him from slamming into the driver's side of the Mercedes. There goes another one, and if I had time I'd visualize more Franklins flying away. We took the hit on the driver's-side rear, and I worry about Arty as I follow through, cut in front of oncoming traffic, and make a U-turn across the divider, causing oncoming traffic to pile up and one car to smash into another, both blocking any attempt by the Renault, whose front end is pretty well smashed up, to follow.

There's a frontage road across the oncoming three lanes that I've blocked, and I complete the maneuver by going on across that center divider, this one with a walkway, scattering a few pedestrians.

More rude gestures, but I'm in the frontage road, and still progressing the way I should be.

"You almost hit that old lady with the cane," Sonya says accusingly.

"The one that gave me the 'up yours' gesture?"

"That is the one. And there was a woman with a stroller not far back."

"I'll send my apologies as a letter to the editor of the French edition of The *New York Times*. But I think I'll wait until we're safe at the embassy."

"Very funny," she says, and this time her tone is not too complimentary. "I guess I should have taken the insurance."

"You didn't take the insurance?"

"No. I never take the insurance."

"Trust me, Sonya, if I'm going to be near the driver's seat, take the insurance." I see more Franklins on the wing. "Are the kids okay?"

She glances back. "Better than me."

"That was bad," Arty says, and I'm assured he's fine.

I'm shooting ahead of the traffic on the thruway, but notice that all the way across it there's another frontage road. One of the Renaults, probably the one that had been in the right lane, is pacing me. Hopefully, the one that hit us is out of the race.

The frontage road is coming to a dead end a couple hundred yards ahead, and I see why. It's the Seine, and all six lanes of the thruway are narrowed to four across the river.

There's one more light and cross street, and I whip to the right, stopping at the light for the cross traffic, waiting for the light to change so I can turn left back onto the thruway, and make it across the bridge. The hell of it is, across the thruway, the second Renault sits, patiently awaiting the change of the light.

"Is everybody strapped in tight?" I ask.

"What are you going—" Sonya manages, before the light changes.

"I'm hoping those boys don't have their belts on, and I'm going to see if German equipment really is far superior to French."

"Oh, my—"

But she doesn't get it out before the light changes, and the Renault and the Mercedes are closing across six lanes of thruway.

I feint right, when my intent is to turn left. He jams

the wheel to his left, trying to cut me off, which is just what I want. I get his front fender and bumper dead center with the Mercedes's front bumper, and the Renault folds like newspaper.

I suddenly get the sensation that I've been shot in the face, then realize I have a face full of airbag, but only for a second. It collapses.

I've turned Sonya's air bag off, which you can do in this model Mercedes, because she's had little Gigi in her lap on and off during the trip. She's not hurt, but a little shaken.

I slam it into reverse, dragging the Renault back for a half dozen yards before the Mercedes breaks free, then cramp it left and am heading up and over the bridge.

The Renault has lost badly, and steam roils from under its crumpled hood.

"How far?" I ask.

"That hurt," Sonya says, rubbing her shoulder under the chest belt.

"Sorry, how far?"

"You can turn left at the next one or the one after that; then it's only a few blocks."

Just as she finishes her sentence, the white Jet Ranger sweeps by so low it has to flare upward to avoid some wires. The Aziz boys have pulled all the stops.

The Mercedes is no longer beautiful, but it's still functioning. Just as I crest the top of the bridge, and glance in the rearview mirror, I lose my elation. The Renault that I cut off at the center divider is back in the game, blowing steam, but coming on fast.

"What a bunch of hardheads," I mumble.

"What?"

"Nothing. How are the kids doing?"

She glances in the back. "Better than me."

"Hang in there. It's only a little bit farther."

Then I'm shocked by a strange voice coming out of

nowhere like an apparition, speaking in rapid French, which I certainly don't understand. Then he calls me by name.

"Mr. Shannon, would you prefer English?"

"Who?"

"OnStar, sir. Your airbag has deployed. May I call an ambulance for you?"

"No," I say with a smile. And I think cell phones are wild and crazy. I guess I'm going to have to get in the twenty-first century. But lying is age-old. I do know, if he wants to, he can turn the Mercedes off cold, and we'll be at the mercy of our pursuers. "It's a mistake, some communications glitch, I guess. My air bag did not deploy."

"Strange, sir. It's never been wrong before."

"Strange things are always happening to me," I say.

"We're here if you need us."

"Good, I may need directions."

"I'll be pleased to provide them, sir."

Big brother is truly watching.

I reach the next light, across the river, at the same time as two cop cars coming from the other direction, each blaring sirens with blue lights flashing. I make a hard left, purposefully cut in front of them, and they follow, cutting off the Renault when they make a hard right turn to pursue me.

The Renault slides to a stop behind them, but the second of the cops sees this, and also puts on the binders on his Citroen. Both of them execute a squealing turn, and it's an all-French affair with the Citroen hot after the Renault.

There's a park to our left, with clear air space, and the Jet Ranger is hovering low, only fifty feet above and on my driver's side. I can clearly see the face of Henri Aziz in the right seat, a very, very angry face. He's talking on the cell phone, yelling it appears, and he's not happy.

This does make me smile. Even though the first cop is hot on my tail, the second is after the remaining bad guy. The Jet Ranger wouldn't dare attempt a landing, even though there are several broad parks in sight that would easily accommodate the aircraft.

I smile again, as I plan to give myself up to the United States Marine Corps, comrades-in-arms, on the front steps of the American embassy.

I manage to wind my way through traffic, only having to run one more light to stay out of the grasp of the cops on my tail, before I swing up to the black and gold ten-foot-high gates of the crescent drive of the American embassy. The red, white, and blue sported by the two marine guards couldn't look any better to me.

The cops slide to a stop at the gates, not following me into the driveway.

By the time they are out of the car and to the steps, Sonya and I are in front of the guards, me carrying Arty Hashim, and she Gigi Hashim. I can see another marine, this one in full battle garb, at the edge of the roof four stories above, tracking the chopper with a hand-held Stinger missile. This has to pucker old man Aziz and the boys.

I glance up, fully extend my arm, and give the finger to well-connected Henri Aziz, then turn to the matter at hand.

"Lance Corporal," I say, letting him know I know something about marines. *"Semper fi.* We're all American citizens. I need to talk to your cultural attaché, or someone with some authority."

With a French police car sitting there with lights blaring, and two very frustrated cops waving their arms and chattering in Frog, a strange chopper *whomp, whomp, whomping* not two hundred feet overhead, his weapon at ready arms, the marine calmly says, "Step into the foyer, sir." It's calm, but it's more of a command than a request.

It's an imposing building, and the fact the French police are stopped cold by the remaining U.S. Marine at the big double doors is even more impressive.

After all, French cops have no authority on American soil. Besides, everyone fears the United States Marines.

# Chapter 18

Being back on American soil means being in the bureaucracy. While the children are escorted away under the protection of some nice lady from the human resources department, I'm led away to wait in an outer office for an attaché. The marine guard has turned me over to two plainclothes types, one of whom has relieved me of my passport, and who stay in close attendance, watching me as if I were an Al Queda suspect. They must be mutes, as they answer my few questions only with a nod or shake of the head, or the well-known shrug.

Knowing something about the marines after five years among them, I'd have preferred being guarded by the lance corporal. At one time I'd considered applying for the Marine Security Guard School. Only a few more than twelve hundred marines are in service at our embassies after receiving this special training. Then I thought it'd be exciting to serve in some foreign country, and then I realized that standing guard, bracketing a door, maybe wasn't my cup of tea. The fact is, it's probably a lot like what I'm doing now, with months of boredom and moments of sheer terror. Besides, after today, I think my life is plenty exciting. But that feeling probably won't last.

After twenty minutes the marine guard does return, carrying a sheaf of papers. He passes me by and enters the inner office, but quickly is back, pausing by my chair.

"Desert Storm. What duty?" he asks.

"Force Recon," I say. "We took out some communication stations way behind the lines . . . as well as taking a few other things out."

"Roger that." He gives me a knowing smile. "Good luck," he says, spins on his heel, and leaves.

The sheaf of papers must be a quick computer look at good old Dev Shannon, if the corporal knew I'd served in Desert Storm.

It's another twenty minutes before I'm called into the attaché's office. The two mute plainclothes types go right along with me.

A small man with a nervous twitch and Coke-bottle glasses, George Twillinger gets my permission before activating a recorder on his desk. I spend an hour relating my story to him, another two hours with his boss, and several hours being interviewed by a cultural attaché who doesn't admit to being, but I'm sure is CIA— Christians In Action, as they are known by many of us who've had to deal with them. It seems the U.S. Government has some interest in Henri Aziz in regard to narcotics and weapons smuggling. That turns out to be a good thing as I don't seem quite such a bad guy for having had a little run-in with the Aziz interests. Not to speak of the fact the embassy seems determined not to return his grandchildren, so long as they have some legal basis to ship them off to their father, an American citizen without a blemish on his record.

It takes two days to get out of the embassy, after a dozen calls to the States and some intense negotiation between Mr. Twillinger and the French police, and my relating the incident in transcribed detail to both the French DCPJ, the Direction Central Police Judiciaire, their equivalent of the FBI, and Interpol. Twillinger has to educate them all as to the status of a bail enforcement agent, and our position as a pseudo police officer in certain situations. It seems the French have great respect for police from almost any country. With Sol's help—thank God he's anxious to get me back on the Haroldstern thing—I post a one-hundred-thousand-dollar performance bond before being allowed to leave French soil. It seems there is the matter of many thousands of dollars in damage to a Mercedes truck and two Mercedes vehicles. At least I'd taken the insurance on the truck and the S340, but Sonya, being an experienced traveler and knowing her personal insurance would cover her, had not. Of course, her insurance will look to me, an unauthorized driver, for reimbursement. Oh, well, maybe the hundred thousand from the good doctor will cover the cost of the rampage from Andorra to Paris.

Sonya and the children are required to hang around, in embassy protection, until a ruling is received from the State Department in Washington, D.C. There is no question in my mind that they'll soon be on a plane to the U.S.

During my long wait, I manage to talk to Cynthia and tell her to gird herself for a battle with Dr. Hashim, and ask her to have her attorney friends prepare a demand for the money, not that I think he'll actually release it until the kids are in Santa Barbara. She reminds me that her "attorney friends" represent Hashim, and that will be unlikely, so I ask her to think of who else might help us.

I also have a long chat with Pug regarding Lenny Haroldstern. The garbage search was almost fruitless. So far, Lenny and the Melinda Haroldstern credit card have been among the missing. No more cash draws, no more charges of any kind. Until we have something more, I decide against flying directly to the Pacific Northwest.

The spectral Oscar visits me in the night, so I call Paul Antone. Julio Sanchez still hasn't turned up, and to be truthful, I am pleased. I still want Julio and his friends for myself.

That will be my first order of business when I get back to Santa Barbara.

After all the t's are crossed and the i's dotted, and my soul is sold to the devil for the performance bond, I receive a personal escort from the cultural attaché who drives me to Charles DeGaulle Airport and turns me over to an American Airlines employee who takes me through a crew's entrance and directly to the plane. It seems when you've spent the last couple of days with the embassy boys, there's a way of circumventing customs.

It's good to be an American.

Pug is waiting at the baggage belt at LAX, which is above and beyond, as I arrive at six A.M.

After relating my Andorran adventures to Pop, I doze all the way home, taking advantage of the old man's liking to drive, and his not minding my fading out on him.

It's also good to sleep in your own bed. I think Futa actually did miss me, as he perches in the sack beside me, purring me to sleep. Oscar awakes me again in the night, and Futa has cut out, I presume to send some wharf rats to rat heaven. With a promise to Oscar that I haven't forgotten him, and that all I need is a good night's sleep, I hit the hay again and sleep until the sun is over the yardarm.

I catch lunch at Café del Sol, a Montecito locals' hangout, with the old man, Cedric, and Iver, and get up to speed on Haroldstern. The only item of interest in

Melinda's garbage was an empty envelope, but because of the return address I know what it contained. My next item of business is a quick trip to Paso Robles, then maybe to Bakersfield, then back to Montecito to see if my hunch on the envelope is right. That means six or seven hours' driving time, but that is fine with me. Even though I hope to find Freddy Branch, all I can do is have a conversation with him, if necessary while squeezing his larynx between thumb and forefinger, so I decide to ride with the wind in my face, and head for Max Howard's boatyard and the Sportster.

I need some clean sea air and a respite from work.

As I plan to do some work if forced to, I drop my hammerless Smith and Wesson in my saddlebags, and as I plan to go to Bakersfield, I don the Bakersfield version of a tux, Levis and T-shirt, with leather jacket and cowboy boots to complete the look.

As always, the faithful bike fires up with a touch.

It's a perfect May day, with puffy clouds scattered in a sky so blue it almost vibrates with color. For some strange reason, when I'm on the bike, on the highway, I get in some really good think time, and this ride is no exception, particularly after I leave the ocean side just past Shell Beach, and the scenery is less spectacular. I review the Spain trip and am not as satisfied as I would be had I got them safely on a plane, but all and all it should work out. My only regrets were crashing so much expensive equipment, and not seeing Sonya on the beach soaking up the sun on 99.5 percent of her body. My thoughts turn to Oscar, Lawanda, and the Branch boys. I'm wondering, with Lawanda finding two kilos of Mexican brown, if Oscar was killed because of his bail enforcement activity, or was it something else? Maybe my guilt in the matter doesn't run as deep as I first thought . . . and maybe Oscar's guilt is deeper?

My first stop will be to see Lawanda—Lalo—then Paul Antone, and then I want to drop by the Butch

Branch dog pound and find out if his brother, Freddy, is back in town. If not, then I'm heading for Bakersfield as it was his home stomping ground, and many times a runner will head for country with which he's familiar, friends, and family.

I wheel off the freeway and idle the bike ten blocks to Lawanda's, kill the bike, and am a little shocked to see yellow crime scene tape sealing off the stairway up to her place. The two kilos of dope goes through my mind, but why would Antone declare a crime scene over dope that was turned in voluntarily? Doesn't figure.

When I get to the stairway, one of the doors on the ground floor opens, and it's the same guy who I saw at Lalo's when I went to see her after Oscar was killed.

"What do you want?" he demands.

I merely give him the hard eye, and start to duck under the tape.

"You can't go up there," he snaps, grabbing me by the wrist.

I rip the hand up, putting pressure against the guy's thumb, and break his grasp. He's way out of his element, and seems to get it. We stand staring at each other, until I break the silence. "What the hell's going on here?"

"Lalo's dead," he says, a blank look on his face.

"What?" I am genuinely shocked, and the bottom falls out of my stomach.

"She shot herself, man. I guess she missed Oscar too much."

"Where's the baby?"

"Lalo's mom came down from Salinas, and went to the county to get her. Protective Services took little Oscar."

"Was the baby there when she did it?"

"Yep."

"But the baby's okay?"

"Yep."

That doesn't ring right to me, a woman shooting herself with her helpless child nearby. "When did this happen?"

"Yesterday. She left a note on my door. My old lady came home and—"

I spin on my heel and head for the bike. Now I have even more reason to go see Antone.

He isn't in, so I head out to see Butch, and hopefully, find the elusive Freddy.

All I get there is dogs, anxious to climb the fence and run me awhile until they can drop me and share the spoils. I guess they smell Futa on me, which makes them extra crazy, not that pit bulls need an excuse.

So it's back to the P.D., where I do find Antone at his desk this time.

"What the hell happened?" I ask.

"Regarding?"

"Regarding Lawanda Lopez."

"Looks pretty cut-and-dry, but I never like it when things are too pat. I've just come from the medical examiner, who says everything is consistent with her shooting herself. The angle of entry is correct, powder burns and powder spackling. The blood spray is indicative of where she did the deed and was found. Powder residue on her hands."

"You know, I didn't know her well, but I knew Oscar, and I don't think he'd tie up with a lady who'd kill herself when she had a new baby to worry about. Where did she shoot herself?"

"In her apartment."

"I know that, where on her body?"

"In the mouth."

I shake my head. "That's not consistent with how a woman does things, even if she was going to kill herself.

Lawanda took really good care of herself. She wouldn't want to be ugly when she was buried. She would have used pills, or something, not a .357 in the mouth."

Antone smiles. "My thoughts exactly. That, and the fact she found two kilos of dope only a few days ago, makes me very, very unhappy with a suicide finding."

"Do you mind if I take a look at the crime scene?"

Again, I get the smile. "Okay, Sherlock. Only because your old man was such a good cop. You think you can see something we didn't, let's go take a look."

We do, with me riding in Antone's unmarked car. After questioning him as to what procedures they used in the investigation, and finding nothing more that I can question, I give up. The blood pattern on the wall indicates that she was standing when she was shot. I've never heard of a shooting suicide where the victim was standing. They're always sitting, usually on the bed or on their favorite chair, or even lying down. But still, I can't make anything of anything, so I ask to go visit the medical examiner's office.

While we're riding, I take the opportunity to ask about the Branch boys.

"I got a bench warrant issued for Freddy," Antone says, then explains, "Material witness."

"So you got any idea where he might be?"

"Nope, but he'll turn up. Routine traffic stop or running a stop sign or something, and we'll have him. Right now, I'm at a standstill on Oscar Sorenson's stabbing."

I don't bother to mention that I have a line on Freddy Branch, his mother's address, as I want to have a chance to have a long talk with Freddy before Antone gets his hands on the boy. But this is good news. If there's a warrant I can put the arm on him, even if he's not an FTA. But now I've got a problem as I'm astride the bike—a good pursuit vehicle in certain situations but a lousy transport one—and don't have any help lined up in Bakersfield, in case he's run home to Mommy.

What the hell, I probably won't find him anyway, and it'll give me the excuse to spend some time on the bike, go back through the Cuyama Canyon. A winding road through some great rock formations.

But even though ill equipped, I can at least have the proper paperwork, and ask Antone to remind me to get a copy of the warrant before I leave.

The medical examiner is a lady, a rather bland tall Pakistani or East Indian woman introduced to me as Dr. Patel, with straight long black hair tied in a ponytail.

Autopsies make a bit of a mess, and Lawanda has been taken apart and badly put back together by the time I see her. My mouth goes dry when I see her lying there, formerly a vibrant girl, now cold and blank, covered by a white sheet. Not that dead bodies bother me, at least no more than the next fella, but this was Oscar's lady, and the mother of his new baby. It's fairly obvious she died from a gunshot wound to the back of the mouth, but her face is in perfect shape. She still has on her makeup, and her nails are long and nicely polished.

Then I notice something and search my mind regarding the short time I'd spent at Lawanda's. And then think I'm on to something.

"Did you notice the exit wound?" I ask Antone. Dr. Patel is leaning against one of her stainless steel counters, obviously bored. She yawns, covering her mouth with a rubber-gloved hand.

"Hard to miss," Antone says. "A .357 exits large."

"Yeah, but it's more on the left side of her upper neck and skull than on the right."

"So?"

"So Lalo was left-handed. I noticed when she poured coffee for me. I noticed because Oscar was left-handed, which gave him some trouble earning his sharpshooter medal. Give me your weapon."

He pulls a little police special out of a holster at the small of his back, unloads it into his palm, and only then hands me the weapon. I demonstrate putting the gun in my mouth using my left hand to hold it. Then think of something I might have missed.

"When they ran the gun, did they check the position of her hand on the weapon? I presume her prints were on the gun?"

"They were. And there is powder residue on her hands."

"Residue on both of them?"

"Yes."

"Were the fingers holding the gun in a normal fashion, or did she reverse her hand on the gun?"

"What do you mean?"

I demonstrate, feigning holding a revolver backward, muzzle facing me, where I'd use my thumb on the trigger rather than my index finger. "If I held it backward in my left hand, thumb on the trigger, I could discharge it at an angle that would cause the left-side exit wound."

This seems to stimulate Dr. Patel, as she stops in midyawn, then moves over to investigate the wound.

"No, the prints were consistent with a normal grip."

"Then she didn't shoot herself, because it would be really unnatural for someone to twist their hand around that much."

"Okay, so she didn't shoot herself. We worked the crime scene hard, and we found a lot of prints, but then she's had more than a dozen different people over. We ran everything through CJIS, and got no hits."

Then I have another brainstorm, thinking about what I would do if I was going to fake a suicide. "Her nails. Did you dust her fingernails?"

"I doubt it." Antone gives Dr. Patel an inquisitive look, but she merely shrugs, then shakes her head. "We normally wouldn't dust the victim's nails . . . particularly when the scene had suicide written all over it."

"How about having it done?"

"Okay, why the nails, Sherlock?"

# Chapter 19

Lt. Paul Antone is looking at me as if I were nuts, me wondering if he'd had the victim's fingernails dusted for fingerprints.

But I'm not nuts, at least I don't think I am.

I hand him his police special, then envelop his hand in mine. "If I had wiped the weapon down, and wanted it to appear that your hand had been holding it when it was fired, I'd wrap my hand around yours, thusly, pressing your fingers firmly onto the grip. Lawanda's nails are long and nicely polished. A good medium to register prints."

"I took scrapings under the nails," Dr. Patel offers, seeing what I'm doing, then looks a little embarrassed. "I may have contaminated the victim's nail surface with my own fingertips."

"Still worth a shot," I say.

"You may have something," Antone admits.

"I'd also like to see a pattern on the blow-back on her hands. It might not be blow-back from her firing the weapon, but rather from her grabbing at the weapon as it was forced into her mouth."

"Okay," Antone says, then looks at Dr. Patel, who

nods, looking not nearly so sheepish as a forensic pathologist should under the circumstance.

Antone goes to make a call to get his print guy back to check. He looks at me with new respect when he returns, so I make it a point *not* to tell him I saw the same solution on TV less than a week ago. Sometimes it's good to keep your mouth shut and go ahead and look smart. Sometimes it's good to physically run out of gas and lie down in front of the TV and crash awhile, particularly if a CSI, *Crime Scene Investigation,* rerun is on the tube. No telling what you'll learn.

He gives me a lift back to the station and the Sportster.

With his promise to let me know about the prints, and with a courthouse-generated copy of the warrant in hand, I head back to the end of Pine Street, and the Branch place. If anything, there's even more junk in the yard than the first time I was there, but this time I notice the Harley is missing. Still no one home but the dogs. They get real feisty and try their best to gnaw through the cyclone fence when I clean out the mailbox, one of those curbside tin ones on a four-by-four, and see that it's probably been a couple or three days since anyone has picked up the mail.

I don't learn a thing from the mail, mostly fliers and advertisements and bills, so I take care of one more piece of business, and set in front of the Branch house and put my cell phone to work.

Patti McAfee, Freddy Branch's ex-girlfriend, is home. I remember Antone saying she said "that cute guy," so I turn on the charm.

"Patti, it's Dev."

"Dev?"

I guess I didn't make all that much impression. "Dev Shannon, you remember? I dropped by to check up on where Fred Branch was."

"Sure, I remember."

"Sorry, but I couldn't find your TV over at Butch's. Freddy probably already sold it."

"The dick-head. That's okay, I didn't expect to get it back."

"Hey, I'd like to drop by and see you sometime."

There's a short silence. "I'm not doing anything tonight."

"Oh, man, I'm traveling, but I'll be in Paso next week sometime. Can I give you a call?"

"Sure."

"Have you heard from the dick-head?"

"Nope. A buddy of his said he cut out in that old Ford pickup he drove sometimes . . . you know, the beige one with the big rip in the upholstery. He better not come back around here." It's the same vehicle Lawanda's friends spotted. I even have the plate number.

"But you don't know where he cut out to? I'd like to send him to the dentist for what he did . . . or didn't do . . . for my buddy Oscar . . . and for stealing your TV," I say as an afterthought.

"Yeah, that was terrible what happened to Oscar."

I chat for a few more minutes so she'll think I'm interested, and then I head out of Paso Robles west on Highway 46. I only go a half dozen miles through the rolling oak- and vineyard-covered hills when I see a sign advertising the Valpredo Winery tasting room. I recall that this is the place Lawanda said she worked, and put the binders on the bike when I reach a drive where a sign with an arrow on it is pointing into the vineyards.

I'm shown into the boss's office in a cedar-shake-roofed ranch-style building overlooking a square mile of vineyards, now bright green with new leaves. Aldo Valpredo is a gentleman, and after I explain that I'm a bail enforcement agent and an old friend of Oscar Sorenson, whom Lawanda lived with and had a child with, and that I'm real interested in finding out who did such a terrible thing to her, he sits me in a deep tan leather chair across his desk from his own and offers me a cup of coffee when I turn down a glass of wine.

But I learn nothing there, only that Lawanda was considered a good employee. We've run out of conversation by the time I finish the coffee. So I ride on.

I stop at Chalome, a wide spot in the road with a single café. It's red-Naugahyde-covered chrome-stool-and-jukebox era, under a pair of broad oaks. I buy a can of Coke and take it outside to sit and finish it on a bench in front of a big marble tribute to James Dean, who was killed just down the road when a student named Turnipseed turned left across the two-lane highway in front of his Porsche Spider, not realizing that Dean was going in the neighborhood of a hundred miles an hour. Roadside marble monuments are not for the likes of me, or Lawanda Lopez, or even for Oscar Sorenson with his well-earned bronze metal. What the hell, I stretch, shake out the kinks, and ride on.

The hills are still green, and even after I leave the oaks behind, then the hills, and ride the long straight highway into the San Joaquin Valley, it's still green. With the sun at my back, the west-side desert at its best with lupine and a few poppies celebrating the late afternoon sun, I find myself taking my time. I have to stop and shed my leather jacket, as now that we're out of the coastal influence, it's in the high eighties. You can always count on the San Joaquin for heat.

The last time I left Paso Robles I had an empty feeling in the pit of my gut; this time there are snakes roiling there, spitting poison. But the ride helps.

It's just past five P.M. when I reach the little community of Oildale, just north of Bakersfield across the Kern River. The wails of Buck Owens and Merle Haggard still echo from its honky-tonks. It's an old part of town surrounded by oil tool and oil well service companies, as on its northeast side are thousands of acres of oil fields. The Branch home place is a tiny clapboard affair about the size of a decent two-car garage located on a street of mostly the same, almost all of them squatted under knotted, fruitless mulberry trees, surrounded by cyclone fences. It's obviously a redneck part of the city, as I see nothing but white faces and they all are in poorly fenced front yards with their share of dogs. Rockers adorn old-style railed front porches, and gardens are staked for tomatoes. This isn't the first time I've been here looking for an FTA, and I know the reputation of this place well. Hardworking oil field roughnecks interspersed with truckers and bikers. A fine mix of folks, if you like beer busts, barbecue, and the occasional black eye or busted lip. And some of the great bar fights in history.

It's a good time to arrive there, as a woman pulls into the unpaved driveway in an old green Oldsmobile with primer spots, about the same time as I kill the bike.

"Mrs. Branch?" I hail her as she exits the car carrying a bag of groceries. She's a round-faced, overweight woman with askew gray hair. Her frumpy flower-print dress has no shape other than the occasional lumps where you figure they might be. It's obvious where Butch and Freddy got their looks.

"Yes, sir," she answers politely. It's not so obvious where Fred and Butch got their lack of manners.

"Looking for Freddy."

"You a friend of Freddy's, young fella?" she asks suspiciously.

"Yes, ma'am. Sure am." I give her my most winning smile.

"He's s'posed to be weeding the garden for me, which is about all he can do with that cast on his wrist, so I imagine he's over at Mugg's."

"Mugg's?"

She motions with a thumb back over her shoulder.

"Beer joint, down that cross street about six or eight blocks."

"Great. But I don't have much time. Tell him Frank dropped by."

"Okay, Frank. You take care."

I leave, heading for Mugg's, the beer joint.

Mine's not the only bike parked in front of the place, there's a pair of Harleys between every pickup. Most of the decent trucks have some kind of oil company sign on their doors, and toolboxes in the back. The others are decorated with dents and primer spots. One has an old bumper sticker, IRAQ WOMEN SHAVE THEIR THING, SAD-DAM IS AGAINST BUSHES. This is a workingman's joint.

I start to head for the door, then have second thoughts. My SOG knife is in my pocket, but I'd hate to be the guy who brought a knife to a gunfight, so I fish the Smith and Wesson out of the saddlebag and clip the holster on the back of my belt, which means I have to wear the leather jacket, which looks a wee bit strange as it's still seventy-five degrees in the shade. While I'm in the bags I rummage around and find a pair of cuffs and slip them into my jacket pocket, and pluck out a black bill cap, with THE POLICE embroidered across its front, but it's the old rock-and-roll group, not the P.D., that it memorializes.

I can hear tinny jukebox music, country-and-western of course, all the way out in the street. Shoving through the door, I'm not a bit surprised to have to squint to see through the smoke down the long bar to the shuffle-board tables. Every seat at the bar is taken, and half the tables. There are at least thirty men in the place, and a half dozen women. One old shaggy-haired boy in cutoff Levis and a torn T-shirt is doing what resembles a dance in the middle of the room with a girl in a red miniskirt, red and white cowboy boots, and a blue blouse unbut-toned well past where the bottom of sad breasts dangle, with her hair piled and ratted high enough so she'd have to duck going out the door. The hair's up proud even if the boobs aren't. And the outfit's patriotic, even if lacking in style.

If there was a place celebrating the song "I've Got Friends in Low Places," this would be it.

The dancers with hands on each other's hips grind personal parts together, with little vigor or style, but obvious intent. It's pretty clear that this dance is a vertical expression of a horizontal desire. I walk around their spot in the world, ignoring them, and make my way to the only opening, the waitress's station at the bar. If the white half-apron's any indicator, she's across the room smoking a cigarette and talking with the shuffleboard players. I make a quick check of all the women in the place, and even as past due as I am, and after being teased for days by the close proximity of a Swedish girl named Sonya, I don't see anything that would even qualify had it been two A.M. and me two six-packs invested. The good news for all of them is the women seem well matched with the men in the place.

So far, I haven't noticed Butch or Freddy anywhere, but I can't see all the way into a room that tees in the back of the place.

As the jukebox screams a lament, "Bubba shot the jukebox last night," I order a long-neck Bud, and it's on the bar almost before I can get my wallet out. The service is fine, and the price is two bucks. Now I know I'm not in Santa Barbara.

"You a little short of tip money there, cowboy?" I'm in Wrangler jeans and cowboy boots, and with my long-sleeve shirt rolled up past the elbows, I somewhat resemble a cowboy.

It's the waitress, who's walked up behind me and seems to be taking umbrage at my ordering from her station.

"Looked like you were kibitzing the shuffleboard game," I say as a lame excuse, "and I've had a long ride across a hot desert."

This does not assuage her. "There're plenty of tables. Have a seat and I'll bring that over." She plans to work her way into that tip somehow. I like ambitious folks, so I leave the beer and walk to the back of the place where I can see the rest of the tables.

Bingo! Butch Branch, in a dark corner, not paying a bit of attention to anything other than cleaning his finger-nails with a switchblade.

He's in a booth, but Freddy's nowhere to be seen. I decide to play it casual, and take a ladder-back chair at a table for four, with my back mostly to Butch, who's a half dozen paces across the room. The rest of the pa-trons are in the front of the place. The Branch boys and I are the only ones back here.

My patience pays off as I hear a hallway door open. I pull the bill cap low over my eyes and with a quick glance over the shoulder I see that Fred A-for-A-hole Branch, fiberglass cast and all, has appeared, and slides into the booth across from his brother. He was in the john, probably packing his nose or shooting up.

It's time to bring the boy to Jesus.

# Chapter 20

Fred is a little wild eyed and emaciated, which means he's probably on the needle. He doesn't appear to be armed, but there's no telling what he's got in his pocket or even stuck up his wrist cast.

I glance over my shoulder again. Both of them have beers in front of them. I'm trying to figure out how to make this come down, while playing it casual with my back to them, when my cell phone and George Strait settle it for me.

The phone rings just as George quits singing, and I have it turned all the way up as I can never hear the damn thing when I'm roaring down the road on the bike. It's so loud it would catch anyone's attention. I should have turned it off before coming into the joint, but I guess I'm off my game. I have to fish it out of my jacket pocket. I do so, and summarily shut it off, hoping I haven't attracted attention I don't want. Up to now, I doubt if they've even glanced my way.

However, there's nothing quite like a ringing cell phone to gain you an unwanted glance—and at the moment I don't even want a casual glance from these guys.

I notice that the table behind me has suddenly gone silent.

Just as I casually turn to check it out, Fred Branch sprints out of the booth and tries to charge past me to a back door, but I'm too quick for him and kick one of the other chairs at the table in front of him.

He tangles up and goes sprawling on his face. Normally I try and make an arrest without the use of the weapon, but somehow, me being alone and Mugg's-the-beer-bar being packed with Butch Branch look-alikes, I make an exception.

I whip out the Smith and Wesson, at the same time yelling "You're under arrest."

Suddenly the place goes quiet, except for some male singer lamenting the truck in her driveway not being his.

As Fred is on his face grabbing the wrist with the cast as if he's in pain, I'm more worried about Butch, who's been cleaning his nails with the six-inch blade of a switchblade, and spin to see what's on his mind. It's a good thing I do as he's up and out of the booth, leading with the switchblade and was only three paces from skewering my spine.

And I thought he and I were buddies.

Normally it's not good bail enforcement agent policy to hit a guy in the head, as it usually does not work out the same way it does on TV. After his eyes roll up in his noggin he may be in a coma for a year while you're fighting a lawsuit for excessive force.

But this seems the exception.

Butch, being no trained knife-fighter, comes in high, with the knife overhead, looping it downward as if he were swinging a hammer. Mistake. I swing my chair up in an equal and opposite motion, and get the seat between me and the knife. The blade buries deep in the black upholstery, I twist, and the cheap blade snaps; then I crack him a good one to the bridge of his wide nose with the butt of the Smith and Wesson. I sidestep, spin, and, while his eyes are still doing an Orphan Annie imitation, give him a low side-kick to the knee with the cowboy boot. The knee folds inward with a crack that sounds like a baseball bat hitting a home run—folding a way knees don't normally fold. The knife goes spinning across the floor, and he goes on his face in a growing puddle of bubbly nose blood.

"Should have had your doggies with you, Butch," I say, then remember my reason for being here as I hear the back door slam.

"You prick, I think you broke my leg," Butch gurgles, between wheezing whines, as he withers on the floor trying to figure out if his knee is busted.

I ignore him and start to head for the back door and my quarry, but one of the roughnecks who's been at the bar steps in front of it. Then I realize that a half dozen of them are up and blocking not only my pursuit of Fred, but my alternative way out the front.

Butch and Fred must still be considered hometown boys. I can readily see the congregation has evil on their beer-soaked brains and pan them with the Smith and Wesson, while giving them my most sadistic smile. "Gentlemen, you're about to get in way over your pointy little heads."

"Who the fuck are you?" It's the one in cutoff Levis and torn T-shirt who was humping on the dance floor when I came in.

With my free hand I fish out my wallet, flip it open, stand a little taller, and flash the brass. I have the biggest badge I could buy out of the NIC catalogue, which is impressive to the uninitiated as they figure I'm P.D. or sheriff, but in fact it says BAIL ENFORCEMENT AGENT. One has to be careful not to impersonate an officer, but of course the print is in very small letters, not that I figure any of these throwbacks can read.

"Move aside, or you're all going downtown."

They look at each other quizzically, no one wanting to be the first to capitulate, but then slowly part. I wait until there's room for me to pass with only a small chance of taking a long-neck beer bottle behind the ear, and head for the front door at a brisk walk.

Then sprint as I clear the crowd.

As I exit, I can see an old cream-colored Ford pickup, already two blocks away, but the way it's smoking out the tailpipe I don't think it would make it far even if I wasn't pursuing. The truck must have been parked in the back of the place.

One kick and I'm able to spin the bike, spit gravel, and am after Fred and the Ford. By the time he's made another block, I'm right on him. He obviously makes me on his tail, as he feints a right turn, then cranks it hard left. The Ford could use some tightening up of the front end, as it drifts off the narrow neighborhood street, sans curbs and sidewalks, wavers into the front yard of the corner house, and takes on a thick old mulberry tree.

The tree wins.

By the time I get to the truck, folks are pouring out of the corner house and a couple more down the block as fast as steam is pouring out of Fred's still-quivering radiator.

I guess the neighborhood folks are a little surprised when I get to the driver's door and find Fred slumped over the wheel. He starts to come around, and I ask him if he's okay.

"Hit my head," he mumbles, and I take that for an "I'm fine."

I yank the door open and jerk Fred out to flop him facedown, spread-eagled in the grass. He's groggy, bleeding from a cut between his eyes and his nose from tangling with the old steering wheel, so he's no problem.

I had visions of maybe using Fred's truck to transport him, but he's eliminated that potential.

I also had visions of squeezing some information out of Fred, but . . .

There's a bear of a man standing over me as I rise, with an open shirt, a beer gut the size of a keg, and enough body and facial hair to testify to his overload of testosterone.

"You a cop or somethin'?" he asks as I pull the cuffs out of my coat pocket.

"Or something," I say. "I'm arresting this guy."

"Good. Sumbitch hit my tree," he says.

"Well, that's not the only reason, but as long as you're happy," I say, while hoping he'll go away so I can put the squeeze on Fred.

"I'm going to call the cops," the big guy says.

"Don't bother." I fish out and show him my cell phone, then a little reluctantly dial 911 and explain that I'm a bail enforcement agent and that I need transportation, and ask for a black-and-white. The operator informs me it'll be a green-and-white, and puts me in touch with the Kern County Sheriff's Department. I take the waiting time to pat Fred down, and come up with a mate to his brother's knife, and more interestingly, a Baggie with at least four ounces of Mexican brown. That will give me a little leverage. I walk over to the bike and drop both the knife and dope in my saddlebags.

In moments, there's a pair of green-and-whites pulling up, and I'm explaining the situation to a big burly sergeant while a five-foot-two-inch brunette lady officer with a cute pug nose escorts a very groggy Fred to the back of her car.

I show my credentials to the sergeant, ask him if he's satisfied, get a tentative nod, then walk over after the female officer's got Fred patted down again and deposited, and has gone across the yard to join her sergeant. Opening the front door, I talk to Fred through the screen. "I found your knife, Fred. Illegal. I found your dope, Fred. Very, very, very illegal. That'll get you at least five to ten where you'll find yourself bent over with some big brothers . . . and I mean twelve-inchers . . . lined up behind to take their turn. You like getting your fudge packed, Freddy?"

"Fuck you," he says, still a little groggy.

"No, I don't think so. But I'll tell you what, I'm not going to rat you out to them, but I'm going to want to have a heart-to-heart with you when you get back to Paso."

"Thanks, man," he says, but I can tell he doesn't believe me.

"I don't want your thanks. I want the truth. You get ready to get straight with me . . . and remember, I've got that Baggie of brown, and your knife, both with your prints all over them. I can always give these boys a call and tell them in the excitement of things I forgot to give them up. You got it?"

"I got it. I got it."

"Remember, I've got your nuts in a vise."

With that, I walk over to the brunette. "Can I have my cuffs?" I ask, then give her a wink, which she ignores, then turns and goes back to the car, unloads Fred, and with good procedure leans him up against the car spread-eagled, and replaces my handcuffs with hers. When she returns, she doesn't wink back, but rather gives me a look like she'd rather be arresting me as she hands me the cuffs.

Can't win 'em all.

I put it off to petty jealously. Cops are to bail enforcement agents what bus drivers are to NASCAR racers. They're city or county employees and we're independent entrepreneurs. They eat the doughnuts, we own the franchise. But I give her an understanding wink anyway.

The sergeant has been carefully surveying the warrant, and asks me, "Was this guy bailed?"

"Nope."

"Is there a reward for him or something?"

"Nope. Personal matter. This is a freebee."

"Didn't know you boys did freebees," he says, looking at me quizzically.

"Hell, Officer, public service is our life's calling," I say with a modest smile, to offset the slightly sarcastic tone.

Seeming satisfied, he gives me directions to the Kern County lockup across the river in downtown Bakersfield, then calls a tow truck.

It takes me an hour to get my business done at the Kern County Jail, but then don't transport him back to Paso Robles. Since there's no money to be made on the deal, I'm not about to rent a car. After I walk out, I call Antone and tell him where he can pick up his material witness, and that he owes me one; then I head out and am on my way back to Santa Barbara.

I probably should go back and check to see that good old Butch Branch has found his way to some medical care, but he had what seemed a house full of buddies, and they may have figured out that I'm a BEA, not a cop, by now.

I really, really wanted to have a little private time with brother Fred, but it wasn't to be. I'll get my chance in Paso, when he's straight after getting wrung out in the lockup. He'll be a whole lot more logical then. I glance at my watch and see that it's only six-thirty. It's too late to make the trip back via the Cuyama road, as it's already getting dark and I couldn't enjoy the scenery, so I decide to go the fastest way and head south on the freeway.

If I can get back to the boat in a little over two hours, I can make the function that I suspect Melinda Haroldstern will be attending. The telltale envelope may have told me how to get next to the ex–Miss Texas runner-up. And if she's what Pug says she is, it sounds like I wouldn't mind getting next to her.


Having a converted broad-beamed fifty-five-foot fishing boat means you can actually have a boat *and* a little closet space, and I have enough that I can keep non-essential things like a tux on board *Aces n' Eights*. I'm happy to note that even though it has a little dust on the shoulders from not being out of the closet for over a year, it's clean and pressed; and tuxes, white shirts, and black bow ties seldom go out of style. The fact is my tux would be in the closet even if I had less room, as I spend my vacations in Palm Beach. To me, most of California is beer and tequila, and Palm Beach champagne and cognac.

I absolutely haul ass all the way, but it's ten o'clock by the time I wheel my oatmeal Chevrolet into the parking area of the Santa Barbara Polo and Racquet Club, hoping to catch the last hour or so of the Rosco Champness Benefit for the Homeless. I park as far from the festivities as possible, so there's little chance of my ride being seen, and so I can work my way around the back and slip in without being asked for my two-hundred-fifty-dollar invitation. With a lot full of Mercedeses, BMWs, Rolls Royces, Bentleys, and Porsches, I'm a little out of place. Rosco Champness is one of the few who can actually sponsor a benefit of this kind and can claim a truly unselfish and highly motivated reason for doing so, as he was actually homeless at one time. That was a short while before he invented some little gizmo that allowed one computer to talk to another. Now, if he truly wanted to, he could house all the homeless in the state in high style.

My opinion of the homeless comes from a different perspective than Rosco's, as I happen to know that most of them are nothing more than old criminals who've worn out their welcome at home because they have rap sheets longer than a polo mallet. Still, it's the party of the year at the polo club.

In order to play polo you need four or more ponies, and a decent polo pony sets one back a minimum of twenty-five grand to buy and several thousand a year to keep. You're expected to field a different pony for each of the six seven-minute chukkers, or periods, of the game, but you can rest a horse a couple of chukkers and bring him back into play. It's an upscale sport, with only four to a team. You probably can't find more than eight accomplished horsemen in the average state who can afford the game. Santa Barbara, of course, fields a dozen teams; then again how many other communities even *have* a polo field?

I know a little about it as I owned a hay-burner when I was a kid and had visions of swinging a mallet with the best of them. I mucked stalls in this place for a summer or two, but wised up about being able to join the club when I saw the member fee of ten grand or so a year, plus miscellaneous.

I doubt if any members here will remember me, as that was twenty years ago.

There's only a small clubhouse at the Santa Barbara Polo and Racquet Club, because most of the functions are outside as the polo season is April through October. The grounds, however, are something else. There's at least a hundred and sixty acres, and it's a stone's throw from the ocean. I have no idea what that would be worth today. A polo field is one hundred fifty yards wide and three hundred yards long, the area of nine football fields. There are condos overlooking the polo grounds, as well as horse barns, hot walkers, workout rings, an Olympic pool for the members, and a workout pool for the horses. If one was to be reborn as a horse, this might just be the place to be. The whole place is surrounded by an eight-foot-high espaliered shrub fence to keep out prying eyes.

I guess the rich don't want to intimidate the poor passersby.

The club is rented out for events such as this one, although Rosco sits on the board and probably gets some kind of a deal, particularly for a benefit.

The ladies are resplendent, some in floor-length gowns, I'm sure with designer labels, and most all of the men in black as am I. There's one of those portable dance floors set up outside the clubhouse, and at least fifty tables spaced about on the grass. A six-piece orchestra is busily at work and the dance floor actually has some action.

There are more folks here than I anticipated, and not ever having seen Ms. Melinda, I may have my work cut out for me. I'm a little surprised that so many of these ladies look as if they could have been Miss Texas runner-ups. The good news is that even though dinner has been served, the hors d'oeuvres have not been completely picked over, and I'm starving.

I load a plate with water crackers spread with goose paté and brie, shrimp and quail eggs, then make a turn around the place, stopping to check out the ladies on the dance floor. There are a half dozen possibles, though all but one of them seem to be with a gentleman. The other is sitting with three other ladies. She's dressed in black, which I doubt is due to her status of fairly recent mourning—as this black dips deep in the front, and is totally void to the low waist in the back. It's an engineering marvel, unless she needs no help from artificial means in keeping the front standing high and proud. Hell, maybe they're holding the dress up, not the other way around.

"Dev?"

I turn to see an old buddy, a part-time bartender from Café del Sol, one of my favorite watering holes near the boat, but on the border between the harbor area and Montecito. I can see he's working, as he's collecting glasses and has no coat over his white shirt and black bow tie. "What's up, Dutch?"

"Working," he confirms. "Trying to earn a living, but I should know better than to try to make any bucks at Montecito fund-raisers. I never saw such a bunch of tight-ass tippers."

I laugh. "That's probably how they got here, stiffing poor suckers like us." He laughs also, then starts back to work. I stop him with a "Hey, help me out."

"What?"

"That blonde, over at the table with the three blue-hairs?"

"Oh, yeah. I worked her house at a party. Mrs. Haroldstern. She's available, since her old man went facedown on State Street last year, but she's way out of your league."

"I'll be the judge of that, thank you. She alone?"

"No, she's with those three ladies." He jabs me, knowing exactly what I meant. "But they're at least three martinis each into the evening, so maybe you'll look fine to her."

"Get me a Jack Daniel's and soda, and I'll even tip."

He fades away toward one of the portable bars, and I work my way over toward the table.

I get the drink, overtip Dutch, and then move another ten feet to the table. "Ladies, may I set my drink here while I dance?"

They look up, then around, wondering why I don't set my drink at one of the nearby empty tables, so I offer, "I'd use one of those, but I'm coming right back here as . . . it's with one of you beautiful ladies I'm dancing." I give them my most mischievous little boy grin. "Now, which one?"

# Chapter 21

I'm happy to say they all have a sense of humor, and laugh. I have to dance with three of them—one twice my age, one twice my size, and one who steps on both my feet—before it's Melinda's turn. I'm happy to say she readily accepts my extended hand, even though I act as if it were a real chore to have to dance just one more time. I'm also happy that it's a slow tune, as it's talk, not dancing, I'm after. And I'm even far more pleased to find she's more than just a little tipsy, as that should loosen her tongue.

We've already been introduced when I returned the first dance partner to the table, so we fall right into conversation.

"Are you a member here?" she asks.

"No, just a supporter. I try and come every year. We have so many homeless. . . ." Hell, if I was homeless, I'd pick Santa Barbara's shrubs to live under. No one said that old criminals were stupid.

"So, do you live in Montecito?"

"Santa Barbara." I'm purposely not asking about her and being elusive with information about myself, knowing that if I come on too strong, I probably won't learn a thing. I figure the strong silent type will be far more fascinating and mysterious. Even a little drunk she's very good on the dance floor, and smells even better than she dances. The eyes are so turquoise they have to be contacts, but those work. She's got more value in rocks on one finger than my total net worth, and more in the necklace she's wearing than all the fancy cars in the parking lot are worth. The center stone has to be ten karats, making the rest of the two dozen or so one-karat stones look like chips.

"So, what do you do?" she asks.

"I have a security company." It's a standard line I use all the time and second only to my favorite, "pest control," but that seems a little plebeian for my current surroundings. Actually, I do perform a little security work once in a while.

"Corporate security?"

"Sort of. Actually, special projects of a discreet nature, for a very select clientele . . . you know, sub-rosa projects." Her eyes light with mischievousness, telling me she's aware of the legal and very ancient term for a covert or secret project.

"My husband . . . he passed away last year, you know . . . my husband used to use some outside security in his company."

"Sorry to hear about your husband. What was his name? Maybe it was my company he used?"

"Jonathan Haroldstern. He was in several things connected with aerospace."

"You know, I've heard of him, but I never had the pleasure." The first time I laid eyes on Melinda, I figured her for early thirties, but on closer inspection, I would guess forty, maybe as old as forty-two, with some excellent reconstructive work. Almost zero worry lines, boobs that are making indentations in the tux jacket.

"You know," I say, as if I've had an epiphany, "I did meet a Haroldstern last week, at the Biltmore . . . or a couple of weeks ago." I shake my head, then let it dawn on me. "Lenny, that's it. Lenny, a nice chap some years younger than me, with a great Porsche . . . red, I think."

A dark veil drops across her face, but only for a moment. Then she smiles, if a little tightly. "Yes, Lenny. He's my husband's nephew. He spent a few days at my place."

"Not *your* nephew? You two look the same age."

"Thank you, liar."

She smiles as if I just told her she won the lottery, not that she needs it. I smile back, and let her continue.

"Jonathan's by a prior marriage. Jonathan and I were only married five years. He liked Lenny a lot. Used to play a lot of golf with him at Birnamwood. Jonathan thought Lenny could go on the tour, but qualifying was too much work for Lenny."

The music ends and I'm forced to return her to her table, but I've gleaned another piece of info: Lenny's a golfer, and a damn good one. One thing that's consistent with skips is that they fall back on old habits. Country club types don't start hanging out in biker bars. Hobbies and habits narrow the trail. And that's how they get caught. If they liked pole dancing in New Mexico, they'll like it in Los Angeles.

On the way back to the table, I decide to force my hand. "Are you ladies up for a drink after this thing ends? The Montecito Inn, or Lucky's, or Café del Sol? I think the invitation said seven to eleven."

She stops before reaching the table. "I doubt if the girls can make it." Then she smiles. "But I'd love one."

"Great, it's a date." I check my watch. "I hate to be a bore, but I have a little business to attend to with a gentleman I haven't seen for a while. Can I drop back by the table in an hour or so?"

"Yes, but I have to have one more dance before we go."

"My pleasure."

I notice there are fresh drinks on the table when I deposit her there. That'll be four martinis for the lady. I would tell my life story after four martinis—I hope she doesn't have so many she can't.

As I walk away I can't help thinking what a cad I am. A sensitive cad of course. Even bounty hunters have a sensitive side. Oh, well, Lenny needs to pay society, and any legal means I can use to help him do so, I will.

The hell of it is, I enjoyed Ms. Melinda's company, not to speak of the fact I still have two major dents in my tux coat. Being a bail enforcement agent is tough, but somebody has to do it.

I stay scarce. When you've made the close, it pays to shut up so you don't mess up. She already said she was going, so if I hang around, all I could do is screw it up.

I completely disappear for forty-five minutes, taking my drink back to Dutch, pouring it down the drain, and filling the glass with straight club soda on the rocks, then losing myself back to the car. I take the opportunity to call Cynthia to check up on how she's doing with the kid's dad, the good doctor. I also left her in charge of following up with Sonya and the children, as I have another row to hoe, and I figured I've already done more than my share.

"You're actually home," I say.

"Curled up with a good book, listening to Kenny G's sweet sax."

"So, what's up with Dr. Hashim and our money?"

"Pissed, but not so much as you might think. Actually, I think he's surprised about the whole thing. Surprised you got the kids away from the Aziz family. I get the impression he didn't think he'd have to ever pay up."

"Come on, he employed Dev Shannon. How could he ever believe—"

"Right. He's more than a little irritated about the

'American soil' thing, as the boys at Ogilvie and Meyers have informed him that you probably performed by getting them to the embassy."

"No probably about it."

"Anyway, I talked to Sonya just an hour or so ago. She says it looks like they may be able to leave inside of a week."

"Great news. If we have the kids in tow, we can unilaterally claim the money. And it's a good thing, as most of mine is probably spent."

"Well . . . maybe we can. Tom Demarco at Ogilvie says Hashim is probably going to get some kind of restraining order to keep us from claiming it even if the kids show up, and that took three drinks to pry out of Tom. But it's all posturing, or so Tom says. I'm in the middle of this, as Olgilvie represents Hashim. I'm walking soft. . . ."

"Why would he get a restraining order if we actually deliver the goods?"

"Because he can. Then he can negotiate a lower fee while we stew and need to pay the rent and phone bill."

"I really don't like that s.o.b. I told you at the get-go, anyone who'll drink Campari—"

"Speaking of drinks, you want to drop by for a nightcap? We can drown our sorrows."

I have to take a deep breath. I haven't been invited to Cynthia's condo in two years. And I have to say no, particularly since it appears that Hashim is going to try and do the worm on us. Lenny Haroldstern, and that recovery fee, becomes even more important.

"I can't. I hate that I can't, Cynthia, but I'm working."

"Okay. It's a really sexy book, a Kat Martin romance, and it's got me really unhappy that Cedric dropped by and interrupted the other night. Oh, well." She laughs so I don't know if she's putting me on or not, and hangs up.

I down the rest of my soda and decide it's time to find Ms. Melinda and give her that dance I promised.

And I discover she's at least as conniving as most women, as they've all conspired against poor old Dev. I have to dance with each of them again before I get to the prize.

They're into their fifth martini, and I get stepped on even more.

But Melinda may just be worth the wait. We hit on another slow dance, and she has another request, with slurred words. "Dev, I hate bars. Can't we just go to my place for a nightcap? You like martinis mixed with a sexy Jacuzzi, don't you?"

# Chapter 22

I do not reply to Melinda's question with "Does a big bear ka-ka in the woods?" as is my first thought, but rather, "You bet, I love them both."

"Good. Do you know Montecito well?"

I can't allow myself to be seen in the oatmeal Chevy, which is not Montecito material, so I think fast. I'm tempted to use that old line, "Actually, I'm in my butler's car . . . my Aston Martin's in the shop, and he's in Monaco." But I don't and say instead, "Actually, I don't have my car. I came with a friend and he had to leave, so how about I ride with you?" It'll seal our mutual fate even more if she thinks I'm depending on her.

"I have to drop a couple of the ladies off, but that's fine. I love to make the girls jealous."

All I can do is smile at that one.

Thank God she allows me to drive her big BMW as she has a little trouble negotiating her way to the parking lot. All of the girls are at least three sheets into a strong wind, and one of them even suggests she join us in the Jacuzzi, but Melinda stops that like the mulberry stopped Freddy. And it's just as well, as I don't think I'm wired to handle an entire AARP chapter.

The winding driveway to the Haroldsterns' is a quarter mile long between native sandpaper oaks and a half million dollars' worth of landscape architecture hoping to look natural. Those little lights line the driveway and lead me to a five-car garage in the back of the place. Melinda obviously hasn't seen fit to sell any of his cars since Jonathan passed on, as a Maserati, a Land Rover, and a stretch limo are still in residence.

I walk around to let her out, and comment as she unloads, "I don't see Lenny's Porsche."

"He's off . . ." She waves a hand, and I learn nothing.

Without ceremony, she begins tossing clothes as we enter a beautifully landscaped area behind the two-story, immaculately maintained house and cross a flagstone patio to one of those infinity swimming pools that has no edge. She's down to nothing but high heels in moments. The view opens up as we near, and we can see all the way to the Santa Barbara harbor to the west and Port Hueneme to the east, not that that's the view I'm admiring. By the time she skirts the pool to a short stairway, she's as God made her, sans even high heels, and He made her well.

There's a small bar built into a rock wall separated from the waterfall and the infinity pool by the stairway. She hits a switch, and the Jacuzzi, which would hold a dozen revelers, fires into action and lights up.

She turns to me, as all I've shed is tie and coat, then leans up against me, refreshing the dents in my shirt, as au naturel they're still erect and proud even without the questionable help of the gown. "You coming in, Doug?"

Doug? Oh, well, I don't give a damn what she calls me, so long as I get some info. Whatever else I get may be in the hands of Bacchus. Already I'm getting turned off mentally, as drunken women are not my forte . . . at least not falling-down drunk.

"Sure, after I make us a drink."

"Okay, turn on the musi . . . music."

Built into the bar is a TV and stereo, and I hit the power switch and without having to worry more, on comes 97.7, Santa Barbara's soft jazz station. She slips into the water, dips under with her face pointing upright, like women do, and smoothes her hair back.

My physical urges are in conflict with my mental, if not moral, reticence about drunken women. I started having an involuntary reaction concurrent with her shedding clothes. After I make us a couple of martinis, showing great panache as they're shaken, not stirred, and begin disrobing, my interest is apparent.

"Nice to see you care," she says, "and even nicer to see your caring is substantial." She's giggling as I hand her the drink.

I slip into the water. It's already hot as hell, but in moments I'm comfortable.

She slips over and sits close enough that we're touching from one end to the other, and whispers, "What do you like, Davy?"

Davy? I hated Doug enough.

"I like to talk a little first. Catholic upbringing."

"So, you like to talk . . . dirty?"

"Only during."

I'm worried she's going to fade before the information phase, even though executing the information phase is rapidly retreating to the back of my mind. I'm considering probing for information in the morning, after my initial probe is, hopefully, well performed.

"How about old Lenny?" I ask. "Where did you say he's off to?"

She backs away a little and eyes me, for the first time with a tiny bit of suspicion.

"I didn't said . . . say. I didn't say, Davy." She downs the martini in two gulps. "But he went . . . uh, let me see . . . south, to play goss . . . golf. He likes to gamble on the golf course. Don't play wis him, he plays rough."

"I'll bet. Where south?"

"Phoenix, or San Diego . . . or some damn place. Who cares?"

"Phoenix is kinda east."

She rises, climbs out of the Jacuzzi, and I'm positioning myself to catch her should she fall backward, but makes it and heads for a cabinet next to the bar, retrieves two towels as big as bedsheets, and clumsily throws me one, which I have to dive for to keep out of the water. "You're a real talker, Davy. I'm going in to my great big playground. You coming . . . or would you like to be?" That makes her giggle again.

I have to help her up the stairs. She reaches the house and we enter a huge master bedroom suite with an oversize bed. She throws the covers back with such vigor they're off the bed, turns, and goes to her back, raises her head, and wiggles an index finger at me, inviting me to join her.

Unfortunately, this just isn't going to happen.

I sit on the edge of the bed, and roll her to her stomach, and begin what I've been told is one of the world's great back rubs. As I suspected, in moments, I can detect the deep steady breathing of sleep.

Not having any interest in resorting to a Lenny approach at sex, I sigh deeply and get back to my feet, find the bathroom, about half the size of my boat, and with some patience as I'm still saluting procreation, finally manage to relieve myself. With mixed emotions that maybe she'll be propped up on one elbow, revived, full of vim and vigor, and waving me over when I return, I do so, but it's not to be. She's snoring loud enough to rattle the windows.

I have to smile at this. I wander over and muss her hair, then take a thumb and with a gentle stroke smear her lipstick, then untuck one corner of the bedsheet and wrinkle the rest, until it looks as if a real party were held there. She'll awaken thinking I've been a bad, bad boy, and that she was successful in seducing me . . . or vice versa. No doubt I'll want some more information from the lady . . . a postcoital talk, if you will, so it's good to have her think we're bosom buds. Then I refit the covers somewhat and tuck her in. As rape and plunder go, I'm an abject failure, and not much better as an interrogator.

Then I notice her address book next to the phone on the bedside table. His number is on the top of a page, and all of Lenny's numbers have been crossed out, and the page is full including most of the margins. But at the bottom is a penciled in number, led by a single L. I note it and tear off a portion of a calendar page and carry it with me back to my clothes.

I find the phone I noticed on the bar near the Jacuzzi and call a cab, then get dressed. The clothes, spread around the Jacuzzi, are wet of course. Just as I finish buttoning up my shirt, my cell phone rings.

It's Pug.

"What are you doing up so late, old man?" I ask.

*"Aces n' Eights.* She's on the bottom."

That stops me cold. "What! What the hell happened?"

"Don't know for sure, and we won't know until we float her."

"Futa? Is Futa okay?"

"Dev, I haven't seen him. No one has."

I run down the driveway, as I told the cab to pick me up at the main gate, and have to pace back and forth for twenty minutes before he arrives. I was going to have him take me to the Santa Barbara Polo and Racquet Club to retrieve the Chevy, but it's the other way from the harbor.

When he finally arrives, I'm not exactly patient. "The harbor, and step on it. I could have walked there by now. It's an emergency."

I have him let me off as close as we can get to the dock, next to Brophy Brothers, and run all the way to the end tie where the boat had been. Pop, Cedric, and Iver are standing at the end of the dock, surveying the miserable sight. The harbor patrol boat is idling nearby, using a dip net to gather up what's become flotsam and jetsam. I know all the harbor patrol officers, and Jake McBean shouts over at me, "How long since you replaced your bilge alarm, Shannon?"

"My bilge alarm and auto bilge pumps were working perfectly, thanks, McBean."

"Not too damn perfectly," he says, and goes back to scooping.

Only the top half of her wheelhouse is sticking up out of the water, and all her antennas and radar bridge.

"Jesus, everything I own." Then I think about the worst of it, unless Futa is down there, trapped and drowned. "My computer. All my records."

"I back them up," Cedric offers, "send them to my server, every time I'm on your computer, remember?"

I do remember something about him saying he was going to do that from time to time.

"My Rolodex. Numbers of agents all over the country. How will I ever—"

"Your Rolodex," Cedric says, a little disgusted I would question him, "was printed off your address book on the computer, remember? It's on my server. I can have you a new one tomorrow."

"Futa, has anyone see Futa?"

"No, son," Pug says, resting a hand on my shoulder. "We walked the docks before you got back, calling for him, but he's nowhere to be found."

I start peeling off my clothes. "Iver, how about getting me some scuba gear from *Copper Glee?* I need to go down and see if Futa's down there."

He starts away, but Pug calls him back. "There's time for all that in the light of day. Right now you're coming back to the house and getting some sleep. We'll face this in the morning."

"Some son of a bitch did this," I say, "and I'll bet I know just who it was. If Futa's down there, I'm going back to Spain to torch a couple of fine houses."

# Chapter 23

"It's probably a bad hose or through-hull, or the packing in your drive shaft's gone bad. Don't start plotting revenge until we know what happened. Let's get some sleep," Pug says. "Things will be better in the morning."

"Revenge, hell, carnage," I say.

He drags me away. I know he's right, but I still have the urge to dive and confirm that Futa is either there or not. If he is, some s.o.b. is going to pay.

I'm tired to the bone, but still I have the old man take me to the Santa Barbara Polo and Racquet Club to get the Chevy, as I'm afraid they'll tow it, and I don't need another fat bill to pay.

My old man lives in the same little California bungalow he's been in for forty years, on Casitas Street in Santa Barbara. The neighborhood's gone a little green over the years, which in S.B. means that folks making less than about a quarter mil a year have to live two or three incomes, and usually families, to the household. It's a good thing the old man's place was bought on the G.I. bill and has been paid for long ago. His eighteen-thousand-dollar home is now in the neighborhood of eight hundred fifty thousand.

I awake with the birds, and give Cynthia a call.

"Jesus, it's early. You need bailing out of jail or what?"

"I need a few answers. Has the good Dr. Hashim heard from his in-laws . . . outlaws in this case?"

"I don't know. Since there's some conflict over the money, I haven't been in touch with him."

"Find out, if you can?"

"Why, what's up?"

"*Aces n' Eights* went to the bottom of the harbor last night, and I doubt if she committed suicide."

"You don't think . . . ?"

"I do, but I'll know more later in the day. Let me hear back, okay?"

My next call is to Cedric. "Hey, man, I need you to take some time away from the Haroldstern thing."

"Sure, what's on the table?"

"I want you to get inside Dr. Mohammad Hashim's computer, and inside his head. I want to hear if he's heard anything from his in-laws in Spain, if he's planning a trip . . . what he had for breakfast. The rumor is his libido is more in tune with interior decorating as a career than head shrinking, and I'd like to see what Web sites and chat groups he's into. Got it?"

"Standard daily rate?"

"You bet."

"I was going to come down and help with the boat today—"

"Iver and Pug and I can handle that. I need you on the keyboard."

"Okay, I wasn't looking forward to diving for the boat anyway. It'll be a little fuliginous down there."

"Right." Then I let him sucker me in. "Haunted, right?"

"Dark and dingy."

"That's a given. Give me a call later and tell me what you've learned."

Even though the sky's just getting light, the old man is sitting at his little breakfast table, coffee in hand, TV news blaring away, the paper already read.

"You ready to go?" I ask.

"I'm not going anywhere with you until you have a cup of coffee and some breakfast. You're grumpy enough."

"Come on, I'll take the coffee with me, and I'll buy us some *pan dulce* on the way." My old man's always been a nut for Mexican sweet bread, and there's a good bakery, Koelsch's, on State Street, on the way to the harbor.

"What's the hurry? Everything's wet and won't get any wetter."

"Futa. I want to see if Futa's on the dock, wondering why his home is a foot deep in the mud at the bottom of the bay."

The old man drives an extended-cab Ford pickup, about as practical in Santa Barbara's narrow streets as a diesel eighteen-wheeler, but it gets us there in good time. Folks in Miatas, Hondas, Volkswagens, and even those in large class-cars who don't want them marred, seem to clear the way for the old man's big rig.

Waterworks is not what it sounds like, but rather is a marine engineering and salvage company, with offices above the Chandlery on the dock. I stop by there and of course the only one in at seven A.M. is the boss. We strike a quick bargain for the use of one of his workboats and some bladders for the day, and then the old man and I stride out down the dock. Iver is sitting on the edge of the dock surveying *Aces n' Eights*, a thermos of coffee beside him, drinking from a plastic cup. Piled on the dock beside him are two complete scuba rigs from the *Copper Glee*.

"Harbor Patrol boat was by," Iver says, climbing to his

feet. "Said they have three or four boxes of junk for you in their yard."

"Let's get below."

In moments, Iver and I are investigating the inside of the boat, underwater. Cedric managed an understatement with "fuliginous," even if it is a mouthful.

I make a couple of tries going down into the engine room, which will give me access to the even tighter bilges, but cannot. Old demons are laughing hysterically at my cowardice, but I just can't bring myself to crawl into that tight a space, particularly underwater.

Iver's known me almost as long as I've been around, so he brushes past me, takes my more powerful waterproof torch out of my hand, and hands me his smaller one and goes down, while I stand by outside the engine room hatch at watch to make sure he doesn't get into trouble.

He's in the bowel of the boat for fifteen minutes by my waterproof Timex, when he finally returns and motions for us to get out of there.

We surface and climb the ladder to the dock. As soon as we get our face masks off, he says, "Coolant water hoses were clearly cut, not worn though, bilge pump wires were snipped, bilge alarm was smashed. You definitely had a visitor."

"I figured. Futa?"

"Not that I could see."

That makes my stomach churn, and my blood go a little icy. Someone has invaded my most personal space.

It takes us the rest of the day with the help of a two-thousand-dollar-a-day salvage boat, some flotation bladders, and the boat's crane, but we get her afloat and get the hoses repaired and automatic bilge pumps hooked back up by cocktail time. We have quite a crowd on the dock as we work, hundreds of tourists gawking from the side rails of the docks nearby. It doesn't thrill me that the sinking of my home is the day's entertainment.

When we get her up, and the water drained away, the identity of my visitors becomes very clear, as they obviously wanted it known. On the bulkhead inside the main salon in four separate places has been spray-painted a big bloodred A. I doubt very seriously if I've offended the Anaheim Athletics to this extent, even if I am a fan of the Dodgers, but know a family with the name of Aziz that has a very big grudge to settle.

It's time for me and mine to watch our backs.


Even though I now can't afford it, I stand all my helpers, including the workboat's three man crew, to drinks at Brophy's.

To my surprise when we enter the place, packed at five-thirty as usual, there are two ladies in attendance whom I know; one whom I know well, one who probably thinks I know her better than I actually do. Cynthia Proffer is sitting at the bar, sipping some kind of rum drink; Melinda Haroldstern is at a table, alone, and it's no surprise she's drinking Perrier.

I stop by Cynthia's bar stool first.

"I didn't want to interfere while you were working," she says.

"Obviously I have been," I say, standing back and spreading my arms so she can see how covered in grime and crud I am.

"You look fine to me."

"I may not look so good to you when you know that my boat was waylaid by the Aziz family. There are big red As painted inside, and she was definitely scuttled."

"You're kidding . . . they're here?"

"I want you to be careful."

"Goes without saying," she says, with a worried continence. "Hashim claims to know nothing about this, although his wife did give him a scathing phone call."

"Hang out with the boys for a while. Looks like we'll

be on the patio as this place is bonkers. Pug and Iver are out there. I've got a tiny bit of work to do, and then I'll join up."

With that, I head across the small dining room to Melinda's two-person table, and take the empty chair. "How are you?" I ask, having no idea what her reaction will be.

"Fine, thanks, except I did some checking on Dev Shannon today." She lowers her voice. "It's always nice to know who's been cavorting in your bed."

"Nice night, thank you."

"Sorry I sort of faded out. I don't do that often."

"I'm sure you don't. Martinis have a way of slamming sensibilities shut, while opening inhibitions wide."

She sits back and eyes me. Even with what must be a hellacious hangover, she's a fine-looking lady. Finally, she smiles, and asks, "Were you only there to find out what you could about Lenny?"

"Lenny is one of my passing interests, admittedly, but I did enjoy your company, until you faded."

"You know I can't tell you anything about Lenny. He's still family, sort of. Even though Jonathan is dead, Lenny was a favorite of his."

"Can't disappoint the dead," I say, and mean it, thinking for the ten thousandth time of Oscar Sorenson. "But to be truthful, I don't have your high opinion of Jonathan's taste in relatives."

"I accept that. Neither do I, to be truthful. Then we don't have to talk about Lenny, if you want to drop by again?"

"Certainly not. We can resume admiring the view from your Jacuzzi."

She's silent for a moment, and I let her be; then she smiles as if the Lenny thing never happened. "You have an interesting job, more interesting than security, I'd think."

"Actually that wasn't a lie. I really try and never lie. I

do do security work . . . but, yes, I have an interesting job."

"Manhunter, I think was what my friend referred to you as. . . ."

"And the occasional woman." I give her my sexiest smile, then glance over as much of her as I can see with her sitting.

She hands me a classy engraved calling card. "I don't know if you bothered to take down my number last night, as the last hour or so of the evening is a little vague. But here it is should you find yourself in the mood for a replay. I'm sure you'd prefer me being an active participant?"

I really do want to tell her that I was the perfect gentleman and in no way took advantage of the situation, but intuition tells me to keep my mouth shut. So I do.

"I'd love to make it tonight—" I start to make an excuse, but she interrupts me.

"God, no. It was all I could do to get down here, hoping I'd run into you. I'm running on pure ibuprofen." She gives me a tight smile. "Dev, I hope you don't turn out to be the prick I suspect you might be, and I know that nephew Lenny is. . . ." Then she gives me a dazzling smile. "Call me."

She flips a five-dollar bill on the table and leaves, giving me a pat on the cheek with a well-manicured, nicely tanned hand on the way by and leaving the wisp of a very expensive scent.

Cynthia only hangs around for one beer, after informing me that the Hashim children and Sonya are due in day after tomorrow, saying she came down to personally give me the good news, and wanted to lend moral support; then, finding out I'm ensconced in the old man's bungalow, in good company, and in relatively good shape, she leaves.

Cedric joins us just as I'm about to drag the old man away from his fourth O'Douls. Cedric orders an Anchor

Steam, his beer of choice, and leans over so I can hear what he has to say while I have one more Corona than I probably should.

"That number that came from Lenny's aunt's address book was a phone booth in Seattle. It could have been him, but we'll never know."

"And the doctor?"

"You know you can't get into someone's home computer unless they have it on, or have left it on?"

"Okay, so you couldn't get on . . . or in . . . or whatever the terminology is."

"Not until about six P.M. I kept trying all day. I got into his office computers earlier. There are two of them, one a secretary's, it seems, but there was nothing I could ferret out but work stuff. When he got home, he turned that one on and left it on for some time. Interesting stuff. But he killed the power before I could get to the meat of things. I need some more time, as he's got a segmented hard drive, or maybe two hard drives, and I haven't found the password for the second part of his system as of yet. The first password was a snap . . . Freud. People are so predictable."

"Is he light in his loafers?"

"Don't find any indication of that, but you can't see a drawer full of pink chiffon through the computer. I get the sneaking hunch he's a whole lot more weird than merely a garden variety swish."

I look at him with interest, and he continues.

"By some of his e-mail, and by one hit he made on a Web site, probably forgetting he was not on the most protected segment of his system. . . ." Cedric sits back, takes a long draw on the Anchor Steam, then drops a bomb on me. "I think the good doctor may be into a little pediatric porn."

# Chapter 24

Just the thought that the father of Arty and little Gigi could be that twisted stops me short, actually breathless. I'm not given to gasping, but I do.

The last thing I want is to bring a couple of kids home to a pedophile. "I hope to hell you're wrong. It could be some research he's doing, or some damn thing. I can't believe . . . don't want to believe . . ."

"I'll know more when I get back in. I'll do better next time, as at least I now know the architecture of his system. The groundwork is laid, and I won't have to start ab ovo." He gives me a condescending smile along with a raised eyebrow, which I've learned to ignore, but as usual he ignores the fact I'm ignoring. "From the egg, for those of you to whom a dictionary is Kafkaesque. Success is not immediately at hand, however . . . when everything's coming your way, you're probably in the wrong lane."

I laugh, which I need at the moment. "I knew we couldn't get through the night without a Cedric-ism. Stay on it, please."

"I will. In the meantime, until I can find the good

doctor's computer cranking again, I'll stay on the trail of the debonair Lenny Haroldstern."

"By the way, he's a golfer. And a damn good one or so Auntie Melinda reports. He makes a living on the golf course. I want you to dig up anything in the Pacific Northwest that would interest a good golfer, a gambling golfer."

"Devlin, do you know how many golf courses there are in the Pacific Northwest? Hundreds."

"Yes, but you're Cedric, the keyboard colossus."

"Humph."

I drag the old man out of there, as he's having a good time regaling the salvage boat crew with tales of the Santa Barbara P.D., and get him home.

Before he hits the sack, he gives me one of my mother's favorite sayings, "This, too, will pass," then adds his own version, "like gas."

"Maybe, but it's sure a pain in the ass while it's here. You're starting to sound like Mom."

"I could have worse problems. You and I and Iver will get your boat sopped out tomorrow, and you'll be back in business in no time."

Futa, rather than Oscar, visits me in the night, and I promise him my search will be endless. Then, with the help of a half dozen Coronas, I get an excellent night's sleep.

As we're on our way back to the harbor, my cell phone demands attention. It's Lt. Paul Antone.

"I've got an officer delivering a prisoner to Bakersfield today, and he'll be bringing our boy Fred Branch back. It's probably not kosher, but do you want to sit in on my interrogation?"

"Nope. I want a few hours alone with the boy."

"Don't think that's going to happen."

"Then I'll visit him in the jail. I'm tied up here for a couple of days."

"Suit yourself."

"But I'd appreciate a call if you learn anything."

"By the way, we got a partial off the Lopez girl's finger-nails. Only one, but it's clear and enough for an ID. That was a good call."

"So . . . whose?"

"We're running it though CJIS in West Virginia. Hope we get a hit."

"How long does the Criminal Justice Information System take?" It's nice to let the cops know I'm up to speed on my cop-isms.

"Not long. Probably tomorrow at the latest."

"Great. I'll probably see you day after tomorrow, when I come up to see Branch."

"That's Monday. No jail visits on Monday."

"Can you get me in?"

"Yeah. It'll cost you, but I'll work it out."

"Okay, you've got a doughnut coming."

"Very funny. See you Monday."

We have a hard day with the scoop shovels, mops, then a gallon of teak oil. It'll be a week of work before she's back to livable, anywhere near where she was when she went down. Not to speak of having to go completely through the engine and generator and clean and check the instrumentation. One item alone, a brand-new GPS tracker, just set me back almost two grand. All in all, it will be another several-thousand-dollar-expense to rack up against the Hashim hundred thousand I have yet to collect. Even though I have insurance, I know it'll be a fight since she was purposely scuttled, and hell, you most always lose with insurance companies. The most immediate problem is that the shore power converter is on the fritz, and we're getting no power on board. Until that's cured, I won't be bunking there, even if I was willing to put up with a place that resembles a dripping cavern at Carlsbad.

The good news is that Cedric wanders in about cocktail time. "I think you're going to like this," he says, a wide smile showing his gold incisors.

"Let's hear it."

"M.G. Greenbaugh is entered in a golf tournament in . . . guess where."

"I'm too tired to guess."

"Would you believe, Eagle Bend Golf Course in Big Fork, Montana?"

"In May? It's probably still freezing in May."

"Sixty-eight degrees yesterday. Toasty warm for Montana."

"When's this tournament?"

"First round is Wednesday. I'll bet the boy is heading for Canada, which is only a couple hundred miles north of Flathead Lake . . . where this golf course resides."

"Outstanding, Cedric. And his auntie told me San Diego or Pheonix. I knew when she said it she was sending me one hundred eighty degrees off course. How in the devil did you find him?"

"Eric Hoffer said that to be fully alive is to believe everything is possible. You have to approach this skip-tracing thing believing that. I didn't find him by searching golf course servers or computers, but in the newspaper. It seems the entrants were listed in the paper and a simple Google search for M.G. Greenbaugh turned up the article in this morning's Big Fork weekly. He was among the list of entrants. Ain't that a gas?"

"A gas."

"Speaking of gas, it didn't hurt that there were two more credit card charges. One at a Conoco gas station in Moses Lake in the middle of Washington, and another in Wallace, Idaho, leaving a trail east."

I don't bother to ask who Eric Hoffer is, knowing I'll get a long lecture. "Still, you're a wizard."

"A wizard in dire need of an Anchor Steam."

"You're on. But first you've got to promise to book

me on a flight to Big Fork or somewhere as close as you can . . . say flying out Tuesday afternoon . . . and you've got to get my Rolodex reprinted so I can find someone to give me a hand up there." It's been driving me crazy, not having my Rolodex at hand, as it's taken me years to build up the two-thousand-plus enforcement bail agents that are listed there.

"Already did it. The Rolodex, I mean. I'll book your flight post Anchor Steam."

And, as we are tired of Brophy's, the Café del Sol is the place of choice, and the place that'll get in my wallet tonight.

We barely are seated when I get a call from Cynthia. "Sonya and the kids are coming in tomorrow, four P.M."

"Does Hashim know?"

"Yes. The embassy informed him. He's going down to meet them."

"So am I. I don't want to lose them back to the mother and the Aziz boys, particularly after what they've done to me. You have time to ride down with me?" I'm doing this, but it's going to bother the hell out of me until that child porn site hit of Dr. Hashim's is explained.

"I can make time."

"Not if you're working on something. Besides, I probably should take someone who can shoot straight."

"Screw you, Shannon. We should leave by noon."

"I'll pick you up at your office."

I put in a call to the Paso Robles P.D. and leave word for Antone that I'm not making it up to see Freddy on Monday.


Cynthia and I arrive at the LAX International Terminal at least forty-five minutes early, and while we're having lunch see Dr. Hashim and a dark-skinned gentleman the size of a Sumo wrestler stroll by heading for the spot where passengers exit customs. Cynthia wants to call him in, and try and patch things up with him, but I tell her absolutely not. She looks at me curiously, but for a change accedes to my wish.

"It seems the doctor brought his muscle with him."

"Seems so," she says, and returns to her lunch.

We're only fifty feet away, still unseen by Hashim, when Sonya and the kids exit, the kids with only a backpack apiece, and Sonya with her Volkswagen-sized bag.

I have my nice new Olympia digital camera in hand, one that replaced the one that got a recent good soaking, and take several pictures of the happy reunion, with time and date imprinted on each. As I do so, Sumo glares at me, his right hand under the tent he wears as a coat. But he makes no move to come over.

I'm very curious how the children relate to their father, and watch while he kneels and they each politely give him a peck on the cheek, then immediately return to each side of Sonya. Actually, it's not what I'd call a happy reunion.

The doctor makes no attempt to pick up his six-year-old daughter, or to hug his son. I get the distinct impression that Dr. Hashim has a very cold relationship with his children, but then many people do. My own mother and father would have been on me like chocolate on a Snicker's bar, particularly when I was six or even eight. My mother's fawning embarrassed me well past high school. I wish she was around to embarrass me now. Damn, I do miss her. . . .

As they turn to head out of the terminal we catch up and pace them. Sumo still has his hand under his coat, hampered a bit by the other hand carrying Sonya's big bag as well as the kids' two backpacks, but the doctor gives him an "It's all right," and he merely drops back so he's following closely behind. But I feel his eyes burning into the back of my neck.

"So, our bargain is complete," I say. It's a statement not a question.

"We will talk about it back in Santa Barbara," he replies.

"Actually, Doc, I was thinking you might want to up the ante, since you didn't bother to mention you were sending me into the lion's den." There's no defense like a good offense, or so my old football coach used to say.

Hashim smiles in his ghoulish way as he trudges along, seeming bemused by the whole thing. I really, really want to clock him one, but that wouldn't be wise, since I want my money and also since there's a Sherman tank dogging my heels. At the moment, I can't afford a hundred grand's worth of ego gratification or a broken knuckle.

"Mr. Devlin, I believe it was you who said, and I quote, 'I'm the best,' or something to that effect. I had no question that you would prevail."

"So, you should then have no question regarding releasing the money."

"As I said, we will discuss that in Santa Barbara."

"Are you going straight back?"

"Yes. I have patients tomorrow."

"If you don't mind . . . actually even if you do . . . we'll stay nearby. It seems your in-laws are in the neighborhood."

That stops him, literally, and he turns to face me. "How do you know this?"

"They sunk my boat . . . my home . . . and have cost me a great deal of money."

"And how do you know it was my in-laws?"

"Do you know anyone else who thinks spray-painted A's all over the place are some kind of interior decorating statement?"

He's silent for a moment, then says, "That is the risk you take, in your business."

"Right," I manage. "Let's get in the cars and on the road before they show up again."

To my great relief, we have no trouble, except for the traffic, on the drive back. The last I see of Sonya, Mohammad, Sumo, and the kids are as Hashim's automatic garage door closes.

As I drive Cynthia back to her place, I call Cedric on the phone. "When do I fly?"

"Eight o'clock in the morning."

# Chapter 25

"Great," I tell Cedric, who's booked my flight to go put the arm on Lenny Haroldstern. "That means I leave for LAX at three A.M. or so?"

"Nope, I got on expedia-dot-com and got a great cheap flight out of Santa Barbara. S.B. to San Fran, to Salt Lake, to Kalispel, where I have a four-wheel-drive SUV reserved at Hertz."

"Great, but I usually use Avis."

"I figured you might be persona non grata with Avis, after the Spain and France thing."

"Actually, I might be persona non grata in all of Europe. Good thinking though. How's it coming with Dr. Hashim?"

"It's not. His computer has to be on, remember. And he was gone all day. I'll stay on it."

"Please. It's really, really important to me."

"By the way, I found you some help in Big Fork."

"Great."

"Yeah, a couple of guys from a place called Polson, nearby, down at the other end of the lake from Kalispel where you're landing. Got them for one fifty a day each if you buy the beer when it's over."

"Well done. Sounds like you've got everything under control."

"Well, maybe. Mario Andretti said that if you have everything under control, you're going too slow."

"Right. How do I tie up with these guys?"

"There's a bar in Big Fork. Willy's, right in the middle of town. They'll be there waiting from four P.M. on. You should make it over there by six."

"Names?"

"Tom Two Poles—"

"You're kidding?"

"Tom Two Poles and Johnny Cutfinger."

"Who's putting who on here?"

"Full-blooded Flathead Indians . . . I believe they prefer to be referred to as Salish, by those of us who are children of a lesser god. You can't miss them, hair to their waist and they eat hay and crap in the street."

"That means they're big?"

"Very. I got a good reference on them from Perry Boggs in Missoula."

"Perry should know."

I hang up, then turn to the lovely redhead on my right. "Cynthia, guess what, I have a free night, and enough room left on the credit card to buy your dinner."

She clears her throat. "I've been meaning to talk to you this whole trip."

I know that tone, and something bad is coming. "So, talk."

"You remember I said it took three drinks to dig some information out of Tom Demarco at Ogilvie and Meyers?"

"Yes, I remember."

"Well . . . we're kind of going steady."

"Ogilvie or Meyers?"

"Ha, ha."

*"Kind* of going steady?"

"Tom asked me if he and I might give it a try . . . not dating anyone else, I mean."

"And I thought you've been working. Silly me. So, are you wearing his ring and letterman sweater?"

"Very funny."

"I've got a whole roster of new lawyer jokes."

"Don't bother."

"Do you know the dif between a dead attorney in the road and a dead snake in the road?"

"No," she says with a big sigh.

"There are skid marks in front of the snake."

"Okay. No more, okay?"

There's silence for a moment and then I break it. "I'll have Cedric print these pictures; then I want you to put in a formal demand at William Bowman's office for the money. Of course he's another prick attorney, so he will do everything he can to not perform, to please his buddies at Ogelvie and Meyers. But deliver the pics and demand, and see what happens."

"Sour grapes. So it's all business now?"

"That was your call."

I drop her off and head down to the boat to see what I can see in the dark, which is not much as the shore power and well-soaked converter on the boat are still not communicating. Until that's fixed, I'll be bunking with the old man unless I want to sleep in the cold and damp.

After an hour of combing the dock and buildings around Brophy's, calling Futa, I find not so much as a dead wharf rat.

I consider giving Ms. Melinda a call, but pass on the idea. I'm off to cuff her nephew in the morning, maybe about the head and shoulders with my leather sap, and it would be kind of shabby to grease my personal sap with the auntie the night before. Anyway, I need to see if the old man had the things cleaned that we salvaged from the boat, so I can pack.

I'm beginning to get what was known in high school and college as blue balls.

With the sincere wish that the boys from Andorra would come face-to-face to give me some trouble, as God knows I'm backed up with testosterone, I hit the hay. But it's a long time before I'm sawing logs, as I'm beginning to feel really guilty about not putting all my time into getting my gun inserted in Julio Sanchez's ear, and performing a lobotomy on the son of a bitch . . . and his buddies. But I guess Oscar understands my problem, as he does not bother to come visit me in the night.

Happily, the flight, with all its short legs, is uneventful. Cedric did not mention that the last leg, from Salt Lake City to Kalispel, involved a stop in Missoula, so actually it's a four-leg flight, which is not bad for buying a cheapey via the Internet. Of course I am up and down so much I'm getting a yoyo complex by the time we land. The last plane is a little on the small side, as in claustro-fucking-phobic, but I concentrate on the scenery as it's a beautiful clear afternoon, and my mind's eye remains on the vista below and not on the aluminum coffin rattling its way to Kalispel.

I burst out of it as if I were free after doing twenty in Alcatraz.

Hertz has a Ford Explorer waiting for me, and by five-thirty I'm on my way to Big Fork, Montana, which I'm informed is only a twenty-five-minute drive. I'm pleased that there's still some light, as Flathead Lake is worth seeing, as big and beautiful as Tahoe, with some interesting islands dotting it.

I'm in the pines, except for a nice drive around the north end of the lake, through some beautiful meadows, where I'm pleased to see a turnoff for Eagle Bend Golf Course. Big Fork lies on the northeast side of the lake, with the magnificent still snowcapped Mission Mountains as its backdrop. The picturesque little town is bisected by the Swan River, which is as beautiful as it sounds, and is snuggled into the hills where the river meets the lake.

I guess the population at a couple of thousand as I turn left at the only light slowing traffic on the highway. I wind into town just as the sun drops behind the mountains to the west, and find my saloon, Willy's, a board-and-batten one-story affair bracketed by tourist shops and boutiques. I get the impression Willy's was there long before the town became a tourist attraction. The town is faithful to a western mountain theme, which makes good marketing sense.

Pool tables and gambling machines—keno and poker—are scattered around a dance floor and the only music gracing the place is from a jukebox. It's blaring out "It's a Hard Day's Night," hardly the country-and-western I'd expect.

There are a half dozen patrons in plaid and Carhart, lace-up lumberjack brogans and cowboy boots. My guys are not hard to spot, as they take up the better part of four stools at the bar and stand out like a dung beetle on a birthday cake.

These Indians look like Indians—dark skin, wide features, raven-black hair—and are the size of Appaloosas. It's a good thing there were a hell of a lot more cowboys than Indians when we invaded their country. Both are wearing jeans, flannel shirts, and worn cowboy boots that have to be size sixteens. I'm a little surprised to find them well spoken, belying the long hair and earrings and five pounds per of silver jewelry. However, I'm not sure these guys are going to fit into the dudes' sport of golf, as picturing them in golf shirts, plaid pants, and two-tone shoes with little tassels is a real stretch. After the introductions and Tom Two Poles ordering me a Moose Drool—no, I'm not kidding, that's a local beer—I pose the question.

"You guys know the Eagle Bend golf course?" Expecting them to say, "Sure, it's just over the hill," I'm surprised.

"Play there quite a bit," Johnny Cutfinger informs me. "It's damned expensive, and not much better than our Polson course, but, yeah, we know it well."

Shows the value of first impressions. "Okay, the guy I'm looking for is supposed to be playing in a tournament there tomorrow."

They laugh. Then Tom says, "The pro there gave me some crap the last time I played, 'cause some tight-ass complained when I chased a ball into his yard—he started to circle the wagons, thought it was a redskin invasion. I told the pro he'd be as green as his golf course after spending a month or so at the bottom of my lake, and he shut up. It'll be a gas to drag some old boy, kickin' and screamin', off his links."

"Your lake?"

"Yeah, you could say that. Half of Flathead is on the rez."

I hand them a set of booking photos. "This guy is a real city boy. I don't expect a bit of trouble, but you never know. He should be a lay-down. . . ."

"You like lay-downs?" Tom asks. "We're meeting some fine ladies tonight down in Polson, if you don't have something for us to do. There's a powwow going on, and these are Crow girls . . . not owls, but I hear they're a hoot. You ever take a woman scalp?"

"Cuffed a few, but can't say as I've scalped any."

"They got a hole in the middle of them."

They both guffaw and slap their big Levi-wrapped thighs.

"Sounds right," I say, after a polite laugh.

"You're welcome to come along," Tom says, and Johnny nods his approval.

I look a little doubtful, so he adds, "You've never lived

until you've had a chubby girl tie her braids around your back and get her spurs into you so you can't dismount till she wants to turn you loose." They both laugh at that.

I envision that, a chubby Indian maiden wearing nothing but a headdress, boots, and spurs piercing my buttocks, and it doesn't seem quite like the way I want to end my drought, so I politely pass.

I'm a little surprised to find Moose Drool about as smooth a dark beer as I've ever tasted. So far, Montana's right up there with France, Andorra, and Spain as a place where I'd like to spend a little quality time.

I find a cheap motel, at least cheap by resort area standards, sleep well, then meet the boys for breakfast at seven in the motel's coffee shop.

I'm pleased to see they both have on duds that would make one think of golf, except it's tennis shoes rather than tasseled golf. I've got on jeans and a dark blue turtleneck, with a lightweight jacket to cover the .38 clipped to the back of my belt. My THE POLICE–emblazoned bill cap is in place.

It's planning time. So I suggest, "I'd like to take him in the parking lot when he shows up."

"No sweat," Tom agrees.

"We'll spot you guys at each end, so if he makes a break . . . You guys can *run*, can't you?"

"Yeah," Johnny says with a grin, "outran many a rez cop when we were growin' up."

I wonder if that wasn't about a hundred pounds ago, but don't question them. "Okay. So this should be simple. I'm armed, you don't need to be."

"What if the perp is?"

"Then act like you're there to play golf, shine him, and let him go on by if he has a weapon and hotfoots it. I don't want you guys shot up or any gunfire in a public parking lot."

"You're paying the bills," Johnny says skeptically, but goes back to his stack of hotcakes.

"Let's finish up, and go take a hard look at the place."

They drive their pickup and I take the rental Explorer. The parking lot is in three levels going up a hill away from the clubhouse. Unfortunately, the lot's bisected by a public road, so there's a getaway both front and rear. And of more concern is the fact the lot is already almost full. After we take a good look at the setup, I go into the spacious clubhouse restaurant and find my way to the rear and the pro shop. I'm a little concerned, as it's not yet eight and the place is packed. Our boy could already be here. I check the crowd out and don't make him, so I wait in line to get to the desk.

"Hey, my cousin, M.G. Greenbaugh, is supposed to meet me here," I tell the tall lanky kid, one of three working the tournament, who waits on me.

"George?"

"Uh, yeah," I say, hoping against hope that I haven't made this trip to find myself face-to-face with a short fat M.G. Greenbaugh, who actually is M. George Greenbaugh.

"He was in an early flight. They teed off"—he checks a sheet—"at seven twenty-eight by the list, but we were running a little late. He should be on, let's see, maybe three by now if things are moving along."

"Thanks." I grab a scorecard, which has a layout of the course, and check it out. Then I turn back to Lanky. "Can I rent a cart?"

"Not unless you're playing, and we don't have a tee time available until three this afternoon. You can't play in the jeans." He looks down his nose at me, and then practical enterprise overcomes class prejudice. "But if you change you can play nine—"

"No, thanks. Too late."

I go out and find my troops, or tribe might be better terminology, and we talk over the situation, while studying the course layout. I know I'd probably be better off to wait until they come in, and simply bust him at the clubhouse, but now I'm worried I might not have the right guy, even though the trail of credit card charges seems to lead this way. So we decide to lay an ambush. Hole number five is as good a place as any, if our quarry hasn't already passed there. It's a very tight uphill hole, so Tom informs me, one of the high-handicap holes on the course. The good news is that a player tees off and cannot really see over the hill he's hitting toward, and it's a steep cart path, so the carts will be slowed down as they move up to their second shot. It's a steep wooded climb up away from the fairway on the east side, with a row of heavily landscaped houses on the west.

Looks good to me.

We drive the Explorer to a spot on the street in front of the houses, park, and I leave the keys on the floorboard. Happy to see the houses are unfenced, we're able to easily move between them where it's almost totally level to the course. The fairway is not more than thirty yards wide here, and we can't see the tee, which is below the line of sight. I look things over and set the boys up sixty yards or so apart on this side and go across to the east side myself where the hill climbs away, heavily wooded, and covered with buck brush. It doesn't look like a runner with any brains would head that way.

Tom Two Poles yells, "Incoming!" at me as I cross, and I have to dive to keep from getting crowned with a ball. I give him a salute and a wave. He must be a Desert Storm vet too, or maybe he's watched *Platoon* too many times.

I take a position in some shrubs, only feet from where I presume Lenny will be coming. I crossed because the paved cart path is on this far side, and I want to be the one to make the FTA. We don't want to put the arm on the wrong guy, particularly some guy who can afford this kind of golf course. All these guys probably have attorneys on retainers.

I fade back into the brush as a green Eagle Bend golf cart approaches. Two fat guys puffing away on Camels . . . then another cart and another two guys, this pair Mutt and Jeff, but the tall one in a very un-golf-like beret has a beak like a bald eagle's and is definitely not my George Hamilton look-alike.

But as soon as they hit up, another ball flies over the hill, then in spaced sequence of a couple or three minutes, three more. Two of these have been hit at least forty yards farther than the first set, one fifty or more and all in the fairway, which would seem to indicate that we've got some good golfers in this flight.

I slip my wallet out and fold it open, so I can flash the brass, but leave the .38 holstered as I don't want to cause some old fart who may be Lenny's sucker, and cart-mate, to have heart failure.

The first cart has a couple of athletic-looking young guys. I raise up a little so I can see farther down the cart path, and see my FTA driving the second cart. It seems M.G. really isn't George, but is posing as Melinda Grace . . . I can understand why a guy wouldn't try and use "Grace." A fiftyish guy is beside him, and is the short ball hitter, so they stop twenty yards back from my position, just a little uphill from me, so he can hit up.

Lenny's attention is on his golfing chum, so I decide to make my move. I charge out of the brush, uphill toward the cart, yelling, "You're under arrest," leading with my badge.

Lenny is a very decisive FTA, and just as my toe catches on a root protruding from the paved cart path, he guns the cart. As I stumble forward, he rams me and I do a face plant on the Plexiglas windshield, bouncing off into a tangle of brush. Letting him have the uphill position was a mistake, as the cart literally leaped forward. He wheels the cart a hard right out onto the fairway, and heads back down the way he came.

My head's swimming, and Lenny's hotfooting it, or I guess, golf-carting it, out of here.

# Chapter 26

Lenny's golfing partner, in the middle of the fairway over his ball, looks up at the commotion, then does a little dance of indecision, as Lenny doesn't seem to mind if he runs him down.

As I recover everything but my dignity, I see Tom Two Poles lumber out from the shrubs across the fairway and make a gallant effort to intercept the cart, but Lenny fakes right, then spins the wheel and clips Tom so hard the cart rattles like Freddy's Ford did when it met the mulberry, and almost comes to a standstill.

Tom does a rather ungraceful backward somersault in the grass.

Sprinting out onto the fairway, I try to overtake the cart, but it's too late, as it's over the crest of the hill and downhill for a long ways. I didn't know a golf cart could go that fast.

Tom is on the ground, sucking wind, looking a little like a beached whale, and Johnny is chugging up, when I yell at them, "Take the car and cut him off at the clubhouse." I charge back up the fairway where the first two golfers are standing near their balls, staring, wondering what the hell is going on.

I flash the badge as I get even with them, but I'm heading for their cart.

"I'm commandeering your cart," I say with authority, and mount up and spin it out on the fairway to follow my quarry.

"My clubs, our clubs . . ." one of them shouts, but I don't have time to worry about the outcome of their game.

It's a wild downhill ride until I reach tee number five, and then it levels out. I can see my boy off to the right and a couple hundred yards ahead, scattering spectators off the cart path as he heads back toward the clubhouse, his vehicle, and then I presume Canada.

I sure as hell don't want to risk another bumper car chase, as I still don't have a total as to what the last one has cost me. As he closes toward the clubhouse, there are so many people milling around that he has to slow the cart almost to a walk, so he jumps out and sprints into the place. There's a double-wide hallway right through the middle of the joint with offices and locker rooms on one side and the restaurant and pro shop on the other.

The crowd is staring after Lenny as I slide to a stop and bail out and am after him.

The hallway is equally crowded, and I'm surprised to get just inside the doorway and see Lenny highballing it back my way, looking back over his shoulder, like John Wayne with the Cheyenne hordes on his tail. My high school football finally pays off and I take him low and hard, pick him up on a shoulder, and drive him to the slate floor.

His "oompf" resounds through the place, now silent as the crowd is fascinated with what's happening, torn between wanting to flee and wanting to observe the action.

I shout, "You're under arrest," while I'm spinning the boy to his belly and cuffing him. The crowd seems relieved until they see a uniformed county mounty close behind Tom Two Poles and Johnny Cutfinger. It's Keystone Cops in the clubhouse.

As they approach, Lenny looks over his shoulder and manages to wheeze, "I'll give you ten grand cash if you let me get to Canada."

I ignore him.

"Hold it!" the sheriff's officer yells, his hand on his Glock with the holster unsnapped. "Back away from him," he demands, and I do so, as Lenny's going nowhere. At the officer's command, Tom, Johnny, and I line up against the wall, under a painting of two battling bull elk.

"I'm a bail enforcement agent," I say quickly. "I've got ID in my wallet and paperwork on this guy."

About that time, the club pro walks up beside the officer. "Pete, this guy took a cart away from some of my players and stole their clubs, and those two caused trouble here a couple of weeks ago."

"Gurgle, gurgle, gurgle," Johnny says to the pro, indicating with a corncob-size finger something spiraling down, down, down. The pro backs away, suddenly going a little green. I guess he hasn't forgotten Johnny's offer to put him in the lake.

I eyeball the pro and the cop, probably Tuesday night poker buddies, and remember Cedric quoting Mark Twain, "Get the facts first, you can distort them later."

"You!" The officer motions at me. "You step away from the other two. I do as he commands, as his hand's still on the butt of the Glock. "Drop the jacket," he commands.

I spread it open carefully so he can see I have no weapon in front, only my cell phone clipped to my belt, and I say, "Cell phone, weapon's in the rear," as I can see he's studying the phone, then turn as I shed the jacket, so he can clearly see the .38 clipped to my belt.

I can't see him, but can clearly hear the whisper of gunmetal on leather as he pulls the Glock on hearing my mention of a weapon. I'm frozen, as I kind of figure if you got shot in a place like Big Fork, by a cop who's known everyone in town since he was in kindergarten, the result on the inquiry would be "shit happens."

"I've got a permit, Officer," I say over my shoulder, "not that you need one here in Montana."

"In some Montana cities you do," he says, his tone small-town cop smart-ass. I feel him relieve me of the .38.

"You two, you got weapons?" he asks Johnny and Tom.

"Pocketknifes," they both say in unison, and I'm glad I've dissuaded them from carrying.

"Now can I get my wallet and ID?" I ask.

"Slowly. Don't turn around."

I dig the badge and ID wallet out of my shirt pocket, and hand it to him, sort of back-ass-wards with my hand behind me.

I can hear him step back, and presume he's studying my National Institute of Bail Enforcement ID.

"So, what's this guy done?"

"I've got the warrant folded up in my back pocket. Can I turn around now?"

"Yeah." Then he says to Tom and Johnny, "You guys stay against the wall until I get this cleared up."

They both nod, but Johnny can't keep his mouth shut, and it would be a good idea to do so as we've got a crowd of thirty or more solid citizens. "You still got a hard-on for Indians, Pete?"

"Shut up, Cutfinger," he says, and then I begin to get it. He's had a run-in, or two, or ten, with my helpers before.

About that time two more sheriff's officers work their way through the crowd. One of these guys looks like he's got some miles on him, and has chevrons on his arm.

"What's up, Pete?" he asks.

Pete looks a little disappointed, as he's enjoying doing his cop thing in front of most of the area's prominent folks. "Bail enforcement agent," he says, like he knows something about the BEA biz.

"Get that guy on his feet," the older guy instructs his officer, Pete, then turns to me. "You got the paperwork?"

"I do," and fish it out of my pocket and hand the copy of the warrant over.

He studies it for a minute, then glances up. "You want to transport him or do you want me to jail him?"

"I'll have to," I say, "unless you want to haul him to Van Nuys, California. He's wanted there, he's got to be booked there."

"Humph," he says, then adds, "Just as well, I've got a plate full."


Lenny and I are back at the airport in Kalispel in time to catch the last flight to Seattle, and then a connecting flight to L.A. Since I can now see how I'm going to pay a few bills, I don't bother calling Cedric to set up a cheapy Internet flight, but lay out the dough to buy the most direct flight to L.A. One stop, Seattle, and only an hour's layover and two gates between flights.

I'm happy to note, after conferring with the Delta station manager, that I can leave the cuffs on my prisoner, so long as I'm discreet. Since Lenny has been a good boy so far, I cuff him in the front so we can keep a magazine or his coat in place to conceal his embarrassment.

Sometimes things are just too easy, if you don't count a sore nose from getting a little close to the cart's Plexiglas.

I call my old friend Sol Goldman, who has recently come to my aid in France and who stands to lose a chunk of change if Lenny had flown. He is pleased to meet me at the airport so we can transport Lenny to the Van Nuys lockup.

Lenny's headed for justice, and I didn't wreck a damned thing, not even a golf cart. I've paid the boys off and given them a hundred extra since I didn't want to hang around and buy the beer. I'll use them again if I can, as they're willing and able, if a little slow on their feet.

My phone rings as we're waiting for the flight.

It's Paul Antone.

"Where the hell are you?" he asks.

"Montana."

"How's the fishing?"

"Good, I caught a two-hundred-pounder this morning."

"This is a courtesy call, 'cause I'm beginning to think you're a lot smarter than you look. We got a hit on the fingerprint."

I still don't tell him about CSI. He's got to do his own television-land homework. "And?"

"And it's a bad boy from Delano, over in the valley. Simon Orozco, who's got a sheet that would shame John Gotti."

"In custody?"

"No way, but I think I have a connection between him and Julio Sanchez."

"No kidding?"

"I don't kid. It seems this Orozco was picked up a couple of years ago, for . . . you'll never guess."

"Probably not."

"Cockfighting."

Actually, I've had some small experiences in the world of chicken WWF, having run down a guy in Louisiana who was into the sport. "So, you got any leads on this guy?"

"He's from Delano, that's about all I know. This two-hundred-pound fish must have made you some dough."

"A nice chunk, and maybe I'll even collect it."

"Anyway, it seems our boy Julio also has a cockfighting charge; actually it was cruelty to animals down there, but I got some detail from the arresting officer who's now a lieutenant. This all happened down in Calexico near the border. We missed it as it was a misdemeanor back when he was arrested, and Julio went by his gang name, Chaco, back then . . . I just didn't dig deep enough."

"So there's some common ground between these guys, other than Oscar Sorenson and Lawanda?"

"Seems so. Cockfighting has to be a pretty small fraternity. I've notified the Delano P.D. and the Kern County Sheriff's Department. And we're putting the forensic guys back on Lawanda's apartment to see what else we can turn up."

"Okay. I'm on my way to scenic Delano myself."

"Be well . . . do well. Bring him down. I'd like to get the Sorenson thing off the books so I can leave the job with a pretty clean slate."

"Do you have a warrant for Simon?"

"No, but I will have in a couple of hours. You want a copy? I've also issued warrants for the guys that I think were with Julio at the fairgrounds . . . Charley 'Chucho' Rodriquez and Cesar 'Raton' Reyes."

"Yeah, I sure would like a certified copy of the warrants, but I may pass through town after hours. How about leaving the copies at the desk for me?"

"I didn't take you to raise."

"I'll owe you one."

"Don't say doughnut or you'll get nothing."

I hang up and before I can put the phone back on its clip, it vibrates again.

"Dev, me lad." It's Cedric.

"So it is?" I say, and my voice must reflect the fact I'm elated, and can begin to see how I'm going to pay some of my many bills. And I've got a lead on Julio Sanchez.

"You sound ecstatic."

"Lenny's cuffed and waiting patiently with me to catch a flight."

"Great! Guess what I just found out?"

"Tell me something good."

"Something good, something bad."

"Give me the good first."

"I've got a lead on Julio Sanchez."

"And that is?"

"He's got an a.k.a., Chaco, and he was arrested for cruelty to animals down in Calexico a few years ago. The guy is into cockfighting."

"Old news."

"You're kidding."

Everyone thinks I'm a kidder today. "Not kidding. See what you can dig up on a guy named Simon Orozco, l.k.a., Delano. What's the bad news?"

"L.k.a. is last known address?"

"Yes."

"Well, the bad news is I penetrated the doctor's hidden hard drive. Smart-ass used d-u-e-r-f as a password . . . Freud spelled backward . . . and guess what?"

And everyone wants me to guess. "No time, they're calling my flight."

"This guy, Hashim, has visited every kiddy porn site on the information superhighway. He must be a real freak."

"No gay stuff?"

"Nope, sick puppy stuff, and plenty of it. He's been doing it for years. I picked up dates as far as three years ago. He's inveterate."

"Right," I say, because it's all I can get out. I think my heart actually stops beating for a moment, as this is the worst news I can get. I've delivered a couple of children to a kiddy porn freak, even if he is their father. I'm heartsick and my stomach is full of snakes. I've got to figure a way to rectify this.

"So," I ask, "can you prove this stuff is on his hard drive?"

"I asked your old man and Iver to come over, then showed them the method I used to get into the doctor's personal computer, and then off-loaded it onto a zip drive. It would stand up in court, I imagine, which is why I got two witnesses when I downloaded it . . . except for the probable cause thing."

"Yeah, there's that." I can't keep the sarcasm out of my tone.

"We could go snatch the computer, if we had some kind of warrant. But, we don't."

"That's the P.D.'s job."

"Still, this should help some enterprising cop get a search warrant, shouldn't it?"

"Ask Pug to get on it. Can Hashim erase it?"

"He might think he has. I doubt if he's computer literate enough to actually get the stuff off."

"What do you mean?"

"I mean when you merely delete files, all that's deleted is the control line that identifies them and keeps them from being overwritten. The actual info is still there until written over, hanging around like a doppelganger."

"A doppel what?"

"A ghost."

"Right. Have you seen Pug?"

"He and Iver are still here."

"Put him on."

I hear Pug's gruff "Yeah?"

"Pop, I've got some really bad boys to go after. All of us, in full gear, the van and the Chevy. Maybe gone a few days. Get it set up, will you?"

He doesn't even bother to ask who or where, and I know we'll be ready to get down and dirty by the time I'm back.

"And let's get one of your old buddies to get a search warrant and go in and grab Hashim's computer."

"That might not be as easy as it sounds."

"Why not?"

"The guy's a psychiatrist. He's going to claim this is work related, that he's studying the psychology of miscreant behavior, or some b.s."

"But it's worth a try?"

"It is, and I will."

As we're in line to board the plane, my phone vibrates for the third time. I don't recognize this voice.

"Mr. Shannon?"

"Yes, how can I help you?"

"Actually, Mr. Shannon, it is I who can help you."

"How's that?" I ask, my curiosity piqued.

"I want to meet with you."

"And this is?"

"Henri Aziz."

# Chapter 27

That stops me in my tracks. Henri Aziz speaks excellent English.

"Henri Aziz from Andorra?" I ask, as if I didn't know.

"Have you had dealings with another? The grandfather of the children you abducted."

I have to collect myself, then decide to take the offensive. "I don't have your grandchildren, Mr. Aziz. They are where they're legally supposed to be . . . compelled to be." It actually turns my stomach to voice that.

"Aww . . . the law. The law is not always, shall we say, sympathetic to those of us who have led hard lives, as have I."

"So, since your grandchildren are where the laws says they should be . . . I guess I cannot help you."

"Then again, Mr. Shannon, you may be able to do so. In fact, when you know the facts regarding Mohammad Hashim, you might desire to help me."

I'm silent for a moment, because I've just learned facts about Hashim that have made me very sick to my stomach. "Since I have returned from Europe, I've learned some things about Dr. Hashim that I didn't know when I took on the assignment. When and where would you like to meet?"

"When are you returning from Montana?"

Henri Aziz is a hard man to get very far ahead of. Still, I don't want to set myself up for this guy, so I lie. "It'll be in a couple of days."

"Then, this weekend?"

"You're here, in the States I mean?"

"Yes. Please do not inform the authorities, or it will not be merely your boat that is at the bottom of the sea. I have many friends, even here in the 'States,' as you say."

"You and your assholes sank my boat."

"And you, Mr. Shannon, made me believe my grandchildren died a violent and horrible death. That was very cruel to an old man, Mr. Shannon." He's silent for a moment. "Sinking your boat was only to get your attention."

"You succeeded." I want to tell him what an absolute unadulterated prick I think he is for sinking my boat, and maybe sending Futa to cat heaven, but that can wait. At the moment, under the new circumstance of Dr. Hashim's abhorrent interests, I want more to meet with Aziz than chastise him, so I keep my mouth shut.

"Call for me, very soon, at the Biltmore in Montecito. I have a friend there who can reach me. Ask, please, to speak with Mr. Poteet."

"Poteet?"

"That is correct. Make sure it is no later than this weekend."

I hang up. It should be an interesting week.


Other than having to listen to Lenny Haroldstern trying to bribe me, it's an uneventful trip home, and the plane is of adequate size so that I'm not clawing at the windows all the way. Sol tries to negotiate me down since we were quickly successful, which fails; then he cries broke, but has a check for me for twenty-five thousand, seventy-five short of what our contract states. He promises to pay me off twenty-five grand a month for the next three, with the last payment being only fifteen thousand, the payment due less the ten-grand cost of the performance bond he helped me post in France. I have no reason to doubt Sol, as he's always been straight with me, if akin to a Lebanese rug merchant.

That's just as well, as if I had the whole amount in my hot little hands at one time I'd probably blow it on bills.

It's a little after nine Saturday morning when I give the Biltmore a call.

Mr. Poteet answers on the first ring. I ask for Mr. Aziz and the man on the phone acts as if he's never heard of anyone named Aziz. Then I tell him who I am and in seconds, after a few clicks as if the call was being transferred, Henri Aziz is on the line.

"Have you had breakfast, Mr. Shannon?"

"I had a bite early, but I could eat."

"In Montecito do you know Tutti's?"

"Of course."

"Be there at ten, please. And be alone."

"No problem."

Pop and Iver are behind me as I speak, both in nylon jackets to cover their weapons and long-sleeve shirts over Kevlar vests, and in jeans and tennis shoes as I'm outfitted. Pug and Iver have the radios. I'm leaving my weapon with Pug as I'm sure I'll be patted down. All three of my team, including Cedric—whom I generally try and leave out of any ops that could get rough—are members of the National Institute of Bail Enforcement at my suggestion, and Iver and Cedric have received many days of training. The old man, of course, needed very little, only on the fine points of bail enforcement law. Strangely enough, most cops are ignorant of that aspect of law enforcement.

We talk the location over. Tutti's is on the main drag in Montecito, and I decide that I'll drive my Chevy, Iver will take his own motorcycle—one of those fancy Honda rice-burners—and the old man will be in his truck. They will take up positions ahead of my arriving, near the restaurant, but bracketing it. People are always on the street in the little burg and they should go relatively unnoticed.

When I park, I'm met by two no-necks, out of place in Montecito in suits and ties, before I reach the front door, and am informed that the meeting place has been changed. Old Henri is taking no chances.

They usher me to a black four-door Mercedes with the windows darkened, parked in Montecito's forty-five-degree street parking, pat me down, and put me in the backseat with one of them. I make eye contact with Iver but we've already discussed this possibility, and he and the old man are ready to follow.

The Mercedes doesn't go far, only across the freeway to the Biltmore's fabulous location on the Pacific. In addition to a couple of main buildings, there are a number of old Spanish-style bungalows, and the Mercedes is driven to the rear of the place and stops at a bungalow the size of a normal three-bedroom house; probably twenty-five hundred a night at the Biltmore. I'm comfortable as I can see Pop wheel his truck into the narrow roadway not a hundred yards from where we've parked, and Iver has idled his bike into the roadway and past us to an employee's entrance to the main building. He actually enters as we exit the car and head for the bungalow, but I can see him turn inside the screen door and stand and watch every move we make.

There's a carved mahogany dining room table that would seat twelve in the dining room just to the right of the entrance, and sitting at that table sipping coffee, is Henri Aziz himself. And to my surprise at his right is a young woman, whom I presume is his daughter, Paloma Hashim.

The two no-necks take up positions beside the dining room door like a pair of carved gargoyles.

Aziz motions for me to set at the table across from him. He introduces himself, and his daughter, without bothering to stand or reach across the table and shake hands. Paloma merely nods, her hands folded demurely in her lap, and it seems to me that her eyes are moist with tears.

Aziz motions for one of the no-necks to pour my coffee, then says, "I took the liberty of ordering eggs Benedict for you, Mr. Shannon . . . unless you would prefer something else? Paloma and I are having cheese and fruit."

As we chat, I notice Pug walk by the dining room window, his glance inside barely noticeable.

When the room service waiter leaves, Aziz continues. "I do not often have," he says, his voice sincere, "how do you say, the wool pulled over my eyes? When my daughter called me from Madrid and told me she and a doctor were discussing marriage, I, to be truthful, was very pleased. I do not want . . . have never wanted . . . my children involved in my business; in fact, I want them all, even my two sons, as far from my business as they can remain. I was very pleased when Paloma brought Mohammad to Costa Brava to meet my wife and me."

"But not so pleased now?"

"Not so. Of course, I had the prospective husband checked out. He seemed a devout Moslem, he paid his bills, he earned good money. He had nothing on his police record. I was very pleased when they married and even when they decided to emigrate to the U.S."

"And now?"

"And now I have discovered he is a madman."

"He seems sane enough to me," I say, but don't really mean it.

"Believe me, he is a madman. He will bring much harm to the children . . . maybe the ultimate harm."

"I can't believe that he doesn't fear you, Mr. Aziz—"

"You do not seem to, Mr. Shannon."

I only smile politely, then continue, "It's my understanding that you are a very powerful and resourceful man. And to be frank, he should know you'll kill him if he harms the children in any way. So, why don't you just take them, as I did?"

"Very simple. I want my daughter and grandchildren to live in peace. I have thoughts of my sons emigrating to the United States. My business interests in Spain and France are tenuous. I do not have the best of relations with another group of . . . how shall I say . . . another group of businessmen, and things there could get very dangerous. I want my grandchildren home in Spain . . . legally. I want it done just so. Then, when the problems in Spain, Andorra, and France are resolved, I want my children and grandchildren to be able to return to the United States, to live out their lives in comfort and peace."

"And if you can't get them legally?"

"Nonetheless, the children will be coming back to Spain. I have to have them near, where I know they are being protected . . . until it's safe for them to be this far from their grandfather."

"So, what do you want of me?"

"You, and Miss Cynthia Proffer, the private investigator, know Mohammad well, do you not?"

"Me, not so well. Cynthia knows him better than I."

"Do you have any loyalty to Mohammad?"

"Truthfully," I say with conviction, "I think he's a lowlife deadbeat prick."

For the first time, Henri Aziz smiles, and Paloma nods with some enthusiasm. "Then if your business is concluded with him, you should have no problem going to work for me."

"Depends on the work."

"I want grounds to have my daughter legally given full custody of the children."

"That might be done, Mr. Aziz." I still haven't dropped the bomb on him that good old Mohammad is a pedophile, and I'm glad I haven't.

"I would pay well, if he could properly be . . . how do you say . . . set up, so any *juez* . . . judge, would give full custody to Paloma."

"I don't think it will require Dr. Hashim being 'set up.' Still, this could take quite a long time."

"It can not, Mr. Shannon."

"And why not?"

"When Mohammad thought he was going to lose his former wife and child, and a good portion of his assets, to divorce . . . I have reason to believe he killed them."

That stops me. "Killed them? How did they die?"

"In an automobile accident, but after long investigation, we believe it was staged."

That sets my mind to reeling and my suspicions have suddenly gone to red alert. I quickly finish my coffee and the last bite of my eggs Benedict, then rise. "I'm leaving, Mr. Aziz. I appreciate your hospitality and the food and coffee."

"I will pay you very well, Mr. Shannon," he says without rising himself.

"I'll tell you what, Mr. Aziz, I have money coming from Mohammad for my trip to Spain, which he has not yet paid. If I can collect that money, and if you reimburse me for all costs I incur from bringing my boat back up to its prior condition, then I will consider that you owe me only a favor, and if I'm ever in Spain or Southern France again . . . Besides, we've both already cost each other a good deal."

I move to the door, tracked by one of the no-necks,

then pause and look back. "There's a good chance Paloma will have her children legally in her hands inside of a week."

If I can get Pug to drop the pedophile bomb on one of his old buddies still at the Santa Barbara P.D., and can get a search warrant generated, then it will be a slam dunk. The children will go immediately into protective custody, and should be released to their mother.

He eyes me with a look that can only be translated as thankful. "If you can do that, I will be greatly indebted."

"I have to take a trip on another matter, but I should return within a week. But don't think I'm not working on this problem of yours. Things will be moving forward, even while I'm out of the area."

Aziz actually rises, as does his daughter, and he puts an arm around her. "It is the end result that matters."

Something has been gouging my psyche since this conversation progressed to Hashim possibly being a murderer. I'm not sure I believe he actually killed a former wife and child. Aziz and Hashim's estranged wife have plenty of reasons to fabricate such a story, but then again . . .

If he did, I'm wondering about something that will make me very, very angry at the good doctor, if true. Even more angry than finding out I've offered up two beautiful children to a pedophile.

Could it be he wants his own children dead?

# Chapter 28

When Pug, Iver, and I are back at the boat, which is drying out with blowers working away now that the shore power is fixed, I pull my old man aside. "I want you to check something out for me."

I go below and fetch a small item that's still in my duffel bag and hand it over, explaining what I want done.

"This'll cost me a favor," Pug says.

"Who better to use up a favor for than your loving son?"

All I get from him is a "humph."

A good time to change the subject. "Are you sure we've got everything we need in the van and Chevy?"

"Yep, except we've got to pick up Cedric."

"Cedric doesn't go on these kinds of things," I say adamantly.

"He wants to go, and I think he should go. How's he ever going to learn?"

I sigh. "These are bad guys, Pop. Cedric shoos flies out of his apartment so he's not tempted to give them a swat. He thinks great whites are one of God's great gifts to the sea, and wants them protected. His head is into computers and other esoteric things, not hand-to-hand kick-ass and handcuffs."

"So, he'll learn. And these guys are no worse than many I've rolled over the hood. Cedric wants to go along."

"Cedric doesn't have a vest."

"Yes, he does, I got him one, and I checked him out on the range while you were gone and he shot a group no bigger than my hand at twenty-five yards."

"Yeah, at a growling paper target. Okay, okay, then Cedric goes. He rides with you in the van, Iver and I are in the Chevy. I don't need any more work on my vocabulary."

"Ha," he says, and I leave it at that.

By three in the afternoon, we're on our way to the less-than-scenic farm community of Delano, with the van loaded with gear and only one stop to slow us down. That's Paso Robles, where we call on the P.D. and pick up a copy of the warrant for Simon Orozco, wanted now only as a suspect in the killing of Lawanda Lopez. At Paso we head east, again past the vineyards and James Dean memorial and into the valley.

The closer I get to the valley, and to the chance of putting my .38 against the temple of Oscar's killers, the more my guts harden and my wits sharpen. I really want these guys, more than I've wanted anything in my life.

It's said the San Joaquin Valley and the Sacramento Valley, which is the great rift between California's Sierras and the costal range, is the most productive agricultural valley in the world, stretching north several hundred miles from the Tehachapi Mountains, sixty miles south of Bakersfield, almost to the Oregon line. It's easy to imagine that estimate of the valley's productivity to be true as you drive across a checkerboard of trees and row crops crisscrossed with irrigation ditches and power lines. Delano rests in its southern quarter, surrounded by orchards, groves, vineyards, and row crops. It's a small town, home of the Cesar Chevez farm labor movement, probably fifteen or twenty thousand population, mostly Mexicans peppered with a few Philippinos, and even fewer Anglos. Like many California towns it's metamorphosed from white to brown over the last three decades. Most of the valley towns bloomed on the east side of the valley, as the higher inland Sierra range sheds a lot of water via a half dozen or more rivers, all of which is funneled into canals and eventually onto crops. So that was where the farming began, and eventually, where the railroad was constructed.

We come into town just at sunset from the south along old Highway 99, which at one time was the main north-south artery in the valley until Interstate 5 was constructed on the west side. Old Highway 99 parallels the railroad, and is lined with packing sheds and silos, and like many upstaged highways, with abandoned businesses and buildings.

Pug and I only have a smattering of Spanish, but both Iver and Cedric are proficient in the language. Our first stop is at a pay phone booth outside a truck stop on the south edge of town. Iver and Cedric flip coins to see who takes the first stint on the phone, and Iver loses. But he gets the phone only after I call both the local P.D. and the Kern County Sheriff's Department and inform them we're in town, describe my vehicles and my crew, and tell them to please advise their officers, particularly their warrant officers and that night's patrolmen, that we may be taking someone down. This is common courtesy and something I should have done in Big Fork, Montana. I would call on them personally but it's Saturday, and they're bureaucrats, which means those in power will be nowhere to be found. It's also good insurance and might keep us from getting shot by a nervous local-yokel cop who doesn't give us time to flash IDs.

While Iver goes to work, the rest of us go inside to

sample truck stop fare, and to order him something to go. And we fit right in. At my suggestion, we're all in clothes that will not offend the valley crowd—jeans, T-shirts and/or plaid shirts, and lace-up or cowboy boots. This is not the Santa Barbara Polo and Racquet Club as to attire or food, but there's plenty of the latter, and it's rib-sticking fare. It's too warm for jackets. All of us wear bill caps; Iver's, the 49ers; Pug's, the Gauchos, University of Santa Barbara; and mine, Raiders, all sports teams. Cedric's, of course, has an intricate embroidery of Minnie Mouse, her image underlined with the very small letters and the apparent question FUCKING GOOFY? Or maybe it's a description of the wearer? It doesn't exactly complement the camouflage T-shirt he wears, not that camo stands out in this crowd.

We would all have done better to have John Deere properly revered on caps of John Deere green.

Iver's job is to call every Orozco in the book to see if he can locate Simon, or even identify his relatives.

He's at the table by the time our food arrives and instructs the waitress to bring his. "Only four," he says, "and nobody has ever heard of a Simon. However, one of the ladies, at the Francisco Orozco residence, was a little quick to answer."

I shrug. Quick may mean she was in the middle of getting laid or doing the laundry. "You can do a drive-by later if you think it's worth it."

No surprise to me that we get no leads, but it's standard procedure. "Then," I suggest, "let's try the Sanchezs and see if any one knows a Julio . . . but after we eat."

And after we sop the last of the gravy the calls to the Sanchezs in the book, over a dozen of them, are bombs also.

"Okay, then let's go split up and work the bars. I wonder if there's a cockfight going down that we can check out. Hell, this town may have a nightly get-together in some barn out in the boondocks. Let's see if anyone's tongue might be loosened by a little booze, and has heard of our boys. I'm sure Mexican brown is a good part of their m.o., so you might ask if you can score some if you're in the right crowd. Ask fairly big time . . . to score a half dozen ounces or more, so you don't get just the average street pusher. Either that, or if somebody is keeping gamecocks, neither can be too hard to find."

"Why's that?" Cedric asks.

"Heroin, because it's everywhere, cocks because it takes a lot of room for even a couple dozen, and that's small potatoes for most breeders. As I recall roosters are staked out well apart, usually each with its own little coop, or they'll fight. That's what they're bred to do, but a breeder can't make any money if they're practicing on each other. It takes a lot of room. Raising birds is legal; fighting them is not. But nobody much tries to hide the fact they're raising gamecocks, just the fact they're fighting them."

We steal the phone book out of the booth and with its map and a list of bars lay out our night's work. We make a short plan, then split up, after I hand out forty bucks to each of them so they can buy a few drinks to loosen tongues. Pug and Cedric take the north side of town, and we take the south. This is a long process, and I don't expect any quick results. But if I'm constantly moving closer than my quarry, I don't have to hurry, so long as the end result is my cold muzzle against a friend's killer's temple.

But it's Saturday night and if we're going to learn anything by canvassing saloons, this will be the night to do it.

There's a campground at a lake, Woolumnes, just southeast of town, and it's there we'll meet after the bars close. All of us have cell phones, so if someone needs help, or gets some critical information, he can inform the others.

Unfortunately, no one bothers to use the phone. It's

three A.M. before we all meet at the campground. We've got sleeping bags among our gear, so for at least this first night, we're going to rough it. Having a day's growth of beard and being a little ripe from no shower will make it easier to cozy up to this crowd.

The night was uneventful, if you can call a knife fight Pug and Cedric witnessed as uneventful. They stayed as far out of it as they could, and none of it ran over onto them.

It's a rough town.

Assisted by some a-hole running a drag boat full throttle up and down the lake, I'm up and out of there early, as I want to see what I can glean from both the Delano P.D. and the local station of the Kern County Sheriff's Department, even if it is Sunday.

I'm sorry to say neither is very helpful, asking me to come back on Monday and talk to lieutenants.

Hundreds of farm workers move in and out of the area with the crops, and just because a house is rented to one family doesn't mean there's not an additional one living with them, or at least a couple of male renters. It's a hard bunch of folks to get a line on.

The boys call my cell phone just after ten and want to meet for lunch. Pug describes a Philippino joint next to the tracks that he and Cedric had noticed the night before. It seems our wandering boy, Cedric, knows something about that ethnic brand of chow, so Delcastillo's it is, at eleven forty-five to beat the lunch crowd.

I was being facetious about beating the lunch crowd, but in fact, the place fills up shortly after we arrive with half the patrons probably post-church in suits and ties. The saloon is full and people are outside waiting to get in. Not only Latinos and Philippinos, but half the Anglo population of the burg. Cedric raves about the food, and in fact, it is delicious. Being Cedric, he insists on giving his personal compliments to the cook, and when things slow down a little, is invited into the kitchen.

Iver reports that they've driven by and checked out the Francisco Orozco place, the "quick answer" Orozco, and knocked on the door asking for Simon, but were again told they'd never heard of the boy . . . but Iver says the woman who answered appeared oddly apprehensive.

Pug, Iver, and I are leaning against the van when Cedric finally makes an appearance.

"Alexandro is the head cook. Great guy. Comes from a little island not far from where I did a treasure dive with some Chinese guys."

This is a story I haven't heard, and am not sure I want to hear now, but then my ears perk up.

"Alexandro says there's a cockfight on Wednesday, Saturday, and Sunday. He says every camp has its own birds . . . camp birds they call them."

"Where?" I ask, alert even with a belly full, as it's Sunday.

"He gets off at four-thirty, and I'm going to pick him up and we're going out to check it out. I said I'd buy the beer and gas."

"Outstanding. It would be better if we knew where so we can reconnoiter the place."

"He wouldn't give up the location . . . said he'd have to take me on out. Seems they're a little spooky as the sheriff's department has been giving them some trouble."

So I go back to the sheriff's department. I use all my charm to get the girl at the desk to call the warrant officer, and I cry the blues to him until he gives me the cell number of an officer who works the area, the east side of the valley, where most of the cockfights take place. It seems they float, like a St. Louis crap game.

I get the guy on the phone and we agree to meet at a coffee shop at his break time, four this afternoon, in the little town of Richgrove, a dozen or so miles northeast of Delano.

The rest of the guys continue doing the barhop while I head for McMurtney's Coffee Shop, which turns out to be the only place open on Sunday afternoon in Richgrove. As it sounds, the place is little more than a wide spot in the road, surrounded by orange and lemon groves.

Officer T.O. Wright, middle name Oliver of course, is county sheriff's deputy to a tee. He's a little overweight with the beginning of his second chin starting to show, a little slow to warm up, and a little reticent about helping a fella whom he considers a city boy and a little outside the law. The good news is, he's heard that bounty hunters can make a lot of money, and before long, we're talking about how he can get into the business, and about my other car being a brand-new Cadillac—lie—and my house being on the Riviera overlooking the ocean in Santa Barbara—lie—and about my sexy girlfriend who is breaking into films—big lie. But at least I've got him talking, and thinking I'm a guy he'd like to know better.

Then again, as it turns out, he may also be a little outside the law, as most of us see the law. At first, he tells me there's no cockfighting going on in his part of the world. Then he really begins to warm up when I discover he too is a Desert Storm vet, not marine but navy shore patrol.

I bear down a little, and stretch the truth of what I know a little more. "This guy, Orozco, tortured and killed a young mother with her child in the room, and Sanchez stuck a good friend of mine, a Desert Storm vet who was only doing his job, and let him bleed out in a parking lot."

"A couple of real lowlifes," Wright agrees, sipping the coffee and eating the apple pie à la mode I've bought him.

"I'm not trying to bust anyone for cockfighting, T.O., I just want to round my guys up and get them out of

your hair. If these guys don't go down, they'll be causing you nothing but grief."

"Hell, you don't even know if these guys hang out
here. . . ."

"Oh, yeah, we do," I lie. "I just can't divulge my source.
I also know there's a floating cockfight that moves from
barn to barn around here."

"Old packing sheds, too," he says, then seems a little
embarrassed that he's spoken up.

"I didn't know that," I exclaim, as if he were a fountain of knowledge.

I lean forward, conspiratorially. "I understand if you
want to leave these boys some room. Hell, man, there's
no reason to stir up a lot of paperwork for you just to
bust some guys for misdemeanors. You want another
piece of pie?"

"Nope . . . I'm on a diet."

"I personally wouldn't blame you if you steered way
clear of cockfights. Keeps the old boys from causing
worse trouble somewhere else."

He looks around to make sure no one's near, then
says in a low voice, "The Polkinghorn place . . . tonight."

# Chapter 29

I can feel the knot in my gut loosen up, as I can finally smell the blood. "And that's where?" I ask.

T.O. Wright, the local sheriff's officer, takes a napkin and draws me a map. It's another five or so miles east, in a farmyard between a citrus grove and a walnut orchard, up against the foothills.

As soon as I have the info, I get up to leave. He ignores the fact I've risen, but not the fact his plate is scraped clean. To his credit, he doesn't lick it.

"Oh, what the heck," he says. "Ethel, bring me another slice of that apple with a gob of ice cream . . . strawberry this time." Then he turns to me. "Don't be causing any trouble out there, other than getting a line on these guys. Some of them ol' boys are good friends of mine."

I nod sincerely, as if trouble is the last thing I want, then wait until Ethel recalculates the check, pay up before T.O. orders another piece of pie, and go to find the Polkinghorn place.

I've only got a little over an hour, as Cedric is picking up his new Philippino friend at four-thirty and should be heading this way. The bad news is he will be using

the van, which is loaded down with gear; then Iver and
Pug won't have a ride. So I decide to risk renting another vehicle and call Pop and fill him in on how things
are progressing.

"Hey," I say, "I've got a position on today's cockfight
and am heading there now. I was thinking about calling
Cedric and his new buddy off, but then again I wonder
if it wouldn't be good to have someone show up with a
local, who'll vouch for him."

"You're right, son. We may not even be able to get
close to the place."

"Good, then go rent a car, a Rent-a-Wreck or—"

"Bull, it'll be a worse wreck when we return it, and
it's on *my* credit card?"

I'm silent for a moment until the exasperation
lessens. "You know, Pop, sometimes you sound just like
somebody's old man."

"Like you've never wrecked a rental car before. . . ."

"If I was there, I'd sign—"

"Forget it, I was just giving you a rash."

"Okay. I'm going to try and get close to the place,
you get a car for Cedric to drive so you and Iver are in
the van with the gear."

"It's Sunday, remember, I may have trouble locating
one."

"If you can't, leave the cook out of it."

I give him directions to the place and tell him to give
me a call when he gets close, then head out.

There are only three or four mailboxes on the
orchard-bracketed road leading out toward the Polkinghorn place. A couple of houses with small barns and
outbuildings and yards with farm equipment are next
to the country road, but a couple are deep in the orchards
out of sight as I'll bet is the Polkinghorn place, and I
turn out to be right. The difference is, at the Polkinghorn mailbox there are native stone flying buttresses
flanking a fancy six-foot-high, twenty-foot-wide, black

wrought-iron gate, with the name POLKINGHORN spelled out in bronze letters inset into the gate. The first N is split in the middle where the gates open. The driveway that disappears into the orange grove is paved, and lined with blooming multicolored rosebushes.

Seems cockfighting is a socially and racially nonprejudicial pastime, if this guy is hosting one, and if folks like a Philippino cook are coming to join the fun. There's a guy on an old pickup, sitting on the tailgate, drinking a beer, just inside the gate, so I give him a honk and wave, but pass on by. He waves, more interested in the beer than the passerby.

I drive a half mile and pass one internal orchard lane, before I reach a dirt path that looks as if it has had some traffic. The only deterrent on this road is a NO HUNTING sign in red, over smaller black letters: POLKINGHORN RANCH. I ignore the sign, even though I definitely am hunting, and turn off the county road and make my way a mile into the ranch before I come up against a canal and foothills beyond, too steep and rocky to farm. There's no tree cover on the hills, not even scrub oak, but there are plenty of boulders.

The canal is flanking the oranges with a good maintenance road on top of its high bank so I wheel up on it and back onto the Polkinghorn place, in the direction of wherever the gated drive might lead.

After I travel a quarter mile a tractor towing a spray rig chugs out of the grove, and stops as I approach. A Mexican farm worker dismounts and walks to the bottom of the bank and waves me down, and like a good law-abiding citizen, I stop, dismount, and walk around the truck where I can look down at him.

He has to remove a face mask with filters in order to talk, pulling it down around his throat so he looks as if he has two huge thyroid goiters. "You know where you are?" he asks.

"Yeah, amigo, looking for the fight."

He eyes me a moment, then says, "Well, you can't get in this way, amigo." His "amigo" is a lot less friendly than mine. "You got to go back and around to the front and check in at the gate."

"I came in from the north and saw a little no-hunting sign that said Polkinghorn Ranch and turned in."

"Hey, man, you got to go back and around."

"Can't turn this toad around up here. Is there another road out up ahead?"

Again there's a silence, and then logic overcomes him and he relents. "There's a quarter-section road about two hundred yards. You can turn it around there."

"How about I take it on out to the county road?"

Again he hesitates, then caves in. "Okay, take it out and go to the front gate. But make sure, man. My ass will be grass. . . ."

"Hate for you to have a grassy ass," I say, whatever that means, and smile and wave.

He's not a trusting soul, and stands and watches me until I make the turn and head down off the embankment out of his sight.

The good news is the road separates the orange grove from a walnut orchard, huge old trees spaced at least forty feet apart.

As soon as I'm down into the trees, I swing a hard left and am driving through the middle of the walnut trees. This time if I'm seen by a farm worker, I'll have a little more 'splaining to do, Lucy.

I bump along, flushing dove and the occasional rabbit for another quarter mile until I see a row of rosebushes blocking my way a little over a hundred yards ahead, then wheel the Chevy a hard left so I'm aiming back at the canal and embankment road, but I don't want to be seen again so I spin the car under the thickest walnut tree I can find with low-hanging branches. I'm pretty well hidden.

I pop the trunk and get my Mossberg twelve-gauge,

stuffing a few double-ought shells in my pockets, and my binocs. My phone and my .38 are on my belt, and I start hoofing it back to the canal.

Now I can see a house on the hillside up ahead a few hundred yards, and the top of a large barn below, its red roof rising up well above the tall walnut trees.

Rather than risk getting spotted, I go down and test the canal water and find it only a little over a foot deep, cross it, and work my way up the boulder-covered hillside. These boulders are truly that, most of them taller than me, and in some places they're stacked randomly.

It takes me the better part of a half hour to get some elevation above the house, barn, and vehicle yard full of farm equipment. I'm maybe forty yards above the house, and a hundred fifty yards from the barn. The view of my subject is not only good from here, but the view of the valley is excellent.

Mr. Polkinghorn picked a nice spot to build. The house is across the canal from barn and equipment, and the wide drive becomes a wrought-iron-railed, two-vehicle-wide bridge where it crosses. The front of the house is grassed and landscaped, including a couple of car-size boulders more easily used than removed, and falls away to the canal. A flat behind the house has been cut and blasted into the hill and it hosts a twenty-by-forty-foot pool and barbecue under a redwood portico. The house itself is lodge-looking stone and redwood, with a lot of glass.

I study the yard below and see that most of the equipment has been moved out into the orchard lanes to make way for cars, and several cars and pickups are already there. It's no surprise that out behind the barn is almost an acre, fenced, with over a hundred little single-chicken coops. Even from here, I can see the roosters staked near them on six-foot tethers. A few of the pickups have camperlike contraptions on their beds, but these are chicken campers with at least sixteen little doors on either side. I've seen dog handlers use these kinds of rigs. Some of them are even pulling trailers with the same configuration.

Somebody will end up with a lot of stewing chickens after this feather-flying battle.

A few men are gathered outside the barn, sipping beer drawn from a keg resting in half a hogshead barrel full of ice.

I'm just getting settled into the crotch of a couple of boulders, where I've got a view of everything but inside the house and barn, when my phone goes off. It startles the hell out of me and I fumble for it as if someone over a hundred yards away could hear it. I've got to remember to put the damned thing on vibrate when I'm working.

It's Pug, who'd promised to call when he got close. I can't see the road even as high above it as I am, as it's well over a half mile away and buried in the orchards.

"You're here?" I ask.

"Yeah, and Cedric and the cook are right behind me. We're passing the front gate right now, and . . . and he's swinging in to chat with the guard."

"Get a half mile away and give me a minute and I'll tell you the best way to get in."

Then I call Cedric.

"Hey," I say.

"Hi, baby doll. You still hot for me?"

I smile as he's on the ball. "When you get to the barn, check it out and see if any of our boys are hanging around, then call me."

"I can't wait either, baby. Cost twenty bucks each to get in this shivaree," and he lowers his voice, "so you owe me. See you under the covers."

Seeing the tractor and spray rig return to the yard— the day's work must be over—I call Pug and Iver and direct them into the walnut orchard, telling them as well as I can where I've hidden the Chevy.

I can see Cedric and the cook come into the yard and park the rental car, a brand-new Toyota Corolla—no way Pop could have found a 1985 model?—then they get a beer and head inside the barn. In the next half hour, thirty or more cars and pickups arrive and find a parking place; then my phone rings again.

"Hi, babe." It's Cedric. "Haven't seen hide nor hair of our friends. They've had a couple of preliminary fights already. You gonna join me tonight?"

"When it gets good and dark," I say, thinking Pop, Iver, and I can slip into the crowd when the action starts and attentions are distracted.

I'm wondering if we should call this whole thing off, as Cedric has seen no one who looks like our FTAs, and FTAs are only a small reason of why I'm really here. I want Julio Sanchez, Charley "Chucho" Rodriquez, and Cesar "Raton" Reyes, also known as Mouse. And almost as much, Simon Orozco, who's suspected of killing Lawanda Lopez, Oscar's lady and the mother of his little girl.

I want revenge for Oscar, Lawanda, and yes, for their orphaned daughter.

It's a warm night as the sun disappears on the western horizon. As soon as it begins to get good and dark, I call Pug and Iver.

"Pop, how about you stay with the car in case we need something—"

"Bullshit. I want in on this."

# Chapter 30

"Pop, you'd serve me better if you were with the gear. Have Iver meet me at the rosebushes and we'll go in together. Make sure he's got his vest on."

"I still think this is bullshit."

"You keep the radio on in case I don't have time to dial you up."

"Okay, okay. He's on his way."

Iver and I meet up, after I wander down and into Polkinghorn's yard so I can cross the bridge and won't have to get wet again. I leave the Mossberg on the hillside, and it's a good thing I do. Just as I reach the yard, the front door of the house opens and a short, stout guy built a lot like Pug exits, adjusting his cowboy hat as he strides across the lawn toward me. Lights come on, and I'm lit up like a deer caught in the headlights.

"Hey!" he yells at me. "You guys are s'posed to stay down below."

"Sorry, I was looking for the head. Somebody said there was some portables up here."

"That's horse crap. What's the matter with the orchard?"

"Not a damn thing," I say, and wave and start down.

"Hold up," he says, and I anticipate trouble, but he jogs up alongside me, and says, "I'll wander on down with you."

I try and make his accent, and figure it's east Texas or Louisiana. "You Polkinghorn?" I ask.

"Sure 'nuf." He extends a hand. "And y're?"

"Shannon, friends call me Shan." That makes him think my first name is Shannon, which is just as well. "That's great beer you're pourin' and that barbecue smells larapin' good."

"I'm Al Polkinghorn. Got both deep-pit beef in Cajun sauce and a pig turnin' out back. Make sure you dig in, only eight bucks for all you can eat." He eyes me a minute as if he's trying to make out where he's met me. "You bring chickens?"

"Nope, my first time at a fight."

That may have been a mistake, and he eyes me a little stronger as we cross the bridge. "So . . . who'd you come with?"

"Old friend of mine, cooks down at Delcastillo's. He brought us out." For the life of me I can't remember what Cedric said was the cook's name. I'm about to get made, I'm thinking, when he smiles.

"Alexandro. He's a chicken bettin' fool. Damn near never wins a gol'darn dime, but sure bets heavy."

Just as we reach the far side of the bridge, he turns toward the barn, and I fade away toward the line of rosebushes. "Got to drain my diddler," I say, trying my best to be a good old country boy, and he gives me a wave and heads away into the growing crowd around the beer. I can hear some shouts from inside the barn, and figure the fights must have started.

I work my way through the thorns and Iver steps out from under a low walnut branch, carrying my stateside-variety M16, which is semiautomatic, not full. Legal, except for its banana clip.

"We going in together?" he asks.

"Probably not. But let's stay in sight of each other. I had to leave my shotgun up on the hill, in the hedgerow near Polkinghorn's house. You want to hide that in the rosebushes." He finds a spot where it can be easily reached from the barn side of the driveway.

I head on toward the barn and beer, stop, and spend three bucks for a plastic cupful, then look back as I head for the doors. Iver, not far behind me, also stops for a beer, as you'd look out of place without one.

There must be two hundred guys in the place, and a dozen or so women.

A pair of Mexican or Philippino fellows are squared off in an opening in the middle of the barn, which is devoid of anything other than some makeshift bleachers built up all around the perimeter of the barn out of bales of straw. The two guys in the open spot, the center of attention, each hold a rooster, facing each other, and are feinting as if they're going to let theirs go, bringing the chickens to a fighting frenzy.

All around the open area guys are squatted down, and behind them, five deep, men stand, most of them with a fistful of money. There's even a few guys and some young kids in the rafters. The noise level would shame a Tyson MGM fight.

There's another guy, a big-bellied white boy, in the ring also, and he yells, "Pit," and the roosters are flung together. Wings and feathers fly, and in less than a three-count one bronze-colored rooster is atop the other, his leg seemingly stuck to the underdog's steel-gray-colored back. The fellow acting as ref starts counting off as if it were a knockdown in a boxing match, reaches five, then steps in and carefully removes the top chicken, and then I see why they are stuck. The one on top has driven one of his three-inch metal spurs into the unfortunate one's back. The steel gray is now streaked with blood.

"Handle," the ref yells at the two who originally had

the chickens in hand, and they step in and again grab up the cocks. The fellow with the struck cock steps back, and allows his chicken's feet to touch the floor, examining his wound and making sure he can even walk, then picks him up and returns to ring center. And again they're feinting the chickens at each other.

"Pit," the ref yells, and they're again flung together. And again, the bronze chicken is atop the other, only this time both knives are driven into the loser, and he definitely is, as he's prostrate on the barn floor, not so much as flicking a feather. Bronze boy poses like a statue, then puffs his chest and crows.

The winning handler fetches his chicken, and the loser turns and stalks away. The ref scoops up the steel-gray now lusterless dead cock and throws it to another white guy, who walks over and unceremoniously drops it in a hogshead barrel.

My mind's eye sees the blade plunge in and out of my old friend Oscar, and my gut again hardens.

I wander around the ring, making a complete circle, carefully looking for my quarry, but none of the four are here. It's a fairly tough job, as I haven't even seen these guys in person, and am only going by descriptions, and 90 percent of the crowd is either Mexican or Philippino.

I spot Polkinghorn standing with a heavyset woman about his height in a simple housedress, and wander over as if I'm just being friendly.

"I got a pocket full a' money, but I need to know a little about what's going on."

"And I'm just the ol' boy to bring you up to speed," he says, winking at the woman, and she laughs and shakes her head.

I stick my hand out to the lady. "Shannon."

"Martha Polkinghorn, welcome to the fun."

Old man Polkinghorn slaps me on the back, then launches into my education.

"It's a lot like any kinda fights. Chickens have to be within two ounces of each other, or you're expected to give odds, say a hundred to eighty if your chicken is four ounces heavier than the other. They weigh from about four pounds eight to six pounds two; anything over that fights as heavyweight, just like boxing."

"How do you bet?" I ask, as if I'm anxious to lose my dough.

"Find an old boy who likes the other chicken, easy as that. Hell, this is the national sport in the Philippines."

"What's the winner get?"

"This here's a cheap fight, costs the ol' boys a thousand to enter their chicken in these early fights, and they get the other guy's money if they win. Couple of fights later it'll be five grand apiece. In places the entry is a hundred thousand and the purse a cool mil. Hell, the DuPont family are big into cockfighting."

"This here's your place?" I ask, in a friendly tone.

"Yep, I get ten percent of the entry money, and I supply the grub and beer, but I don't do it for that. It's the fun Martha and I like."

"You sound like you're from down Louisiana way?"

"Sunset, Louisiana, home of some of the biggest cockfights in the country. Course it's legal down in Louisiana and Oklahoma."

The next fight is about to start, and he wanders off to get a bet down, so I pick up the conversation with Martha. "So, which one is gonna win?"

"If I knew that, young fella, I'd bet the farm, but this here chicken fighting is about like bettin' on where a fly's gonna land. Course, Albert would disagree."

I visit with her for a while, then wander away and sidle up to Cedric, facing slightly away from him so it's not obvious we're talking. "You make anybody?"

He shakes his head, and concentrates on the fight, so I wander halfway around the barn and move alongside Iver. "Anything up?" I ask.

"Old boy across the room, a white guy, has been giving me a dirty look since I walked in."

"Which one?"

"The one over there standing on the first row of bales."

"Talking to the lady?"

"Yes, something's bothering him."

I walk away and head around the crowd, as the guy Iver's concerned about is talking to Martha Polkinghorn. So I wander up and put the charm on. "Mrs. Polkinghorn, can I get you a beer?"

"That's right kindly of you, young man, but I don't partake."

So I stick my hand out to the one Iver was worrying about. "Howdy, I'm Shan."

He shakes. "Delbert Polkinghorn," he says, eyeing me a little suspiciously.

"You must be Al's son?" I ask, with my best good old boy grin. I wish I was missing a front tooth, as I'd look more like one of the locals.

"Yep." Then he turns to his mother. "Ma, there sure are a lot of guys here I don't know. I don't remember letting no black guy through the gate."

Then I realize that Delbert had been the guy sitting on the pickup tailgate when I passed and waved.

"Come to think of it," he says, "I don't remember you paying and coming in the front way."

I get the impression they have some trouble with guys trying to beat them out of the twenty bucks, and laugh, and offer, "I came right in behind that white Ford pickup"—there's always a white Ford pickup—"and you got my twenty," I say, happy that Cedric had bitched about using his own dough to get in so I knew the entry amount.

"Well, maybe, but I'd remember that there black guy. Wasn't no black guys coming in here tonight."

"That guy over there?" I point across the room at Iver.

"That's the one."

"Hell, he's probably a dark-skinned Mex."

"Black as Hardy's ass," he says.

I don't bother to ask who Hardy is or how Delbert knows his ass is black, but rather, picking up on the colloquialism say, "He don't seem to be bothering nobody."

"Bothers the hell out of me if he don't pay," he says, then strides out around the crowd toward where Iver stands watching the feathers fly.

I pace ol' Delbert, not two strides behind.

He stops behind Iver, puts a mitt on Iver's shoulder, and tries to pull him around. Now, Iver's not a guy to be jerked around, but he turns slowly, and glares down at the much shorter Delbert.

"You didn't pay," Delbert accuses, glaring up at the six-foot-six Iver as if he were a banty rooster.

"And you are?" Iver says, in a voice that rumbles as if he were announcing for CNN.

"I am Delbert Polkinghorn, an' my daddy owns this place, and I work the gate, and you didn't pay."

Iver merely eyes the little man, thick in the chest, but short, then glances at me and sees I'm at his back, so he says, "I've got money on this fight," and turns back to the action.

"Like hell," Delbert says, and puts a hand on Iver's biceps, and tries to drag him back to face him. Mistake. Iver spins, whips an arm under Delbert's, and bars him up on his toes. Delbert is dancing on tiptoes like he'd look better wearing a tutu, looking wide-eyed up into Iver's dark flaring ones.

"You're bothering me, little man. You keep bothering me, and I'll jerk your fat little arm off and beat the hell out of you with it, understand?"

"I . . . I . . . I still don't think you paid," Delbert says while dancing on his tiptoes, but he's brave enough, almost as brave as he is stupid.

"I'm going to let you go, little man, and you're going to go away and not bother me." He jacks Delbert up a little higher. "Would that be acceptable?"

"Ye . . . ye . . . yes," Delbert stutters, and Iver lets him back down to his flat feet, and he spins on his heel and beats it out of there.

I shrug, and Iver turns back to the fights.

Making another round of the room, I come back to find Iver with his back to the barn wall, and a half dozen big old ugly farm boys in a half circle around him, having an animated conversation with my friend and associate. Two of these guys have ax handles in hand, although they are being held behind them, and are not used to threaten Iver . . . as of yet.

Delbert is in the middle of the half circle, showing a good deal more bravado now that he has several hundred pounds of lard and a couple of shillelaghs backing him up.

I've seen Iver in action, and these six guys are severely outnumbered.

I tap Delbert on the shoulder, and he stops his yap flapping long enough to turn and see who's bothering him.

"What's up?" I ask.

He glares at me, but seeing as how I'm a friend of Al's, gives me a moment. "We're fixing to take this old boy down and dig a twenty out of his wallet, then throw his black ass out of here."

He starts to turn back, then stops as I say, "Mistake."

"What?" He turns to face me, now glaring at me as if I've just lost friendship status with Papa Polkinghorn, or worse. "What the hell are you talking about?" he slathers.

I pull my badge wallet out of my front pocket and shove it in his face. We've hung around here long enough as it doesn't look as if our boys are going to show. So all I want to do is make a strategic exit. This time the mistake is mine, as I say, "He's with me."

"Cops!" yells one of the farm boys, and you'd have thought someone had set a tear gas bomb off in the place. It's assholes and elbows and chicken feathers everywhere as cockfighters and crowd are scattering and dropping out of the rafters, hotfooting it for the doors.

It couldn't be a worse time for me to realize that Simon Orozco is across the room, staring at me, his hand inside an overshirt.

I can feel my eyes narrow and the muscles in my shoulders and thighs tense. The roar of the running crowd goes silent, at least to me. Every sense of mine is now attuned to a single purpose—Simon Orozco.

# Chapter 31

Orozco wears a red do rag around his head, and is wearing a T-shirt that's tight across a muscular chest under a loose overshirt.

I feign ignoring him, but casually keep an eye on him while watching the rest of the turmoil.

He moves rather casually, the only one among the two-hundred-plus to do so, toward a pair of six-foot-wide sliding barn doors that are separated in the middle enough for a man to pass through.

At the front door, men are running all over each other, fighting and yelling to get out. Cedric has retreated up on some hay bales and looks a little amused at the whole scene.

Iver steps up beside me. "That worked well."

"Orozco is here."

"Where?"

"Going out the end of the barn, between the doors. I think he's carrying, and he knows I'm the guy with the brass."

"I'm on him," Iver says, and jogs out to follow Orozco.

I grab the radio out of my jacket pocket, waving Cedric over, talking as I head for the front doors, which have begun to clear. "Pop, Orozco is here, just exited the barn. Get out to the front and see if you can make him if he gets to the car and out before we bring him down."

I get no answer.

When I get out to the front, dust and gravel are flying as cars and trucks are peeling out in every direction. Cedric and I now both have our badges hanging from our belts so they can be clearly seen.

"That car," Cedric yells at me, and I see he's pointing at a cherry-black-on-black brand-new Chevy SS Monte Carlo that's been lowered. Two guys are hustling to get inside, and I make at least two of them, Simon Orozco, who's getting behind the wheel, and the other, who I'm sure is Julio Sanchez. Orozco is driving and Julio's riding shotgun, which is probably more than a mere description of his position in the vehicle. Two others are already in the backseat.

Iver is closing the distance between himself and the drivers door, when a Mac-10 barrel pokes out the rear window, and as Iver dives to the side, it chatters and spits flame.

The Chevy, thirty or forty yards from us, throws barnyard dirt and fishtails as it heads for the lane, as both Cedric and I drop to one knee, side arms in hand and being leveled.

We both get off a shot, then hold up as there are cars behind the SS, and we don't want to take out a bystander.

Orozco fits the Chevy nicely between a couple of pickup trucks and is heading out, getting clean away, when to my great surprise, the rosebushes part in a cloud of dust, and my van crashes through and smacks into the fore quarter panel of the Chevy SS, knocking it off the lane, and both vehicles shudder to a standstill.

Cedric yells, "That SS was parked at the Orozco place in town," as he runs for the rental car, and I run for the

wreck, a hundred yards from where I stand in the barnyard. It has to be my old man behind the wheel.

Just as I get about fifty yards from them, another gun
barrel sticks out of the passenger side of the Chevy, and
fires twice with a shotgun report, flame licking out in
the darkness, and in the light of a road full of cars and
headlights, I see the front window of the van disappear
in a cloud of glass.

I hope to God my old man was not sitting in that
driver's seat.

Before I can get close enough to get a good clear
shot off at the SS, it slams into gear and takes off into
the orange grove, with barely enough room between
the trees to pass.

In seconds, they are out of sight.

I reach the van, slowly approach, and sick with ap-
prehension peek inside, just as the rear doors fly open
and the old man rounds the side, his face covered with
blood, and levels a Mossberg twelve-gauge at my gut.

"Hold on!" I shout, happy to see he's mobile but
hardly happy that he's leveling a weapon at me that
would cut me in half.

"Where'd they go?" he gasps.

"Into the oranges."

"Take the bike and I'll try and go around and head
them off."

"You're hurt."

"I was down in the seat. Spraying glass . . . it's nothing."

My Sportster is strapped into the back, and I hustle
around and am barely able to gun it out of the van bed
when the old man is back in the driver's seat and hits
the gas and spins the van onto the lane.

Just as I make the orange grove, Cedric and Iver
catch up in the rental car.

"Follow the old man," I yell, and head into the oranges.

Thank God, the SS has broken some branches out of the way, but I'm still not able to move very fast through the grove as it's so thick it tries to sweep me out of the seat when I try to get up any speed, not to speak of the dust and darkness.

In a short time, I break out of the oranges, cross a narrow orchard lane, and am into a walnut orchard that's much more open. Almost three hundred yards ahead, I can see the taillights of the SS, fishtailing back and forth in the soft orchard ground, and then he turns back toward the country road. I now have the advantage as I can cut diagonally across the orchard on the bike. I gun it hard enough that it does a wheely, and turn into the same lane the SS has taken, when I realize it's now only a hundred yards ahead.

Then I see another vehicle turn off the county road, a quarter mile in front of the SS, heading this way.

It's chicken time as the two cars bear down on each other, closer, closer, until the SS tries to crank a hard left, and dust and big walnut leaves fly as the Chevy doesn't make the turn and catches the thick trunk of a walnut tree, which collapses the front right, and then the car careens off, still under power, but can't recover before it crashes into another tree trunk with the left front, then swings back into the opening between the trees, but the SS is badly wounded.

It seems to have knocked a front wheel way out of kilter, and I can see that the driver is trying hard to keep correcting; then he lets it go and it slides to the right between two trees and comes to a stop.

The car that had confronted them turns out to be the Toyota, and it's taken a lane that's bringing it down on the SS, one orchard row away from me. I'm within forty yards when I realize the boys in the SS have piled out and my headlight picks up a pair of them beside the SS, and both of them are leveling weapons at me. I gun the Sportster toward them from thirty yards, but launch myself at the same time, taking the key with me, hit, and somersault through the deep orchard soil. By the time I stop rolling, I have my Smith and Wesson in hand, but am wishing I had the Mossberg I had to leave behind.

I can hear the chatter of the Mac-10 and the boom of a shotgun, and see the Corolla sliding to a stop.

With a thick walnut trunk as cover, I fire as quickly as I can pull them off with my target hopefully eighteen inches behind the muzzle blast of the Mac-10, then use my speed loader to load up.

Then I scramble to another tree toward the SS, using another walnut trunk as cover. I'm only ten yards from the SS, its lights still on, and in the other lane not more than twenty-five yards away, is the Corolla with its lights on and its doors open.

It was very dark when we left the barn, but now a cloud moves away from a full moon, and we've got a little light.

It's suddenly very silent, eerily so, as dust and gun smoke settles in the lights of the cars. I have no idea where Iver and Cedric are, which is a bad thing, but then I hear a sound to my left, maybe twenty yards away. And in the growing moonlight, I can make out a hand holding a Mac-10, just barely sticking out from behind one of the same row of walnuts I occupy.

My damned cell phone has betrayed me many times, so I decide it's time it paid its dues. I slip it off the belt clip, pick a spot, and throw it twenty or more yards into the next lane, then pull my little Motorola radio from my pocket and hit the send button. In less than the count of two, Pug comes back.

"Where are you guys? I can see your lights, but the shots don't seem to be coming from there."

"Sit tight and stay out of it," I whisper. "Call me on the cell phone."

I get into a firing position, leveling my .38 at the tree with the hand sticking out. My phone rings, behind the guy with the Mac-10, and he scrambles around the tree trunk to keep it between him and the sound. Mistake.

The .38 bucks in my hand and he goes sprawling, slinging the Mac-10 aside. I'm out from behind the tree and on the weapon before he can recover. Then shove it under Simon Orozco's chin.

"I'm hurt bad, man," he manages, holding a hand over a chest wound, blood flowing between his fingers.

Without saying a thing, I roll him over and cuff him. His wound is going to have to wait.

Then shots ring out from a hundred yards away, and I sprint toward them, and dive under a tree when I figure I'm close. My radio vibrates, but I ignore it for the moment.

"Iver? Cedric?" I call out.

Iver's deep voice rings out from twenty or so yards ahead of me. "Here, a couple of these old boys are over in the next row, under a tree, I think. Careful, they're shooting at everything that moves."

I move so I can see where I think Iver is talking about, just as one of the Mexicans, wearing a white do rag around his head, breaks from the tree cover, but before I can fire, Cedric springs from the tree just ahead and tackles the guy. They both roll in the dirt, then come up facing each other. The big Mexican, who has to be Cesar "Raton" Reyes, as he must be the better part of three hundred pounds, has at least a hundred forty edge on Cedric. To add insult to poundage, he jerks a switchblade and I see it flash in the moonlight. Just as I decide to risk a shot, I'm amazed as Cedric's foot shoots out and the knife goes flying; then he spins and, way higher than his head, the same foot comes up beside the big boy's oversized melon.

I'm momentarily distracted by another set of gunshots a hundred or more yards back toward the barn.

Mouse staggers back from the first blow; Cedric spins again. I can clearly hear the crack of his foot against the

Mexican's head, and Mouse goes down as if he were poleaxed with one of the farm boys' ax handles, but he's tough, and starts to struggle back up. This time Cedric performs a soccer kick and the big man's head snaps back and he goes to his face. I knew Cedric was a yoga freak and flexible as hell, but I had no idea he was proficient in the martial arts.

I have a new respect for my compatriot.

"Cuff him," I yell, and wait until I can see that Cedric has him under control; then I sprint off toward where I heard the other set of gunshots.

As I near the spot I figure had the action, which has to be Iver, I yell out again, not wanting to be shot by my own people. "Iver?"

He stumbles out of the cover of a tree nearby, and sinks to his knees. "Bastard got me with a lucky blind shot," he says, holding his side, but blood oozes through his fingers.

I grab up my radio. "Pop, get an ambulance out here."

"You hit?" the radio comes back.

"Iver took one in the side."

"I've already got them coming. I'm bringing the kit in."

"Stay out there and make sure nobody gets out of this orchard," I instruct the old man, but he never has obeyed worth a damn.

"I'm coming in, in the van. Tell Iver to see if he can make it back to where the car lights are."

"You need help?" I ask my big friend.

"That's Julio Sanchez out there. Get him," he says.

I can hear movement off in the trees, then the sound of rapid footfalls.

Sprinting over a few yards, I can see someone running dead-out fifty yards away from me, and I holster my weapon and take off. I'm not as fast as some, but I'm used to running on the beach, and I'd be real surprised if Julio Sanchez can outlast even if he can outrun me for a hundred yards. It takes me a hundred and fifty yards, but I'm only a few paces behind him when he looks back over his shoulder, cuts to the side, and spins with an automatic in hand.

I careen to the side under a low walnut branch, pulling my own weapon as he fires. The side of my neck suddenly burns as if someone's laid a red-hot iron across it, and I wonder if he's killed me, as I return fire.

Julio Sanchez is knocked backward, but still with gun in hand, so I fire again, this time more calmly. I don't want him dead, yet, and pick a knee and see it flinch and him drop his weapon and grab for it. I plunge forward, kick the automatic spinning away, kick him in the bloodied knee, then step back and aim again. His eyes flare as he thinks I'm about to blow his head off, but I drop the muzzle and blow the hell out of his other knee.

It spasms and he withers in pain as he clasps the knee. "Man, you're crazy, I give up! I give up! Don't shoot me again, please, please!" he begs, his voice full of fear.

I move forward and kick him in the mouth, putting him on his back, then put a knee in his chest and shove the hot muzzle in his mouth, and he grabs my wrist with both hands, trying to wrench away from the hot barrel but adrenaline is on my side and he can't pull the gun hand away.

"You stuck my buddy Oscar, and you killed his lady and I'm going to blow your ugly head off, Julio."

He tries to say something, but can't with the muzzle in his mouth. So I pull it back a couple of inches, enjoying his fear.

"I didn't kill no woman. Mouse and Chucho and Simon did that."

I shove the gun back in his mouth. "That leaves Oscar, and I know you stuck him. Freddy Branch was there and saw it."

I cock the weapon just as car lights sweep over me, making me hesitate in acting on my sworn promise to kill this son of a bitch.

The old man's voice rings out. "Don't do it, Dev."

"Bullshit," I say, as I hear his door slam shut.

"Don't do it, Devlin."

"I promised myself . . . ."

"That's right . . . it's not about him . . . it's about you."

"I can live with it," I say, shoving the muzzle deeper into his mouth until he gags.

"Maybe you can," Pug says, and then his voice softens. "But I can't. Give me a break here."

I look up at him and in the light of the headlamps, see anguish in his eyes.

He repeats his plea. "Don't do it, Devlin. I can hear your mother's heavenly cries. This goes against all she taught you. All I've taught you."

I sigh deeply, then slowly pull the weapon back, uncock it, then with all the strength I can muster, sweep it across Julio's already ugly mug. Blood splatters from a two-inch gash on his cheekbone, but he doesn't know it as he's crumpled . . . out cold.

"Roll him," Pug orders, and I do as Pug cuffs him. "Then get a dressing on that crease in your neck. That was close."

We can hear sirens out on the county road, and Pug instructs me. "You walk out and lead them in . . . after you dress that wound. I'm going to load this prick, then go find Iver and Cedric."

I smile sardonically at him. "You don't trust me alone with ol' Julio?"

"Sure I do, but you're the boss here and you need to make peace with the county boys, who I'm sure are a little ill at ease about now."

I shrug, and head for the van.

To my great pleasure, I run into Officer T.O. Wright, who doesn't look too happy.

"You call this 'causin' no trouble'?" he asks, hunkering forward with a brow-furrowed frown as if he were about to bust a schoolkid for shoplifting.

"It was their call," I say, and brush right on past him. I can hear him grumble as I move away, but that's the extent of it. It's amazing what five bucks in pie and ice cream can buy you.

We did okay, it turns out—the only bad news is that Chucho managed to beat a trail. Chucho is such a little guy he probably managed to hide in the weeds better than the rest of them. The worst of it is the EMT says Orozco is going to live. That is a real bummer.

The best of it is that Iver's wound is through and through, and the EMT says it hasn't hit anything vital. He's going to be sore for a month or so, but he's tough as the hubs of hell and will heal.

As it happens, we make a major bust, but then so does the Kern County Sheriff's Department. I find eight kilos of smack in the trunk of Simon's SS, and a wad of cash, and while no one's looking, I manage to hide a handful of green in the van. The cops are on the hunt for Mouse.

The sheriff's department, on the guise of pursuing a felon, Mouse, pushes their way into Albert Polkinghorn's lodge-style redwood home, and turn up a couple of kilos, the wrappers of which match the wraps on Simon's horde. It seems Simon has been doing a little business with Al and Martha Polkinghorn. And it also seems the sheriff has been waiting a good long while for the right opportunity to bust the old Louisiana farm boy.

It takes Pop and me a couple of days to transport our boy, Mouse, to San Bernardino, where he's wanted for a few traffics and an assault with a deadly weapon. I run the bail bondsman down and tell him I've delivered his FTA and would like to be paid. Somehow, I've lost my leverage with Orozco already in jail, so he lays only 1C percent on me. Julio Sanchez is cuffed to a hospital bed in the Kern Medical Center jail unit, but I go ahead and drive down to Costa Mesa and hit up the bondsman there for a fee. He's a gentleman, and is glad to lay the normal 20 percent on me, and buys me a Jack Daniel's before we start back.

The Toyota Corolla has been returned to the rental joint with only a few branch scratches in the paint, and it costs me a couple hundred to have it buffed out, and of course some grief from the old man about it being scuffed while on his beat, and more importantly on his credit card.

I pass through Santa Barbara only long enough to drop the old man off. He offers to go on north with me, but he doesn't know my mission, and I don't want him to.

I make a three-hour trip to Salinas in the Chevy. La-wanda Lopez's mother and father live in a single-wide mobile home on a ranch outside of town.

Her father, Enrico, and her mother, Maria, and I hit it off just fine, and when I'm convinced he's an all right guy—and with Oscar Jr. bouncing on my knee—I hand the old man twelve thousand six hundred and eighty-seven bucks in small well-worn bills that I filched from Simon Orozco's trunk, after getting Mr. Lopez's sworn promise that he'll never say where the money came from, and that he'll use it to educate Oscar Jr.

I consider that the best day's work I've performed in a long time.


I come home to a shock.

Pug's buddy at the crime lab, Dr. Tobias Crawford, has a report on the pediatric sleeping pills that the good doctor provided me to "calm the children." It seems Dr. Hashim did figure he would never have to pay out the hundred eighty grand after the twenty he advanced, as he thought the children would never make it back from Spain.

Dr. Tobias invites us to the Santa Barbara County Crime Lab, where he gives us a short education.

The pills tested as *Conium maculatum* . . . hemlock. The Socrates poison. It has a toxicity rating of six, the highest, and paralyzes the muscles much like curare, eventually causing death from paralysis of the lungs. The poison takes several hours, numbing the body. The hemlock was combined with a heavy sedative, and we would have assumed the children were merely asleep, until their breathing stopped.

The dirty, dirty son of a bitch.

Pug quickly had the small plastic container tested for fingerprints, but the good doctor had wiped the container clean before handing it to me.

As we leave, and are riding away in Pug's pickup, he asks, "What now?"

"Take me to Hashim's, I'm breaking in and getting the kids out of there, and then I'm gonna gut that dirty bastard and dump him out at sea."

"All that will do is get the Santa Barbara P.D. after your dumb butt."

"Then what?"

"Breaking in is good, but taking the kids and filleting the doc is not . . . even though tempting. We have to figure a way to set him up so he goes away for a long time."

"How?"

Pug smiles. "Let's give the S.B. boys a reason to bust in, and to give his computer a look."

"How?"

"He's a freak who has a lot to lose if he's discovered, right?"

"Right."

"Let's outfreak him. Does he know Cedric?"

"No reason he should."

"Good, Cedric is freaky enough to pull this off."

The old man drops me off at the boat, and heads off to meet up with a couple of old buddies in the vice division of the S.B. Police Department, while I run Cedric down and get him up to speed on the program.

At a little before five P.M., Cedric calls Dr. Hashim's office from the boat, which finally has its phone and recording equipment back in order, and asks to speak to him, recorder running and me on the line as well. His secretary tells Cedric that's impossible until Cedric tells her it's in regard to Gigi and Arty, and he immediately comes on the line.

"You interested in buying a zip disk, Doctor?" Cedric asks.

"Why would I be?" Hashim asks in his usual haughty manner.

"It's the only copy of everything I took off your home hard drive . . . the hidden section on your hard drive."

"What are you talking about?"

"You know, Doc, the section with Freud spelled backward as the password."

"Who is this?" he snaps, but I can hear his voice break a little.

"Just your average everyday hacker, Doc, but I hacked out a jewel this time."

"What do you want?"

"Five grand, cash, and you can have the zip drive, e-mails, and pictures I copied from your hard drive."

"I can't talk here. . . ."

"There's a pay phone at the station down the street from your office. Go there and I'll give you a call in ten minutes."

"I have a patient."

"Tough titty. Go now."

"No, let me ask my patient to leave."

I know he's put his hand over the receiver, and I can hear him arguing with the patient. Then he comes back on-line. "He's gone. Where can we meet?"

"How about the harbor, say down behind Brophy's in the parking lot?"

"What time?"

"Seven P.M. I have a date at seven-thirty with a little chicken I know, and now I'll have a lot of money to take him to dinner. Bring five grand, small bills, in a plain brown paper sack. You got it?"

"How do I know it's the only copy?"

"You don't, Doc, you'll just have to take my word."

"How will I know you?"

"You don't have to, I'll know you. I've seen your picture, remember. The one with that kid about fourteen that was on your hard drive. Of course, I may not recognize you with your skinny ass dressed. You better hurry . . . you've just got time to get to the bank."

"I have a new red Cadillac. Look for that."


Cedric is leaning up against a Dumpster in plain view. Pug is in his car, and Detectives Alverez and Thompson are waiting in their unmarked one. I'm in jeans and a sweatshirt and as I'm the only one the doctor should recognize, I'm well hidden behind the Dumpster that Cedric leans upon, waiting.

I can hear Cedric call out to Hashim as the car brakes.

"You the guy?" I hear Hashim ask.

"Yep."

"You got my things?" Hashim asks, his voice so low I can barely hear him.

"You bet. You got my money?" Cedric replies.

"Come over to the car," the doctor instructs.

Then I hear the roar of a gunshot. Jesus, I never suspected. . . . I break out from behind the Dumpster and round it just as Hashim is out of the car bending over Cedric, who's flat on his back, seemingly unconscious but alive and gasping. Hashim is trying to put a small automatic in Cedric's hand, I presume with the idea that he's going to say that Cedric was trying to rob him.

Hashim looks up just as I reach him and tries to recover the weapon, but my kick takes him in the ribs and he rolls away, holding the brown paper bag close to his chest as if it contained the Holy Grail. Kicking the son of a bitch is good, so I walk along giving him three or four more as he's rolling, then flopping away, before Pug gets to us and pulls me off him.

I spin back to Cedric as Pug puts Hashim on his face and cuffs him, just as the two detectives get to them.

"Cedric?" I yell.

But Cedric is already sitting up, rubbing his chest, still gasping for breath.

"You okay?" I ask.

"Vests really work, 'cept I feel like I've been kicked by a mule."

I can hear Detective Alverez compliment the old man. "You're still okay with those cuffs, Pug."

"Had enough practice. You got probable cause?"

"Hell, him firing his weapon at an unarmed man in a public parking lot . . . while trying to buy some kiddy porn. You bet we do."

"And we didn't set him up . . . no entrapment?"

"Entrapment? Hell, Pug, we were just coming to Brophy's for a beer when some asshole started shooting . . . ."

By nine that evening, Gigi and Arty are in protective custody. My call to the Biltmore is a real pleasure. Aziz is effusive with his praise and pleasure, and tells me to contact Mr. Poteet any time during the next week with my bill for the boat repairs . . . just as soon as Paloma gets the kids.

That night, I sleep the sleep of the innocent, without a spectral visit from Oscar, I'm happy to note, or from Futa, I'm very unhappy to note.

# Epilogue

It's a beautiful morning and way past due when I decide to ride north and call on Paul Antone and my old buddy Freddy Branch, who's still being held as a material witness.

"You broke my brother's leg," he says accusingly from across the jail visiting table.

"Shit happens," I say, unrepentant.

"So, what happened to your neck?"

My dressing is down to a wide Band Aid. "Not as much as happened to Simon and Julio."

"So, what do you want?"

"The truth."

"Fuck you."

"Fuck me? Fuck the guy who still has six ounces of your smack and your pig sticker. I think you're the fuckee here, Freddy. Is that wrist about healed? 'Cause if it is, I'm gonna break it again."

"Okay, okay. What?"

"What was Oscar doing with two kilos and why did Lawanda take a hit?"

"You wired?"

"Nope."

"You won't rat me out?"

"Probably not, but if you don't give me all of it, I will rat you definitely for sure and in about three minutes."

"I hid it in Oscar's attic."

"Why?"

"In a weak moment, I filched it from Julio, who worked for Simon. Julio figured out who'd gotten into his stash and heard I was going to the concert with Oscar, and that Oscar was going to try and put the arm on him. I thought Oscar could do it . . . put Julio away, I mean . . . and I'd be home free with Julio in the can."

"How did Julio hear all that?"

"Butch told him. Butch always did run off at the mouth, and he was a customer of Julio's . . . smack and nose candy."

"And of course you told Butch. So, why didn't Julio kill your dumb ugly ass in the parking lot?"

"He wanted his smack back. He hurt me bad, and told me to bring the stuff on over to Delano when I healed up. When he figured that Oscar was going to bleed out, he figured he'd better hotfoot it out of there and that he'd settle up with me later."

"And Lawanda?"

"Simon and his buddies came and rousted me after I got out of the hospital. Julio still owed Simon for the buy and Simon wasn't going to wait for me, and I had to tell them where I hid it. When they found out Lawanda had found it and turned it over to the cops, Simon lost it and popped her. He's a crazy man."

I sit back in my chair, relieved that Oscar was not into the dope biz, and that Lawanda had only tried to do what was right.

"You gonna rat me?" Freddy asks.

"You're a low-priority item . . . not worth my time," I say, and sincerely mean it.

Freddy looks as if I've hurt his feelings.

I spend a little time with Antone, filling him in on

the bust and what had really happened to Lawanda. His people had managed to gather some fibers and DNA from Lawanda's place. Seems Simon and his buddies had helped themselves to a few beers from Lawanda's fridge, and left spittle and prints on the cans.

Satisfied as much as I can be after losing a good friend and buddy, and his lady whom I would've liked to know better, I head for home.

I'm exhausted, and don't even feel the need for a beer before I hit the sack.


It's midmorning and I've just returned from my run on the beach.

The good news is I've awakened to one of those perfect days that God bestows on Santa Barbara so much more often than lesser places.

I'm on the deck, still feeling exhausted even after an invigorating run, and even more so after receiving the demand from Andorra, Spain, and France, and deducing that I've come out only eleven thousand to the good, and only that because Pug, Iver, and Cedric have refused the twenty-five grand I said I'd pay them as part of the Lenny Haroldstern payout. As Cedric was the only one to participate and that was only a couple of days on the keyboard, he agrees to accept twenty-five hundred bucks. Pop and Iver settle on a steak dinner at Chuck's for the Dumpster diving.

Cynthia has advised me that we'll probably never collect the money from Hashim, as he's promised it to his attorneys as a fee if they can recover it, and they'll bury us with paperwork for years. It's not worth the grief, and besides, it's blood money and I don't really give a damn.

I'm enjoying a cup of too thick coffee and the Santa Barbara *News Press*, when I look up to see a thirty-four-foot Catalina sloop putting by on its auxiliary, the

*Seabird,* with a figurehead that makes me rise and stare to make sure I'm seeing what I think I'm seeing.

Futa, in regal splendor, is sitting at the very point of the bow as if he were a Siamese Magellan looking for a route around the world.

Almost as surprising, I know the very tan and well-proportioned person at the tiller.

I scramble to the rear of *Aces n' Eights* where my dingy is tied, jump aboard, and fire up the little six-horse Mercury outboard. By the time the Catalina is making the turn toward the harbor exit, I've caught up with them.

"Back it off," I yell.

Sonya Johanson, in bikinied glory, eases the throttle back and lets the boat come to a drift. I throw her a bowline, we get the dingy alongside, and I manage to scramble over.

"Fancy seeing you here," I say. As soon as I board, she shoves the throttle back to the wall.

She spreads her arms and looks a little sheepish. "I am out of a job, so I thought I would take a few days and visit the islands."

"My cat?"

"Pardon me."

"My cat. You've got my cat."

"Snookums is your cat?"

"Futa is my cat."

"Futa, what an ugly name for so beautiful an animal."

"I think it's a studly name . . . Snookums is a pussy name."

"Well?"

She's got me there. "Okay, but it's still Futa."

"A few days ago, he came on board my boat, wet and hungry and—"

"This is your boat?"

"Of course. I owned her long before I went to work for Dr. Hashim."

I remember then that I know little about Sonya's background, and never asked where she lived, presuming she lived only at Hashim's house.

"So, you've lived at the harbor?"

"Yes, for a few months, on board my *Seabird* until Mrs. Hashim and the doctor started having problems; then I agreed to move into Dr. Hashim's home to take full-time care of the children as he thought she'd be leaving without them."

Futa has disdained to come back to say hello. "Traitor," I murmur as I glance down, chastising him, not that I can fault his choice of shipmates. He ignores my growl and gives me the old glad-to-see-you ankle rub, purring so loud I can hear him while standing. I'm a lay-down. He's forgiven.

"I want my cat back," I demand.

"Of course," she says, flashing me that mesmerizing smile of hers.

"Can I return him after we get back from the islands?"

"No. . . . We?"

"Yes, you and I and Futa. Is that okay then?"

"I don't have any clothes." Sometimes I say the stupidest things.

"So, the sun is shining . . . why would you need clothes?" She points out the obvious, then demonstrates. About that time we reach the end of the breakwater and she reaches a hand to the middle of her back and pops the clasp on her bikini top, a double-jointed move only a woman can accomplish, and lets it drift away to the floor of the cockpit. "They frown on topless in the harbor," she says, again with the faultless smile.

"The fools," I manage in a loud and very preoccupied whisper.

"You have time to go?" she asks.

"The time, and the inclination," I manage to mumble, hoping she doesn't notice that my inclination is beginning to show.

"Then, it is settled. Let us get some canvas up and this stinky engine turned off."

One of the good things about a thirty-four-foot Catalina is its forward bunk, about the size of a queen tapering to a full size at the anchor locker.

It's got a lot of headroom . . . and yes . . . that's a pun.

It's dangerous to be below with the autopilot and your traitor cat the only ones on watch while you're crossing the freighter lanes in what's known as the Santa Barbara Canal, the channel between the harbor of Santa Barbara and the Channel Islands. Of course, curing a long drought with the help—expert help as it turns out—of a beautiful *Svenska flicka* is well worth the risk.

One should never be out of sight of palm trees and beach, with this one notable exception.

We hope you enjoy a peek at the
next Bob Burton novel,
*Bullet Blues,*
coming soon from Pinnacle Books.

Grief is a funny thing.

And that, of course, is a bit oxymoronic; much like jumbo shrimp, army intelligence, rap music, act naturally; or in my business, found missing.

True grief manifests itself, early on, in most of us by our enwrapping ourselves in our arms, bending double, and splattering the floor with teardrops. In the case of the more demonstrable you might add wailing to the mix.

Not, however, in my old friend Mason Fredrich.

Mason, for the first couple of months, maintained his smile and gregarious manner with slaps on the back and encouragement that, yes, June would show up. Not June the month, but June his wife of a dozen years. A marriage so apparently happy it made others uncomfortable as the two of them clung inseparable and giggled like schoolkids, their smiles only fading when momentarily apart.

In Mason, grief was insipid. It descended upon him slowly, like a tapeworm, until if you pierced his formerly tan and healthy hide, which over the past year had gone placid, you felt as if you'd be sprayed with pus before the lack of it revealed a palled pulsating worm silently feasting on now feckless flesh. A vital outgoing human slowly subsiding to a cloistral chrysalis where a man had been. Having before looked ten years younger than his fifty, he now appeared twenty years older.

I'd never seen such a change in a person.

When he came to me on my boat, directly from being bailed from the Santa Barbara County Jail, it was apparent he'd lost thirty or more pounds. His Armani suit hung on his frame almost as if it graced a coat-hook in the hall. His eyes, formerly flashing with a glimmer of joy, stared jaundiced, hollow, and slaked with remorse. I read in yesterday's Santa Barbara *News Press* about his arrest the day before that, and, at the time, had to smile, if tightly, at the ludicrousness of that action by the Santa Barbara County District Attorney. Another oxymoron, an amusing arrest. But Mason was the last guy on earth whom I'd picture killing his wife.

Notwithstanding the fact he is an old friend, how could I say no to the request of someone so blatantly pitiful? I couldn't, and didn't.

I will find her, if she's to be found.

Being in the bail enforcement business brings you all sorts of opportunities, mostly recoveries of other sorts, and at the moment, besides a list of Failure to Appears, I am retained to recover a bichon frisé. That sounds very impressive, as if it were a rare piece of art, but in fact, that's a dog, if you can call a slathering puffball a dog. A bit of fluff, but still chattel, which the court ordered to remain with the male side of a rather nasty divorce. . . . It doesn't take a Sherlock to figure who might be the dirty dognapper. Futa, my ten-pound Siamese, yowled with disdain when I accepted that particular assignment.

My second current non-FTA assignment is the recovery of an eighty-eight-foot yacht, which was purloined from a gentleman who divides his time between Montecito—a neighboring community to my own Santa Barbara—Coral Gables, and Costa Rica.

Why a lapdog might be worth a twenty-thousand-dollar recovery fee is a little beyond my ken—even though his master's settlement was several million—but it's easy to deduce why an eighty-eight-foot, twin-diesel, Italian-built Benetti might be worth a cool hundred to the party who recovered her. And I plan that party to be Dev Shannon, my father's best-looking—and of course, only—son.

Mason and I didn't talk money, and unless helping him means I incur a lot of out-of-pocket expense, we won't, if I have anything to say about it.

For June also was, and I hope still is, a friend of mine.

In normal circumstances, the above would constitute a full plate, and would consume my total attention and effort; however, there is one other small item that's distracting.

Someone's trying to kill me.

# More Nail-Biting Suspense From Your Favorite Thriller Authors

# More Thrilling Suspense From Your Favorite Thriller Authors

| | | |
|---|---|---|
| **If Angels Fall**<br>by Rick Mofina | 0-7860-1061-4 | $6.99US/$8.99CAN |
| **Cold Fear**<br>by Rick Mofina | 0-7860-1266-8 | $6.99US/$8.99CAN |
| **Blood of Others**<br>by Rick Mofina | 0-7860-1267-6 | $6.99US/$9.99CAN |
| **No Way Back**<br>by Rick Mofina | 0-7860-1525-X | $6.99US/$9.99CAN |
| **Dark of the Moon**<br>by P.J. Parrish | 0-7860-1054-1 | $6.99US/$8.99CAN |
| **Dead of Winter**<br>by P.J. Parrish | 0-7860-1189-0 | $6.99US/$8.99CAN |
| **Paint It Black**<br>by P.J. Parrish | 0-7860-1419-9 | $6.99US/$9.99CAN |
| **Thick Than Water**<br>by P.J. Parrish | 0-7860-1420-2 | $6.99US/$9.99CAN |

*Available Wherever Books Are Sold!*

Visit our website at **www.kensingtonbooks.com**